THE HISTORY OF

MR. POLLY

THE
HISTORY OF
Mr. Polly

BY

H. G. WELLS

WITH A FOREWORD BY
SINCLAIR LEWIS

THE PRESS OF THE READERS CLUB
NEW YORK: 1941

was first published, and
country by Duffield and
ngements for the publi-
cation of this edition for THE READERS
CLUB have been made with Mr. Wells
and his present publishers, Dodd Mead
and Co.

The special contents of this edition are copyright,
1941, by THE READERS CLUB

This edition has been designed by W. A. DWIGGINS;
it has been composed in linotype Scotch
and printed on paper especially made for
this book by the West Virginia Pulp and
Paper Company; the composition, printing and binding has been done by The
Kingsport Press of Kingsport, Tennessee

PRINTED IN THE UNITED STATES OF AMERICA

FOREWORD

THERE IS no such thing as a "greatest" novelist, for
how can you compare Lewis Carroll with Proust or
Willa Cather with Dreiser? But it seems probable
to me that just now, in 1941, there is no *greater*
novelist living than Mr. H. G. Wells. On the moun-
tainous slopes of Thomas Mann, there are too many
fogs of magic for the bulk of him to overshine the
quick, plump, gaily trotting human figure of Wells.

Of all the gallery of Wells novels, from such
early fantasies as *The First Men in the Moon,*
through that panorama of Edwardian folly and
ambition, *Tono-Bungay,* down to the last tired re-
iterations that it really is just too bad that Mankind won't gather in a still and spacious library and
determine to do something about it all, there is no
book so deeply reaching into contemporary character, so funny yet so moving, as THE HISTORY OF

MR. POLLY. And nowadays it does not seem to "date", not one paragraph of it, though it was first published in 1909, and has for a decade been neglected, instead of having the five or six hundred thousand new readers every year that it deserves.

I saw POLLY first in the month of its original American publication. I was a cub editor in New York, but I knew nothing of this undistinguished Mr. Wells except that he had written tales about food which turned brats into giants, and about Martians invading Earth. He was to me the Orson Welles of his day — a fancy fellow, pretty exciting but of doubtful future.

I was enamored, then, of a young lady with black eyes, and, with luck beyond the deserts of a $17.50-a-week literary grub, I had snared an invitation to call on her. She had a flat with a cat. While she was scolding the cat, I picked up from her table a new book with the drab title, THE HISTORY OF MR. POLLY, glanced in, and discovered the plump little man sitting on a stile in the east wind, a midget martyr to indigestion and to dreams. I was instantly his captive.

My hostess was cheerful, and full of the choicest Greenwich Village conversation of the 1910's. She chanted, "Aren't Emma Goldman and anarchism wonderful!" She beamed at me, and moved over on the hard little settee. But I had again glanced into the book. I wanted to know more about Mr. Polly's waking up to find that he was apparently married to a young woman whom he didn't know and didn't much like.

The amiability of my hostess thinned, but she suggested breaking a bottle of beer. When she returned with the two glasses, she had to speak twice before she roused me from the cyclopean battle of Mr. Polly and Uncle Jim and the flying eel, at the Potwell Inn. I left that flat as soon as possible, with no reluctance at all from my hostess, and it took me three more weeks to save up enough to buy THE HISTORY OF MR. POLLY.

I have just read it again, and it is as contagious a comedy as ever — the eternal story of the kind, imaginative, friendly Little Man, whose heart and courage would anywhere, in Shanghai or Penn Yan as readily as in Foxbourne, lift him from behind the counter of the Gents' Furnishings Shoppe, and lead him out to find a wayside world that is perpetually new and surprising.

SINCLAIR LEWIS

CHAPTER
THE FIRST

BEGINNINGS,

AND THE BAZAAR

BEGINNINGS,

AND THE BAZAAR

"Hole!" said Mr. Polly, and then for a change, and with greatly increased emphasis: "Ole!" He paused, and then broke out with one of his private and peculiar idioms. "Oh! Beastly Silly Wheeze of a Hole!"

He was sitting on a stile between two threadbare looking fields, and suffering acutely from indigestion.

He suffered from indigestion now nearly every afternoon in his life, but as he lacked introspection he projected the associated discomfort upon the world. Every afternoon he discovered afresh that life as a whole and every aspect of life that presented itself was "beastly." And this afternoon, lured by the delusive blueness of a sky that was blue because the wind was in the east, he had come out in the hope of snatching something of the joyousness

1

of spring. The mysterious alchemy of mind and body refused, however, to permit any joyousness whatever in the spring.

He had had a little difficulty in finding his cap before he came out. He wanted his cap — the new golf cap — and Mrs. Polly must needs fish out his old soft brown felt hat. " *'Ere's* your 'at," she said in a tone of insincere encouragement.

He had been routing among the piled newspapers under the kitchen dresser, and had turned quite hopefully and taken the thing. He put it on. But it didn't feel right. Nothing felt right. He put a trembling hand upon the crown of the thing and pressed it on his head, and tried it askew to the right and then askew to the left.

Then the full sense of the indignity offered him came home to him. The hat masked the upper sinister quarter of his face, and he spoke with a wrathful eye regarding his wife from under the brim. In a voice thick with fury he said: "I s'pose you'd like me to wear that silly Mud Pie for ever, eh? I tell you I won't. I'm sick of it. I'm pretty near sick of everything, comes to that. . . . Hat!"

He clutched it with quivering fingers. "Hat!" he repeated. Then he flung it to the ground, and kicked it with extraordinary fury across the kitchen. It flew up against the door and dropped to the ground with its ribbon band half off.

"Shan't go out!" he said, and sticking his hands

2

into his jacket pockets discovered the missing cap in the right one.

There was nothing for it but to go straight upstairs without a word, and out, slamming the shop door hard.

"Beauty!" said Mrs. Polly at last to a tremendous silence, picking up and dusting the rejected headdress. "Tantrums," she added. "I 'aven't patience." And moving with the slow reluctance of a deeply offended woman, she began to pile together the simple apparatus of their recent meal, for transportation to the scullery sink.

The repast she had prepared for him did not seem to her to justify his ingratitude. There had been the cold pork from Sunday and some nice cold potatoes, and Rashdall's Mixed Pickles, of which he was inordinately fond. He had eaten three gherkins, two onions, a small cauliflower head and several capers with every appearance of appetite, and indeed with avidity; and then there had been cold suet pudding to follow, with treacle, and then a nice bit of cheese. It was the pale, hard sort of cheese he liked; red cheese he declared was indigestible. He had also had three big slices of greyish baker's bread, and had drunk the best part of the jugful of beer. . . . But there seems to be no pleasing some people.

"Tantrums!" said Mrs. Polly at the sink, struggling with the mustard on his plate and expressing the only solution of the problem that occurred to her.

And Mr. Polly sat on the stile and hated the whole scheme of life — which was at once excessive and inadequate as a solution. He hated Foxbourne, he hated Foxbourne High Street, he hated his shop and his wife and his neighbours — every blessed neighbour — and with indescribable bitterness he hated himself.

"Why did I ever get in this silly Hole?" he said. "Why did I ever?"

He sat on the stile, and looked with eyes that seemed blurred with impalpable flaws at a world in which even the spring buds were wilted, the sunlight metallic and the shadows mixed with blue-black ink.

To the moralist I know he might have served as a figure of sinful discontent, but that is because it is the habit of moralists to ignore material circumstances, — if indeed one may speak of a recent meal as a circumstance, — with Mr. Polly circum. Drink, indeed, our teachers will criticise nowadays both as regards quantity and quality, but neither church nor state nor school will raise a warning finger between a man and his hunger and his wife's catering. So on nearly every day in his life Mr. Polly fell into a violent rage and hatred against the outer world in the afternoon, and never sus-

4

pected that it was this inner world to which I am
with such masterly delicacy alluding, that was thus
reflecting its sinister disorder upon the things without. It is a pity that some human beings are not
more transparent. If Mr. Polly, for example, had
been transparent or even passably translucent, then
perhaps he might have realised from the Laocoon
struggle he would have glimpsed, that indeed he
was not so much a human being as a civil war.

Wonderful things must have been going on inside Mr. Polly. Oh! wonderful things. It must have
been like a badly managed industrial city during
a period of depression; agitators, acts of violence,
strikes, the forces of law and order doing their best,
rushings to and fro, upheavals, the *Marseillaise*,
tumbrils, the rumble and the thunder of the tumbrils. . . .

I do not know why the east wind aggravates life
to unhealthy people. It made Mr. Polly's teeth
seem loose in his head, and his skin feel like a misfit,
and his hair a dry, stringy exasperation. . . .

Why cannot doctors give us an antidote to the
east wind?

"Never have the sense to get your hair cut till
it's too long," said Mr. Polly catching sight of his
shadow, "you blighted, degenerated Paintbrush!
Ugh!" and he flattened down the projecting tails
with an urgent hand.

5

⇢≫ II ≪⇠

MR. POLLY'S age was exactly thirty-five years and
a half. He was a short, compact figure, and a little
inclined to a localised embonpoint. His face was not
unpleasing; the features fine, but a trifle too pointed
about the nose to be classically perfect. The corners of his sensitive mouth were depressed. His eyes
were ruddy brown and troubled, and the left one
was round with more of wonder in it than its fellow.
His complexion was dull and yellowish. That, as I
have explained, on account of those civil disturb-
ances. He was, in the technical sense of the word,
clean shaved, with a small sallow patch under the
right ear and a cut on the chin. His brow had the
little puckerings of a thoroughly discontented man,
little wrinklings and lumps, particularly over his
right eye, and he sat with his hands in his pockets,
a little askew on the stile and swung one leg.

"Hole!" he repeated presently.

He broke into a quavering song. "Ro-o-o-tten
Be-e-astly Silly Hole!"

His voice thickened with rage, and the rest of his
discourse was marred by an unfortunate choice of
epithets.

He was dressed in a shabby black morning coat
and vest; the braid that bound these garments was
a little loose in places; his collar was chosen from

stock and with projecting corners, technically a
"wing-poke"; that and his tie, which was new and
loose and rich in colouring, had been selected to en-
courage and stimulate customers — for he dealt in
gentlemen's outfitting. His golf cap, which was also
from stock and aslant over his eye, gave his misery
a desperate touch. He wore brown leather boots —
because he hated the smell of blacking.

Perhaps after all it was not simply indigestion
that troubled him.

Behind the superficialities of Mr. Polly's being,
moved a larger and vaguer distress. The elementary
education he had acquired had left him with the impression that arithmetic was a fluky science and
best avoided in practical affairs, but even the absence of book-keeping and a total inability to distinguish between capital and interest could not
blind him for ever to the fact that the little shop in
the High Street was not paying. An absence of re-
turns, a constriction of credit, a depleted till, the
most valiant resolves to keep smiling, could not pre-
vail for ever against these insistent phenomena.
One might bustle about in the morning before dinner, and in the afternoon after tea and forget that
huge dark cloud of insolvency that gathered and
spread in the background, but it was part of the
desolation of these afternoon periods, these grey
spaces of time after meals, when all one's courage
had descended to the unseen battles of the pit, that

life seemed stripped to the bone and one saw with a hopeless clearness.

Let me tell the history of Mr. Polly from the cradle to these present difficulties.

"First the infant, mewling and puking in its nurse's arms."

There had been a time when two people had thought Mr. Polly the most wonderful and adorable thing in the world, had kissed his toe-nails, saying "myum, myum," and marvelled at the exquisite softness and delicacy of his hair, had called to one another to remark the peculiar distinction with which he bubbled, had disputed whether the sound he had made was just da da, or truly and intentionally dadda, had washed him in the utmost detail, and wrapped him up in soft, warm blankets, and smothered him with kisses. A regal time that was, and four and thirty years ago; and a merciful forgetfulness barred Mr. Polly from ever bringing its careless luxury, its autocratic demands and instant obedience, into contrast with his present condition of life. These two people had worshipped him from the crown of his head to the soles of his exquisite feet. And also they had fed him rather unwisely, for no one had ever troubled to teach his mother anything about the mysteries of a child's upbringing — though of course the monthly nurse

8

and her charwoman gave some valuable hints — and
by his fifth birthday the perfect rhythms of his
nice new interior were already darkened with perplexity. . . .

His mother died when he was seven.

He began only to have distinctive memories of
himself in the time when his education had already
begun.

I remember seeing a picture of Education — in
some place. I think it was Education, but quite con-
ceivably it represented the Empire teaching her
Sons, and I have a strong impression that it was a
wall painting upon some public building in Manchester or Birmingham or Glasgow, but very pos-
sibly I am mistaken about that. It represented a
glorious woman with a wise and fearless face stooping over her children and pointing them to far
horizons. The sky displayed the pearly warmth of
a summer dawn, and all the painting was marvellously bright as if with the youth and hope of the
delicately beautiful children in the foreground. She
was telling them, one felt, of the great prospect of
life that opened before them, of the spectacle of the
world, the splendours of sea and mountain they
might travel and see, the joys of skill they might
acquire, of effort and the pride of effort and the
devotions and nobilities it was theirs to achieve.
Perhaps even she whispered of the warm triumphant mystery of love that comes at last to those

9

who have patience and unblemished hearts. . . .
She was reminding them of their great heritage as
English children, rulers of more than one-fifth of
mankind, of the obligation to do and be the best
that such a pride of empire entails, of their essential nobility and knighthood and the restraints and
the charities and the disciplined strength that is becoming in knights and rulers. . . .

The education of Mr. Polly did not follow this
picture very closely. He went for some time to a
National School, which was run on severely economical lines to keep down the rates by a largely
untrained staff, he was set sums to do that he did
not understand, and that no one made him understand, he was made to read the catechism and Bible
with the utmost industry and an entire disregard
of punctuation or significance, and caused to imi-
tate writing copies and drawing copies, and given
object lessons upon sealing wax and silk-worms and
potato bugs and ginger and iron and such like
things, and taught various other subjects his mind
refused to entertain, and afterwards, when he was
about twelve, he was jerked by his parent to "finish
off" in a private school of dingy aspect and still
dingier pretensions, where there were no object lessons, and the studies of book-keeping and French
were pursued (but never effectually overtaken)
under the guidance of an elderly gentleman who
wore a nondescript gown and took snuff, wrote cop-

perplate, explained nothing, and used a cane with remarkable dexterity and gusto.

Mr. Polly went into the National School at six and he left the private school at fourteen, and by that time his mind was in much the same state that you would be in, dear reader, if you were operated upon for appendicitis by a well-meaning, boldly enterprising, but rather over-worked and under-paid butcher boy, who was superseded towards the climax of the operation by a left-handed clerk of high principles but intemperate habits,—that is to say, it was in a thorough mess. The nice little curiosities and willingnesses of a child were in a jumbled and thwarted condition, hacked and cut about—the operators had left, so to speak, all their sponges and ligatures in the mangled confusion—and Mr. Polly had lost much of his natural confidence, so far as figures and sciences and languages and the possibilities of learning things were concerned. He thought of the present world no longer as a wonderland of experiences, but as geography and history, as the repeating of names that were hard to pronounce, and lists of products and populations and heights and lengths, and as lists and dates—oh! and boredom indescribable. He thought of religion as the recital of more or less incomprehensible words that were hard to remember, and of the Divinity as of a limitless Being having the nature of a schoolmaster and making infinite

11

rules, known and unknown rules, that were always ruthlessly enforced, and with an infinite capacity for punishment and, most horrible of all to think of! limitless powers of espial. (So to the best of his ability he did not think of that unrelenting eye.) He was uncertain about the spelling and pronunciation of most of the words in our beautiful but abundant and perplexing tongue, — that especially was a pity because words attracted him, and under happier conditions he might have used them well — he was always doubtful whether it was eight sevens or nine eights that was sixty-three — (he knew no method for settling the difficulty) and he thought the merit of a drawing consisted in the care with which it was "lined in." "Lining in" bored him beyond measure.

But the indigestions of mind and body that were to play so large a part in his subsequent career were still only beginning. His liver and his gastric juice, his wonder and imagination kept up a fight against the things that threatened to overwhelm soul and body together. Outside the regions devastated by the school curriculum he was still intensely curious. He had cheerful phases of enterprise, and about thirteen he suddenly discovered reading and its joys. He began to read stories voraciously, and books of travel, provided they were also adventurous. He got these chiefly from the local institute, and he also "took in," irregularly but thoroughly, one of those inspiring weeklies that dull people used to call "penny dreadfuls," admirable weeklies crammed with imagination that the cheap boys' "comics" of to-day have replaced. At fourteen, when he emerged from the valley of the shadow of education, there survived something, indeed it survived still, obscured and thwarted, at five and thirty, that pointed — not with a visible and prevailing finger like the finger of that beautiful woman in the picture, but pointed nevertheless — to the idea that there was interest and happiness in the world. Deep in the being of Mr. Polly, deep in that darkness, like a creature which has been beaten about the head and left for dead but still lives, crawled a persuasion that over and above the things that are jolly and "bits of all right," there was beauty, there was delight, that somewhere — magically inaccessible perhaps, but still somewhere, were pure and easy and joyous states of body and mind.

He would sneak out on moonless winter nights and stare up at the stars, and afterwards find it difficult to tell his father where he had been.

He would read tales about hunters and explorers, and imagine himself riding mustangs as fleet as the wind across the prairies of Western America, or coming as a conquering and adored white man into the swarming villages of Central Africa. He shot bears with a revolver — a cigarette in the other hand — and made a necklace of their teeth and claws for the chief's beautiful young daughter. Also he killed a lion with a pointed stake, stabbing through the beast's heart as it stood over him.

He thought it would be splendid to be a diver and go down into the dark green mysteries of the sea.

He led stormers against well-nigh impregnable forts, and died on the ramparts at the moment of victory. (His grave was watered by a nation's tears.)

He rammed and torpedoed ships, one against ten.

He was beloved by queens in barbaric lands, and reconciled whole nations to the Christian faith.

He was martyred, and took it very calmly and beautifully — but only once or twice after the Revivalist week. It did not become a habit with him.

He explored the Amazon, and found, newly exposed by the fall of a great tree, a rock of gold.

Engaged in these pursuits he would neglect the work immediately in hand, sitting somewhat slackly on the form and projecting himself in a manner tempting to a schoolmaster with a cane. . . . And twice he had books confiscated.

Recalled to the realities of life, he would rub himself or sigh deeply as the occasion required, and resume his attempts to write as good as copperplate. He hated writing; the ink always crept up his fingers and the smell of ink offended him. And he

14

was filled with unexpressed doubts. *Why* should writing slope down from right to left? *Why* should downstrokes be thick and upstrokes thin? *Why* should the handle of one's pen point over one's right shoulder?

His copy books towards the end foreshadowed his destiny and took the form of commercial documents. *"Dear Sir,"* they ran, *"Referring to your esteemed order of the 26th ult., we beg to inform you,"* and so on.

The compression of Mr. Polly's mind and soul in the educational institutions of his time, was terminated abruptly by his father between his fourteenth and fifteenth birthday. His father — who had long since forgotten the time when his son's little limbs seemed to have come straight from God's hand, and when he had kissed five minute toe-nails in a rapture of loving tenderness — remarked:

"It's time that dratted boy did something for a living."

And a month or so later Mr. Polly began that career in business that led him at last to the sole proprietorship of a bankrupt outfitter's shop — and to the stile on which he was sitting.

⇥≫ III ≪⇤

Mr. Polly was not naturally interested in hosiery and gentlemen's outfitting. At times, indeed, he

urged himself to a spurious curiosity about that
trade, but presently something more congenial came
along and checked the effort. He was apprenticed
in one of those large, rather low-class establishments which sell everything, from pianos and furniture to books and millinery, a department store in
fact, The Port Burdock Drapery Bazaar at Port
Burdock, one of the three townships that are
grouped around the Port Burdock naval dockyards.
There he remained six years. He spent most of the
time inattentive to business, in a sort of uncomfortable happiness, increasing his indigestion.

On the whole he preferred business to school;
the hours were longer but the tension was not nearly
so great. The place was better aired, you were not
kept in for no reason at all, and the cane was not
employed. You watched the growth of your mous-
tache with interest and impatience, and mastered
the beginnings of social intercourse. You talked,
and found there were things amusing to say. Also
you had regular pocket money, and a voice in the
purchase of your clothes, and presently a small
salary. And there were girls. And friendship! In
the retrospect Port Burdock sparkled with the
facets of quite a cluster of remembered jolly times.

("Didn't save much money though," said Mr.
Polly.)

The first apprentices' dormitory was a long bleak
room with six beds, six chests of drawers and look-

ing glasses and a number of boxes of wood or tin; it
opened into a still longer and bleaker room of eight
beds, and this into a third apartment with yellow
grained paper and American cloth tables, which
was the dining-room by day and the men's sitting-
and smoking-room after nine. Here Mr. Polly, who
had been an only child, first tasted the joys of social intercourse. At first there were attempts to
bully him on account of his refusal to consider face
washing a diurnal duty, but two fights with the apprentices next above him, established a useful repu-
tation for choler, and the presence of girl apprentices in the shop somehow raised his standard of
cleanliness to a more acceptable level. He didn't
of course have very much to do with the feminine
staff in his department, but he spoke to them casu-
ally as he traversed foreign parts of the Bazaar,
or got out of their way politely, or helped them to
lift down heavy boxes, and on such occasions he
felt their scrutiny. Except in the course of business
or at meal times the men and women of the establishment had very little opportunity of meeting;
the men were in their rooms and the girls in theirs.
Yet these feminine creatures, at once so near and
so remote, affected him profoundly. He would watch
them going to and fro, and marvel secretly at the
beauty of their hair or the roundness of their
necks or the warm softness of their cheeks or the
delicacy of their hands. He would fall into pas-

17

sions for them at dinner time, and try and show devotions by his manner of passing the bread and margarine at tea. There was a very fair-haired, fair-skinned apprentice in the adjacent haberdashery to whom he said "good-morning" every morning, and for a period it seemed to him the most significant event in his day. When she said, "I *do* hope it will be fine to-morrow," he felt it marked an epoch. He had had no sisters, and was innately disposed to worship womankind. But he did not betray as much to Platt and Parsons.

To Platt and Parsons he affected an attitude of seasoned depravity towards womankind. Platt and Parsons were his contemporary apprentices in departments of the drapery shop, and the three were drawn together into a close friendship by the fact that all their names began with P. They decided they were the Three Ps, and went about together of an evening with the bearing of desperate dogs. Sometimes, when they had money, they went into public houses and had drinks. Then they would become more desperate than ever, and walk along the pavement under the gas lamps arm in arm singing. Platt had a good tenor voice, and had been in a church choir, and so he led the singing; Parsons had a serviceable bellow, which roared and faded and roared again very wonderfully; Mr. Polly's share was an extraordinary lowing noise, a sort of flat recitative which he called "singing seconds."

They would have sung catches if they had known how to do it, but as it was they sang melancholy music hall songs about dying soldiers and the old folks far away.

They would sometimes go into the quieter residential quarters of Port Burdock, where policemen and other obstacles were infrequent, and really let their voices soar like hawks and feel very happy. The dogs of the district would be stirred to hopeless emulation, and would keep it up for long after the Three Ps had been swallowed up by the night. One jealous brute of an Irish terrier made a gallant attempt to bite Parsons, but was beaten by numbers and solidarity.

The Three Ps took the utmost interest in each other and found no other company so good. They talked about everything in the world, and would go on talking in their dormitory after the gas was out until the other men were reduced to throwing boots; they skulked from their departments in the slack hours of the afternoon to gossip in the packing-room of the warehouse; on Sundays and Bank holidays they went for long walks together, talking.

Platt was white-faced and dark, and disposed to undertones and mystery and a curiosity about society and the *demi-monde*. He kept himself *au courant* by reading a penny paper of infinite suggestion called *Modern Society*. Parsons was of an

19

ampler build, already promising fatness, with curly hair and a lot of rolling, rollicking, curly features, and a large blob-shaped nose. He had a great memory and a real interest in literature. He knew great portions of Shakespeare and Milton by heart, and would recite them at the slightest provocation. He read everything he could get hold of, and if he liked it he read it aloud. It did not matter who else liked it. At first Mr. Polly was disposed to be suspicious of this literature, but was carried away by Parsons' enthusiasm. The Three Ps went to a performance of "Romeo and Juliet" at the Port Burdock Theatre Royal, and hung over the gallery fascinated. After that they made a sort of password of: "Do you bite your thumbs at Us, Sir?"

To which the countersign was: "We bite our thumbs."

For weeks the glory of Shakespeare's Verona lit Mr. Polly's life. He walked as though he carried a sword at his side, and swung a mantle from his shoulders. He went through the grimy streets of Port Burdock with his eye on the first floor windows —looking for balconies. A ladder in the yard flooded his mind with romantic ideas. Then Parsons discovered an Italian writer, whose name Mr. Polly rendered as "Bocashieu," and after some excursions into that author's remains the talk of Parsons became infested with the word "amours," and Mr. Polly would stand in front of his hosiery fixtures trifling with paper and string and thinking of perennial picnics under dark olive trees in the everlasting sunshine of Italy.

And about that time it was that all Three Ps adopted turn-down collars and large, loose, artistic silk ties, which they tied very much on one side and wore with an air of defiance. And a certain swashbuckling carriage.

And then came the glorious revelation of that great Frenchman whom Mr. Polly called "Rabooloose." The Three Ps thought the birth feast of Gargantua the most glorious piece of writing in the world, and I am not certain they were wrong, and on wet Sunday evenings where there was danger of hymn singing they would get Parsons to read it aloud.

Towards the several members of the Y. M. C. A. who shared the dormitory, the Three Ps always maintained a sarcastic and defiant attitude.

"We got a perfect right to do what we like in our corner," Platt maintained. "You do what you like in yours."

"But the language!" objected Morrison, the white-faced, earnest-eyed improver, who was leading a profoundly religious life under great difficulties.

"*Language*, man!" roared Parsons, "why, it's LITERATURE!"

"Sunday isn't the time for Literature."

"It's the only time we've got. And besides ——"

The horrors of religious controversy would begin. . . .

Mr. Polly stuck loyally to the Three Ps, but in the secret places of his heart he was torn. A fire of conviction burnt in Morrison's eyes and spoke in his urgent persuasive voice; he lived the better life manifestly, chaste in word and deed, industrious, studiously kindly. When the junior apprentice had sore feet and homesickness Morrison washed the feet and comforted the heart, and he helped other men to get through with their work when he might have gone early, a superhuman thing to do. Polly was secretly a little afraid to be left alone with this man and the power of the spirit that was in him. He felt watched.

Platt, also struggling with things his mind could not contrive to reconcile, said "that confounded hypocrite."

"He's no hypocrite," said Parsons, "he's no hypocrite, O' Man. But he's got no blessed Joy de Vive; that's what's wrong with him. Let's go down to the Harbour Arms and see some of those blessed old captains getting drunk."

"Short of sugar, O' Man," said Mr. Polly, slapping his trouser pocket.

"Oh, *carm* on," said Parsons. "Always do it on tuppence for a bitter."

"Lemme get my pipe on," said Platt, who had

recently taken to smoking with great ferocity. "Then I'm with you."

Pause and struggle.

"Don't ram it down, O' Man," said Parsons, watching with knitted brows. "Don't ram it down. Give it Air. Seen my stick, O' Man? Right O."

And leaning on his cane he composed himself in an attitude of sympathetic patience towards Platt's incendiary efforts.

–»»   IV   «‹–

Jolly days of companionship they were for the incipient bankrupt on the stile to look back upon.

The interminable working hours of the Bazaar had long since faded from his memory — except for one or two conspicuous rows and one or two larks — but the rare Sundays and holidays shone out like diamonds among pebbles. They shone with the mellow splendour of evening skies reflected in calm water, and athwart them all went old Parsons bellowing an interpretation of life, gesticulating, appreciating and making appreciate, expounding books, talking of that mystery of his, the "Joy de Vive."

There were some particularly splendid walks on Bank holidays. The Three Ps would start on Sunday morning early and find a room in some modest inn and talk themselves asleep, and return singing

23

through the night, or having an "argy bargy" about the stars, on Monday evening. They would come over the hills out of the pleasant English country-side in which they had wandered, and see Port Burdock spread out below, a network of interlacing street lamps and shifting tram lights against the black, beacon-gemmed immensity of the harbour waters.

"Back to the collar, O' Man," Parsons would say. There is no satisfactory plural to O' Man, so he always used it in the singular.

"Don't mention it," said Platt.

And once they got a boat for the whole summer day, and rowed up past the moored ironclads and the black old hulks and the various shipping of the harbour, past a white troopship and past the trim front and the ships and interesting vistas of the dockyard to the shallow channels and rocky weedy wildernesses of the upper harbour. And Parsons and Mr. Polly had a great dispute and quarrel that day as to how far a big gun could shoot.

The country over the hills behind Port Burdock is all that an old-fashioned, scarcely disturbed English country-side should be. In those days the bicycle was still rare and costly and the motor car had yet to come and stir up rural serenities. The Three Ps would take footpaths haphazard across fields, and plunge into unknown winding lanes between high hedges of honeysuckle and dogrose.

24

Greatly daring, they would follow green bridle paths through primrose studded undergrowths, or wander waist deep in the bracken of beech woods. About twenty miles from Port Burdock there came a region of hop gardens and hoast crowned farms, and further on, to be reached only by cheap tickets at Bank Holiday times, was a sterile ridge of very clean roads and red sand pits and pines and gorse and heather. The Three Ps could not afford to buy bicycles and they found boots the greatest item of their skimpy expenditure. They threw appearances to the winds at last and got ready-made working-men's hob-nails. There was much discussion and strong feeling over this step in the dormitory.

There is no country-side like the English country-side for those who have learnt to love it; its firm yet gentle lines of hill and dale, its ordered confusion of features, its deer parks and downland, its castles and stately houses, its hamlets and old churches, its farms and ricks and great barns and ancient trees, its pools and ponds and shining threads of rivers; its flower-starred hedgerows, its orchards and woodland patches, its village greens and kindly inns. Other country-sides have their pleasant aspects, but none such variety, none that shine so steadfastly throughout the year. Picardy is pink and white and pleasant in the blossom time, Burgundy goes on with its sunshine and wide hill-sides and cramped vineyards, a beautiful tune re-

peated and repeated, Italy gives salitas and wayside chapels and chestnuts and olive orchards, the
Ardennes has its woods and gorges — Touraine
and the Rhineland, the wide Campagna with its
distant Apennines, and the neat prosperities and
mountain backgrounds of South Germany, all
clamour their especial merits at one's memory. And
there are the hills and fields of Virginia, like an
England grown very big and slovenly, the woods
and big river sweeps of Pennsylvania, the trim New
England landscape, a little bleak and rather fine
like the New England mind, and the wide rough
country roads and hills and woodland of New York
State. But none of these change scene and character in three miles of walking, nor have so mellow a
sunlight nor so diversified a cloudland, nor confess
the perpetual refreshment of the strong soft winds
that blow from off the sea as our Mother England
does.

It was good for the Three Ps to walk through
such a land and forget for a time that indeed they
had no footing in it all, that they were doomed to
toil behind counters in such places as Port Burdock for the better part of their lives. They would
forget the customers and shopwalkers and department buyers and everything, and become just
happy wanderers in a world of pleasant breezes
and song birds and shady trees.

The arrival at the inn was a great affair. No

one, they were convinced, would take them for
drapers, and there might be a pretty serving girl
or a jolly old lady, or what Parsons called a "bit
of character" drinking in the bar.

There would always be weighty enquiries as to
what they could have, and it would work out always at cold beef and pickles, or fried ham and
eggs and shandygaff, two pints of beer and two
bottles of ginger beer foaming in a huge round-
bellied jug.

The glorious moment of standing lordly in the
inn doorway, and staring out at the world, the
swinging sign, the geese upon the green, the duck-
pond, a waiting waggon, the church tower, a sleepy
cat, the blue heavens, with the sizzle of the frying
audible behind one! The keen smell of the bacon!
The trotting of feet bearing the repast; the click
and clatter as the tableware is finally arranged! A
clean white cloth!

"Ready, Sir!" or "Ready, Gentlemen." Better
hearing that than "Forward Polly! look sharp!"

The going in! The sitting down! The falling to!

"Bread, O' Man?"

"Right O! Don't bag all the crust, O' Man."

Once a simple mannered girl in a pink print
dress stayed and talked with them as they ate; led
by the gallant Parsons they professed to be all des-
perately in love with her, and courted her to say
which she preferred of them, it was so manifest she

did prefer one and so impossible to say which it
was held her there, until a distant maternal voice
called her away. Afterwards as they left the inn
she waylaid them at the orchard corner and gave
them, a little shyly, three keen yellow-green apples
— and wished them to come again some day, and
vanished, and reappeared looking after them as
they turned the corner — waving a white handkerchief. All the rest of that day they disputed over
the signs of her favour, and the next Sunday they
went there again.

But she had vanished, and a mother of forbidding aspect afforded no explanations.

If Platt and Parsons and Mr. Polly live to be a
hundred, they will none of them forget that girl as
she stood with a pink flush upon her, faintly smiling and yet earnest, parting the branches of the
hedgerows and reaching down apple in hand.
Which of them was it, had caught her spirit to attend to them? . . .

And once they went along the coast, following it
as closely as possible, and so came at last to Foxbourne, that easternmost suburb of Brayling and
Hampsted-on-the-Sea.

Foxbourne seemed a very jolly little place to
Mr. Polly that afternoon. It has a clean sandy
beach instead of the mud and pebbles and coaly de-
filements of Port Burdock, a row of six bathing
machines, and a shelter on the parade in which the

Three Ps sat after a satisfying but rather expensive lunch that had included celery. Rows of verandahed villas proffered apartments, they had feasted in an hotel with a porch painted white and gay with geraniums above, and the High Street with the old church at the head had been full of an agreeable afternoon stillness.

"Nice little place for business," said Platt sagely from behind his big pipe.

It stuck in Mr. Polly's memory.

→» V «←

MR. POLLY was not so picturesque a youth as Parsons. He lacked richness in his voice, and went about in those days with his hands in his pockets looking quietly speculative.

He specialised in slang and the disuse of English, and he played the rôle of an appreciative stimulant to Parsons. Words attracted him curiously, words rich in suggestion, and he loved a novel and striking phrase. His school training had given him little or no mastery of the mysterious pronunciation of English and no confidence in himself. His schoolmaster indeed had been both unsound and variable. New words had terror and fascination for him; he did not acquire them, he could not avoid them, and so he plunged into them. His only rule was not to be misled by the spelling. That

29

was no guide anyhow. He avoided every recognised phrase in the language and mispronounced everything in order that he shouldn't be suspected of ignorance, but whim.

"Sesquippledan," he would say. "Sesquippledan verboojuice."

"Eh?" said Platt.

"Eloquent Rapsodooce."

"Where?" asked Platt.

"In the warehouse, O' Man. All among the table-cloths and blankets. Carlyle. He's reading aloud. Doing the High Froth. Spuming! Windmilling! Waw, waw! It's a sight worth seeing. He'll bark his blessed knuckles one of these days on the fixtures, O' Man."

He held an imaginary book in one hand and waved an eloquent gesture. "So too shall every Hero inasmuch as notwithstanding for evermore come back to Reality," he parodied the enthusiastic Parsons, "so that in fashion and thereby, upon things and not *under* things articulariously He stands."

"I should laugh if the Governor dropped on him," said Platt. "He'd never hear him coming."

"The O' Man's drunk with it — fair drunk," said Polly. "*I* never did. It's worse than when he got on to Raboloose."

CHAPTER
THE SECOND

THE DISMISSAL OF

PARSONS

THE DISMISSAL OF PARSONS

→»» I «←

SUDDENLY Parsons got himself dismissed.

He got himself dismissed under circumstances of peculiar violence, that left a deep impression on Mr. Polly's mind. He wondered about it for years afterwards, trying to get the rights of the case.

Parsons' apprenticeship was over; he had reached the status of an Improver, and he dressed the window of the Manchester department. By all the standards available he dressed it very well. By his own standards he dressed it wonderfully. "Well, O' Man," he used to say, "there's one thing about my position here, — I *can* dress a window."

And when trouble was under discussion he would hold that "little Fluffums" — which was the apprentices' name for Mr. Garvace, the senior partner and managing director of the Bazaar — would think twice before he got rid of the only man in the

33

place who could make a windowful of Manchester goods *tell*.

Then like many a fellow artist he fell a prey to theories.

"The art of window dressing is in its infancy, O' Man — in its blooming Infancy. All balance and stiffness like a blessed Egyptian picture. No Joy in it, no blooming Joy! Conventional. A shop window ought to get hold of people, *grip* 'em as they go along. It stands to reason. Grip!"

His voice would sink to a kind of quiet bellow. "*Do* they grip?"

Then after a pause, a savage roar; "*Naw!*"

"He's got a Heavy on," said Mr. Polly. "Go it, O' Man; let's have some more of it."

"Look at old Morrison's dress-stuff windows! Tidy, tasteful, correct, I grant you, but Bleak!" He let out the word reinforced to a shout; "Bleak!"

"Bleak!" echoed Mr. Polly.

"Just pieces of stuff in rows, rows of tidy little puffs, perhaps one bit just unrolled, quiet tickets."

"Might as well be in church, O' Man," said Mr. Polly.

"A window ought to be exciting," said Parsons; "it ought to make you say: El-*lo!* when you see it."

He paused, and Platt watched him over a snorting pipe.

"Rockcockyo," said Mr. Polly.

"We want a new school of window dressing,"

said Parsons, regardless of the comment. "A New School! The Port Burdock school. Day after to-morrow I change the Fitzallan Street stuff. This time, it's going to be a change. I mean to have a crowd or bust!"

And as a matter of fact he did both.

His voice dropped to a note of self-reproach. "I've been timid, O' Man. I've been holding myself in. I haven't done myself Justice. I've kept down the simmering, seething, teeming ideas. . . . All that's over now."

"Over," gulped Polly.

"Over for good and all, O' Man."

≫ II ≪

PLATT came to Polly, who was sorting up collar boxes. "O' Man's doing his Blooming Window."

"What window?"

"What he said."

Polly remembered.

He went on with his collar boxes with his eye on his senior, Mansfield. Mansfield was presently called away to the counting house, and instantly Polly shot out by the street door, and made a rapid transit along the street front past the Manchester window, and so into the silkroom door. He could not linger long, but he gathered joy, a swift and fearful joy, from his brief inspection of Parsons' unconscious back. Parsons had his tail coat off and was working with vigour; his habit of pulling his waistcoat straps to the utmost brought out all the agreeable promise of corpulence in his youthful frame. He was blowing excitedly and running his fingers through his hair, and then moving with all the swift eagerness of a man inspired. All about his feet and knees were scarlet blankets, not folded, not formally unfolded, but — the only phrase is — shied about. And a great bar sinister of roller towelling stretched across the front of the window on which was a ticket, and the ticket said in bold black letters: "LOOK!"

So soon as Mr. Polly got into the silk department and met Platt he knew he had not lingered nearly long enough outside. "Did you see the boards at the back?" said Platt.

He hadn't. "The High Egrugious is fairly On," he said, and dived down to return by devious subterranean routes to the outfitting department.

Presently the street door opened and Platt, with an air of intense devotion to business assumed to cover his adoption of that unusual route, came in and made for the staircase down to the warehouse. He rolled up his eyes at Polly. "Oh *Lor!*" he said and vanished.

Irresistible curiosity seized Polly. Should he go through the shop to the Manchester department, or risk a second transit outside?

He was impelled to make a dive at the street door.

"Where are you going?" asked Mansfield.

"Lill Dog," said Polly with an air of lucid explanation, and left him to get any meaning he could from it.

Parsons was worth the subsequent trouble. Parsons really was extremely rich. This time Polly stopped to take it in.

Parsons had made a huge symmetrical pile of thick white and red blankets twisted and rolled to accentuate their woolly richness, heaped up in a warm disorder, with large window tickets inscribed in blazing red letters: "Cosy Comfort at Cut Prices," and "Curl up and Cuddle below Cost." Regardless of the daylight he had turned up the electric light on that side of the window to reflect a warm glow upon the heap, and behind, in pursuit of contrasted bleakness, he was now hanging long strips of grey silesia and chilly coloured linen dusterings.

It was wonderful, but —

Mr. Polly decided that it was time he went in. He found Platt in the silk department, apparently on the verge of another plunge into the exterior world. "Cosy Comfort at Cut Prices," said Polly. "Allittritions Artful Aid."

He did not dare go into the street for the third time, and he was hovering feverishly near the window when he saw the governor, Mr. Garvace, that is to say, the managing director of the Bazaar, walking along the pavement after his manner to assure himself all was well with the establishment he guided.

Mr. Garvace was a short stout man, with that air of modest pride that so often goes with corpulence, choleric and decisive in manner, and with hands that looked like bunches of fingers. He was red-haired and ruddy, and after the custom of such complexions, hairs sprang from the tip of his nose. When he wished to bring the power of the human eye to bear upon an assistant, he projected his chest, knitted one brow and partially closed the left eyelid.

An expression of speculative wonder overspread the countenance of Mr. Polly. He felt he must *see*. Yes, whatever happened he must *see*.

"Want to speak to Parsons, Sir," he said to Mr. Mansfield, and deserted his post hastily, dashed through the intervening departments and was in position behind a pile of Bolton sheeting as the governor came in out of the street.

"What on Earth do you think you are doing with that window, Parsons?" began Mr. Garvace.

Only the legs of Parsons and the lower part of his waistcoat and an intervening inch of shirt were visible. He was standing inside the window on the steps, hanging up the last strip of his background from the brass rail along the ceiling. Within, the Manchester shop window was cut off by a partition rather like the partition of an old-fashioned church pew from the general space of the shop. There was a panelled barrier, that is to say, with a little door like a pew door in it. Parsons' face appeared, staring with round eyes at his employer.

Mr. Garvace had to repeat his question.

"Dressing it, Sir — on new lines."

"Come out of it," said Mr. Garvace.

Parsons stared, and Mr. Garvace had to repeat his command.

Parsons, with a dazed expression, began to descend the steps slowly.

Mr. Garvace turned about. "Where's Morrison? Morrison!"

Morrison appeared.

"Take this window over," said Mr. Garvace pointing his bunch of fingers at Parsons. "Take all this muddle out and dress it properly."

Morrison advanced and hesitated.

"I beg your pardon, Sir," said Parsons with an immense politeness, "but this is *my* window."

"Take it all out," said Mr. Garvace, turning away.

Morrison advanced. Parsons shut the door with a click that arrested Mr. Garvace.

"Come out of that window," he said. "You can't

dress it. If you want to play the fool with a window——"

"This window's All Right," said the genius in window dressing, and there was a little pause.

"Open the door and go right in," said Mr. Garvace to Morrison.

"You leave that door alone, Morrison," said Parsons.

Polly was no longer even trying to hide behind the stack of Bolton sheetings. He realised he was in the presence of forces too stupendous to heed him.

"Get him out," said Mr. Garvace.

Morrison seemed to be thinking out the ethics of his position. The idea of loyalty to his employer prevailed with him. He laid his hand on the door to open it; Parsons tried to disengage his hand. Mr. Garvace joined his effort to Morrison's. Then the heart of Polly leapt and the world blazed up to wonder and splendour. Parsons disappeared behind the partition for a moment and reappeared instantly, gripping a thin cylinder of rolled huckaback. With this he smote at Morrison's head. Morrison's head ducked under the resounding impact, but he clung on and so did Mr. Garvace. The door came open, and then Mr. Garvace was staggering back, hand to head; his autocratic, his sacred baldness, smitten. Parsons was beyond all control—a strangeness, a marvel. Heaven knows

40

how the artistic struggle had strained that richly endowed temperament. "Say I can't dress a window, you thundering old Humbug," he said, and hurled the huckaback at his master. He followed this up by hurling first a blanket, then an armful of silesia, then a window support out of the window into the shop. It leapt into Polly's mind that Parsons hated his own effort and was glad to demolish it. For a crowded second Polly's mind was concentrated upon Parsons, infuriated, active, like a figure of earthquake with its coat off, shying things headlong.

Then he perceived the back of Mr. Garvace and heard his gubernatorial voice crying to no one in particular and everybody in general: "Get him out of the window. He's mad. He's dangerous. Get him out of the window."

Then a crimson blanket was for a moment over the head of Mr. Garvace, and his voice, muffled for an instant, broke out into unwonted expletive.

Then people had arrived from all parts of the Bazaar. Luck, the ledger clerk, blundered against Polly and said, "Help him!" Somerville from the silks vaulted the counter, and seized a chair by the back. Polly lost his head. He clawed at the Bolton sheeting before him, and if he could have detached a piece he would certainly have hit somebody with it. As it was he simply upset the pile. It fell away from Polly, and he had an impression of somebody

41

squeaking as it went down. It was the sort of impression one disregards. The collapse of the pile of goods just sufficed to end his subconscious efforts to get something to hit somebody with, and his whole attention focussed itself upon the struggle in the window. For a splendid instant Parsons towered up over the active backs that clustered about the shop window door, an active whirl of gesture, tearing things down and throwing them, and then he went under. There was an instant's furious struggle, a crash, a second crash and the crack of broken plate glass. Then a stillness and heavy breathing.

Parsons was overpowered. . . .

Polly, stepping over scattered pieces of Bolton sheeting, saw his transfigured friend with a dark cut, that was not at present bleeding, on the forehead, one arm held by Somerville and the other by Morrison.

"You — you — you — you annoyed me," said Parsons, sobbing for breath.

⇒⇒ III ⇐⇐

THERE are events that detach themselves from the general stream of occurrences and seem to partake of the nature of revelations. Such was this Parsons affair. It began by seeming grotesque; it ended disconcertingly. The fabric of Mr. Polly's daily life was torn, and beneath it he discovered depths and terrors.

Life was not altogether a lark.

The calling in of a policeman seemed at the moment a pantomime touch. But when it became manifest that Mr. Garvace was in a fury of vindictiveness, the affair took on a different complexion. The way in which the policeman made a note of everything and aspirated nothing impressed the sensitive mind of Polly profoundly. Polly presently found himself straightening up ties to the refrain of " 'E then 'It you on the 'Ed and——"

In the dormitory that night Parsons had become heroic. He sat on the edge of the bed with his head bandaged, packing very slowly and insisting over and again: "He ought to have left my window alone, O' Man. He didn't ought to have touched my window."

Polly was to go to the police court in the morning as a witness. The terror of that ordeal almost overshadowed the tragic fact that Parsons was not only summoned for assault, but "swapped," and packing his box. Polly knew himself well enough to know he would make a bad witness. He felt sure of one fact only, namely, that " 'E then 'It 'Im on the 'Ed and——" All the rest danced about in his mind now, and how it would dance about on the morrow Heaven only knew. Would there be a cross-examination? Is it perjoocery to make a slip? People did sometimes perjuice themselves. Serious offence.

Platt was doing his best to help Parsons, and inciting public opinion against Morrison. But Parsons would not hear of anything against Morrison. "He was all right, O' Man — according to his lights," said Parsons. "It isn't him I complain of."

He speculated on the morrow. "I shall 'ave to pay a fine," he said. "No good trying to get out of it. It's true I hit him. I hit him" — he paused and seemed to be seeking an exquisite accuracy. His voice sank to a confidential note; — "On the head — about here."

He answered the suggestion of a bright junior apprentice in a corner of the dormitory. "What's the Good of a Cross summons?" he replied; "with old Corks, the chemist, and Mottishead, the house agent, and all that lot on the Bench? Humble Pie, that's my meal to-morrow, O' Man. Humble Pie."

Packing went on for a time.

"But Lord! what a Life it is!" said Parsons, giving his deep notes scope. "Ten-thirty-five a man trying to do his Duty, mistaken perhaps, but trying his best; ten-forty — Ruined! Ruined!" He lifted his voice to a shout. "Ruined!" and dropped it to "Like an earthquake."

"Heated altaclation," said Polly.

"Like a blooming earthquake!" said Parsons, with the notes of a rising wind.

He meditated gloomily upon his future and a

colder chill invaded Polly's mind. "Likely to get another crib, ain't I—with assaulted the guvnor on my reference. I suppose, though, he won't give me refs. Hard enough to get a crib at the best of times," said Parsons.

"You ought to go round with a show, O' Man," said Mr. Polly.

Things were not so dreadful in the police court as Mr. Polly had expected. He was given a seat with other witnesses against the wall of the court, and after an interesting larceny case Parsons appeared and stood, not in the dock, but at the table. By that time Mr. Polly's legs, which had been tucked up at first under his chair out of respect to the court, were extended straight before him and his hands were in his trouser pockets. He was inventing names for the four magistrates on the bench, and had got to "the Grave and Reverend Signor with the palatial Boko," when his thoughts were recalled to gravity by the sound of his name. He rose with alacrity and was fielded by an expert policeman from a brisk attempt to get into the vacant dock. The clerk to the Justices repeated the oath with incredible rapidity.

"Right O," said Mr. Polly, but quite respectfully, and kissed the book.

His evidence was simple and quite audible after one warning from the superintendent of police to "speak up." He tried to put in a good word for

Parsons by saying he was "naturally of a choleraic disposition," but the start and the slow grin of enjoyment upon the face of the grave and Reverend Signor with the palatial Boko suggested that the word was not so good as he had thought it. The rest of the bench was frankly puzzled and there were hasty consultations.

"You mean 'E 'As a 'Ot temper," said the presiding magistrate.

"I mean 'E 'As a 'Ot temper," replied Polly, magically incapable of aspirates for the moment.

"You don't mean 'E ketches cholera."

"I mean — he's easily put out."

"Then why can't you say so?" said the presiding magistrate.

Parsons was bound over.

He came for his luggage while every one was in the shop, and Garvace would not let him invade the business to say good-by. When Mr. Polly went upstairs for margarine and bread and tea, he slipped on into the dormitory at once to see what was happening further in the Parsons case. But Parsons had vanished. There was no Parsons, no trace of Parsons. His cubicle was swept and garnished. For the first time in his life Polly had a sense of irreparable loss.

A minute or so after Platt dashed in.

"Ugh!" he said, and then discovered Polly.

Polly was leaning out of the window and did not look around. Platt went up to him.

"He's gone already," said Platt. "Might have stopped to say good-by to a chap."

There was a little pause before Polly replied. He thrust his finger into his mouth and gulped.

"Bit on that beastly tooth of mine," he said, still not looking at Platt. "It's made my eyes water, something chronic. Any one might think I'd been doing a blooming Pipe, by the look of me."

CHAPTER
THE THIRD

CRIBS

CRIBS

→»» I «←

PORT BURDOCK was never the same place for Mr.
Polly after Parsons had left it. There were no
chest notes in his occasional letters, and little of
the "Joy de Vive" got through by them. Parsons
had gone, he said, to London, and found a place
as warehouseman in a cheap outfitting shop near
St. Paul's Churchyard, where references were not
required. It became apparent as time passed that
new interests were absorbing him. He wrote of so-
cialism and the rights of man, things that had no
appeal for Mr. Polly. He felt strangers had got
hold of his Parsons, were at work upon him, making him into someone else, something less picturesque. . . . Port Burdock became a dreariness full
of faded memories of Parsons and work a bore.
Platt revealed himself alone as a tiresome compan-
ion, obsessed by romantic ideas about intrigues and
vices and "society women."

51

Mr. Polly's depression manifested itself in a general slackness. A certain impatience in the manner of Mr. Garvace presently got upon his nerves. Relations were becoming strained. He asked for a rise of salary to test his position, and gave notice to leave when it was refused.

It took him two months to place himself in another situation, and during that time he had quite a disagreeable amount of loneliness, disappointment, anxiety and humiliation.

He went at first to stay with a married cousin who had a house at Easewood. His widowed father had recently given up the music and bicycle shop (with the post of organist at the parish church) that had sustained his home, and was living upon a small annuity as a guest with this cousin, and growing a little tiresome on account of some mysterious internal discomfort that the local practitioner diagnosed as imagination. He had aged with mysterious rapidity and become excessively irritable, but the cousin's wife was a born manager, and contrived to get along with him. Our Mr. Polly's status was that of a guest pure and simple, but after a fortnight of congested hospitality in which he wrote nearly a hundred letters beginning:

Sir:

Referring to your advt. in the "Christian World" for an improver in Gents' outfitting I beg

*to submit myself for the situation. Have had six
years' experience.* . . .

and upset a bottle of ink over a toilet cover and
the bedroom carpet, his cousin took him for a walk
and pointed out the superior advantages of apartments in London from which to swoop upon the
briefly yawning vacancy.

"Helpful," said Mr. Polly; "very helpful, O'
Man indeed. I might have gone on there for
weeks," and packed.

He got a room in an institution that was partly
a benevolent hostel for men in his circumstances
and partly a high minded but forbidding coffee
house and a centre for pleasant Sunday afternoons.
Mr. Polly spent a critical but pleasant Sunday
afternoon in a back seat, inventing such phrases
as:

"Soulful Owner of the Exorbiant Largenial Development." — An Adam's Apple being in question.

"Earnest Joy."

"Exultant, Urgent Loogoobuosity."

A manly young curate, marking and misunder-
standing his preoccupied face and moving lips,
came and sat by him and entered into conversation
with the idea of making him feel more at home.
The conversation was awkward and disconnected
for a minute or so, and then suddenly a memory of
the Port Burdock Bazaar occurred to Mr. Polly,

and with a baffling whisper of "Lill' dog," and a reassuring nod, he rose up and escaped, to wander out relieved and observant into the varied London streets.

He found the collection of men he found waiting about in wholesale establishments in Wood Street and St. Paul's Churchyard (where they interview the buyers who have come up from the country) interesting and stimulating, but far too strongly charged with the suggestion of his own fate to be really joyful. There were men in all degrees between confidence and distress, and in every stage between extravagant smartness and the last stages of decay. There were sunny young men full of an abounding and elbowing energy, before whom the soul of Polly sank in hate and dismay. "Smart Juniors," said Polly to himself, "full of Smart Juniosity. The Shoveacious Cult." There were hungry looking individuals of thirty-five or so that he decided must be "Proletelerians" — he had often wanted to find someone who fitted that attractive word. Middle-aged men, "too Old at Forty," discoursed in the waiting-rooms on the outlook in the trade; it had never been so bad, they said, while Mr. Polly wondered if "De-juiced" was a permissible epithet. There were men with an overweening sense of their importance, manifestly annoyed and angry to find themselves still disengaged, and inclined to suspect a plot, and men so faint-hearted

54

one was terrified to imagine their behaviour when
it came to an interview. There was a fresh-faced
young man with an unintelligent face who seemed
to think himself equipped against the world beyond all misadventure by a collar of exceptional
height, and another who introduced a note of gaiety by wearing a flannel shirt and a check suit of
remarkable virulence. Every day Mr. Polly looked
round to mark how many of the familiar faces had
gone, and the deepening anxiety (reflecting his
own) on the faces that remained, and every day
some new type joined the drifting shoal. He realised how small a chance his poor letter from Easewood ran against this hungry cluster of competi-
tors at the fountain head.

At the back of Mr. Polly's mind while he made
his observations was a disagreeable flavour of dentist's parlour. At any moment his name might be
shouted, and he might have to haul himself into the
presence of some fresh specimen of employer, and
to repeat once more his passionate protestation of
interest in the business, his possession of a capacity for zeal — zeal on behalf of anyone who would
pay him a yearly salary of twenty-six pounds a
year.

The prospective employer would unfold his
ideals of the employee. "I want a smart, willing
young man, thoroughly willing — who won't object to take trouble. I don't want a slacker, the

sort of fellow who has to be pushed up to his work
and held there. I've got no use for him."

At the back of Mr. Polly's mind, and quite beyond his control, the insubordinate phrasemaker
would be proffering such combinations as "Chubby
Chops," or "Chubby Charmer," as suitable for the
gentleman, very much as a hat salesman proffers
hats.

"I don't think you'd find much slackness about
me, sir," said Mr. Polly brightly, trying to disregard his deeper self.

"I want a young man who means getting on."

"Exactly, sir. Excelsior."

"I beg your pardon?"

"I said excelsior, sir. It's a sort of motto of mine.
From Longfellow. Would you want me to serve
through?"

The chubby gentleman explained and reverted
to his ideals, with a faint air of suspicion. "Do *you*
mean getting on?" he asked.

"I hope so, sir," said Mr. Polly.

"Get on or get out, eh?"

Mr. Polly made a rapturous noise, nodded appreciation, and said indistinctly: "*Quite* my style."

"Some of my people have been with me twenty
years," said the employer. "My Manchester buyer
came to me as a boy of twelve. You're a Christian?"

"Church of England," said Mr. Polly.

"H'm," said the employer a little checked. "For

good all round business work I should have preferred a Baptist. Still——"

He studied Mr. Polly's tie, which was severely
neat and businesslike, as became an aspiring outfitter. Mr. Polly's conception of his own pose and
expression was rendered by that uncontrollable
phrasemonger at the back as "Obsequies Defer-
ence."

"I am inclined," said the prospective employer
in a conclusive manner, "to look up your reference."

Mr. Polly stood up abruptly.

"Thank you," said the employer and dismissed
him.

"Chump chops! How about chump chops?" said
the phrasemonger with an air of inspiration.

"I hope then to hear from you, sir," said Mr.
Polly in his best salesman manner.

"If everything is satisfactory," said the prospective employer.

⇒ II ⇐

A MAN whose brain devotes its hinterland to making odd phrases and nicknames out of ill-conceived
words, whose conception of life is a lump of aurif-
erous rock to which all the value is given by rare
veins of unbusinesslike joy, who reads Boccaccio
and Rabelais and Shakespeare with gusto, and

uses "Stertoraneous Shover" and "Smart Junior" as terms of bitterest opprobrium, is not likely to make a great success under modern business conditions. Mr. Polly dreamt always of picturesque and mellow things, and had an instinctive hatred of the strenuous life. He would have resisted the spell of ex-President Roosevelt, or General Baden Powell, or Mr. Peter Keary, or the late Dr. Samuel Smiles, quite easily; and he loved Falstaff and Hudibras and coarse laughter, and the old England of Washington Irving and the memory of Charles the Second's courtly days. His progress was necessarily slow. He did not get rises; he lost situations; there was something in his eye employers did not like; he would have lost his places oftener if he had not been at times an exceptionally brilliant salesman, rather carefully neat, and a slow but very fair window-dresser.

He went from situation to situation, he invented a great wealth of nicknames, he conceived enmities and made friends—but none so richly satisfying as Parsons. He was frequently but mildly and discursively in love, and sometimes he thought of that girl who had given him a yellow-green apple. He had an idea, amounting to a flattering certainty, whose youthful freshness it was had stirred her to self-forgetfulness. And sometimes he thought of Foxbourne sleeping prosperously in the sun. And he began to have moods of discomfort and lassitude and ill-temper due to the beginnings of indigestion.

Various forces and suggestions came into his life and swayed him for longer and shorter periods.

He went to Canterbury and came under the influence of Gothic architecture. There was a blood affinity between Mr. Polly and the Gothic; in the middle ages he would no doubt have sat upon a scaffolding and carved out penetrating and none too flattering portraits of church dignitaries upon the capitals, and when he strolled, with his hands behind his back, along the cloisters behind the cathedral, and looked at the rich grass plot in the centre, he had the strangest sense of being at home — far more than he had ever been at home before. "Portly capons," he used to murmur to himself, under the impression that he was naming a characteristic type of medieval churchman.

He liked to sit in the nave during the service, and look through the great gates at the candles and choristers, and listen to the organ-sustained voices, but the transepts he never penetrated because of the charge for admission. The music and the long vista of the fretted roof filled him with a vague and mystical happiness that he had no words, even mispronounceable words, to express. But some of the smug monuments in the aisles got a wreath of epithets: "Metrorious urnfuls," "funererial claims," "dejected angelosity," for ex-

ample. He wandered about the precincts and speculated about the people who lived in the ripe and
cosy houses of grey stone that cluster there so
comfortably. Through green doors in high stone
walls he caught glimpses of level lawns and blazing
flower beds; mullioned windows revealed shaded
reading lamps and disciplined shelves of brown
bound books. Now and then a dignitary in gaiters
would pass him, "Portly capon," or a drift of
white-robed choir boys cross a distant arcade and
vanish in a doorway, or the pink and cream of
some girlish dress flit like a butterfly across the
cool still spaces of the place. Particularly he responded to the ruined arches of the Benedictine's
Infirmary and the view of Bell Harry tower from
the school buildings. He was stirred to read the
Canterbury Tales, but he could not get on with
Chaucer's old-fashioned English; it fatigued his
attention, and he would have given all the story
telling very readily for a few adventures on the
road. He wanted these nice people to live more and
yarn less. He liked the Wife of Bath very much.
He would have liked to have known that woman.

At Canterbury, too, he first to his knowledge
saw Americans.

His shop did a good class trade in Westgate
Street, and he would see them go by on the way
to stare at Chaucer's "Chequers," and then turn
down Mercery Lane to Prior Goldstone's gate. It

impressed him that they were always in a kind of quiet hurry, and very determined and methodical people,—much more so than any English he knew.

"Cultured Rapacicity," he tried.

"Vorocious Return to the Heritage."

He would expound them incidentally to his attendant apprentices. He had overheard a little lady putting her view to a friend near the Christchurch gate. The accent and intonation had hung in his memory, and he would reproduce them more or less accurately. "Now does this Marlowe monument really and truly *matter?*" he had heard the little lady enquire. "We've no time for side shows and second rate stunts, Mamie. We want just the Big Simple Things of the place, just the Broad Elemental Canterbury praposition. What is it saying to us? I want to get right hold of that, and then have tea in the very room that Chaucer did, and hustle to get that four-eighteen train back to London."

He would go over these precious phrases, finding them full of an indescribable flavour. "Just the Broad Elemental Canterbury praposition," he would repeat. . . .

He would try to imagine Parsons confronted with Americans. For his own part he knew himself to be altogether inadequate. . . .

Canterbury was the most congenial situation

Mr. Polly ever found during these wander years, albeit a very desert so far as companionship went.

→»» III «←

IT WAS after Canterbury that the universe became really disagreeable to Mr. Polly. It was brought home to him, not so much vividly as with a harsh and ungainly insistence, that he was a failure in his trade. It was not the trade he ought to have chosen, though what trade he ought to have chosen was by no means clear.

He made great but irregular efforts and produced a forced smartness that, like a cheap dye, refused to stand sunshine. He acquired a sort of parsimony also, in which acquisition he was helped by one or two phases of absolute impecuniosity. But he was hopeless in competition against the naturally gifted, the born hustlers, the young men who meant to get on.

He left the Canterbury place very regretfully. He and another commercial gentleman took a boat one Sunday afternoon at Sturry-on-the-Stour, when the wind was in the west, and sailed it very happily eastward for an hour. They had never sailed a boat before and it seemed simple and wonderful. When they turned they found the river too narrow for tacking and the tide running out like a sluice. They battled back to Sturry in the course of six hours (at a shilling the first hour and sixpence for each hour afterwards) rowing a mile in an hour and a half or so, until the turn of the tide came to help them, and then they had a night walk to Canterbury, and found themselves remorselessly locked out.

The Canterbury employer was an amiable, religious-spirited man and he would probably not have dismissed Mr. Polly if that unfortunate tendency to phrase things had not shocked him. "A Tide's a Tide, Sir," said Mr. Polly, feeling that things were not so bad. "I've no lune-attic power to alter that."

It proved impossible to explain to the Canterbury employer that this was not a highly disrespectful and blasphemous remark.

"And besides, what good are you to me this morning, do you think?" said the Canterbury employer, "with your arms pulled out of their sockets?"

So Mr. Polly resumed his observations in the Wood Street warehouses once more, and had some dismal times. The shoal of fish waiting for the crumbs of employment seemed larger than ever.

He took counsel with himself. Should he "chuck" the outfitting? It wasn't any good for him now, and presently when he was older and his youthful smartness had passed into the dulness of middle age it would be worse. What else could he do?

He could think of nothing. He went one night to a music hall and developed a vague idea of a comic performance; the comic men seemed violent rowdies and not at all funny; but when he thought of the great pit of the audience yawning before him he realised that his was an altogether too delicate talent for such a use. He was impressed by the charm of selling vegetables by auction in one of those open shops near London Bridge, but admitted upon reflection his general want of technical knowledge. He made some enquiries about emigration, but none of the colonies were in want of shop assistants without capital. He kept up his attendance in Wood Street.

He subdued his ideal of salary by the sum of five pounds a year, and was taken at that into a driving establishment in Clapham, which dealt chiefly in ready-made suits, fed its assistants in an underground dining-room and kept them until twelve on Saturdays. He found it hard to be cheerful there. His fits of indigestion became worse, and he began to lie awake at night and think. Sunshine and laughter seemed things lost for ever; picnics and shouting in the moonlight.

The chief shopwalker took a dislike to him and nagged him. "Nar then Polly!" "Look alive Polly!" became the burthen of his days. "As smart a chap as you could have," said the chief shopwalker, "but no *Zest*. No *Zest!* No *Vim!* What's the matter with you?"

During his night vigils Mr. Polly had a feeling— A young rabbit must have very much the feeling, when after a youth of gambolling in sunny woods and furtive jolly raids upon the growing wheat and exciting triumphant bolts before ineffectual casual dogs, it finds itself at last for a long night of floundering effort and perplexity, in a net — for the rest of its life.

He could not grasp what was wrong with him. He made enormous efforts to diagnose his case. Was he really just a "lazy slacker" who ought to "buck up"? He couldn't find it in him to believe it. He blamed his father a good deal — it is what fathers are for — in putting him to a trade he wasn't happy to follow, but he found it impossible to say what he ought to have followed. He felt there had been something stupid about his school, but just where that came in he couldn't say. He made some perfectly sincere efforts to "buck up" and "shove" ruthlessly. But that was infernal — impossible. He had to admit himself miserable with all the misery of a social misfit, and with no clear prospect of more than the most incidental happiness ahead of him. And for all his attempts at self-reproach or self-discipline he felt at bottom that he wasn't at fault.

As a matter of fact all the elements of his troubles had been adequately diagnosed by a certain high-browed, spectacled gentleman living at Highbury, wearing a gold pince-nez, and writing for the most part in the beautiful library of the Reform Club. This gentleman did not know Mr. Polly personally, but he had dealt with him generally as "one of those ill-adjusted units that abound in a society that has failed to develop a collective intelligence and a collective will for order, commensurate with its complexities."

But phrases of that sort had no appeal for Mr. Polly.

CHAPTER
THE FOURTH

MR. POLLY AN ORPHAN

MR. POLLY AN ORPHAN

⇒⇒⇒ I ⇐⇐⇐

THEN a great change was brought about in the life of Mr. Polly by the death of his father. His father had died suddenly — the local practitioner still clung to his theory that it was imagination he suffered from, but compromised in the certificate with the appendicitis that was then so fashionable — and Mr. Polly found himself heir to a debateable number of pieces of furniture in the house of his cousin near Easewood Junction, a family Bible, an engraved portrait of Garibaldi and a bust of Mr. Gladstone, an invalid gold watch, a gold locket formerly belonging to his mother, some minor jewelry and bric-a-brac, a quantity of nearly valueless old clothes and an insurance policy and money in the bank amounting altogether to the sum of three hundred and ninety-five pounds.

Mr. Polly had always regarded his father as an

immortal, as an eternal fact, and his father being
of a reserved nature in his declining years had said
nothing about the insurance policy. Both wealth
and bereavement therefore took Mr. Polly by surprise and found him a little inadequate. His mother's death had been a childish grief and long forgotten, and the strongest affection in his life had
been for Parsons. An only child of sociable tenden-
cies necessarily turns his back a good deal upon
home, and the aunt who had succeeded his mother
was an economist and furniture polisher, a knuckle
rapper and sharp silencer, no friend for a slovenly
little boy. He had loved other little boys and girls
transitorily, none had been frequent and familiar
enough to strike deep roots in his heart, and he
had grown up with a tattered and dissipated affectionateness that was becoming wildly shy. His father had always been a stranger, an irritable stranger with exceptional powers of intervention and
comment, and an air of being disappointed about
his offspring. It was shocking to lose him; it was
like an unexpected hole in the universe, and the
writing of "Death" upon the sky, but it did not
tear Mr. Polly's heartstrings at first so much as
rouse him to a pitch of vivid attention.

He came down to the cottage at Easewood in response to an urgent telegram, and found his father
already dead. His cousin Johnson received him
with much solemnity and ushered him upstairs, to

look at a stiff, straight, shrouded form, with a face unwontedly quiet and, as it seemed, with its pinched nostrils, scornful.

"Looks peaceful," said Mr. Polly, disregarding the scorn to the best of his ability.

"It was a merciful relief," said Mr. Johnson.

There was a pause.

"Second — Second Departed I've ever seen. Not counting mummies," said Mr. Polly, feeling it necessary to say something.

"We did all we could."

"No doubt of it, O' Man," said Mr. Polly.

A second long pause followed, and then, much to Mr. Polly's great relief, Johnson moved towards the door.

Afterwards Mr. Polly went for a solitary walk in the evening light, and as he walked, suddenly his dead father became real to him. He thought of things far away down the perspective of memory, of jolly moments when his father had skylarked with a wildly excited little boy, of a certain annual visit to the Crystal Palace pantomime, full of trivial glittering incidents and wonders, of his father's dread back while customers were in the old, minutely known shop. It is curious that the memory which seemed to link him nearest to the dead man was the memory of a fit of passion. His father had wanted to get a small sofa up the narrow winding staircase from the little room behind the shop to

71

the bedroom above, and it had jammed. For a time
his father had coaxed, and then groaned like a soul
in torment and given way to blind fury, had sworn,
kicked and struck at the offending piece of furniture and finally wrenched it upstairs, with considerable incidental damage to lath and plaster and
one of the castors. That moment when self-control
was altogether torn aside, the shocked discovery
of his father's perfect humanity, had left a singular impression on Mr. Polly's queer mind. It was
as if something extravagantly vital had come out
of his father and laid a warmly passionate hand
upon his heart. He remembered that now very vividly, and it became a clue to endless other memories
that had else been dispersed and confusing.

A weakly wilful being struggling to get obdu-
rate things round impossible corners — in that
symbol Mr. Polly could recognise himself and all
the trouble of humanity.

He hadn't had a particularly good time, poor
old chap, and now it was all over. Finished. . . .

Johnson was the sort of man who derives great
satisfaction from a funeral, a melancholy, serious,
practical-minded man of five and thirty, with great
powers of advice. He was the up-line ticket clerk
at Easewood Junction, and felt the responsibilities
of his position. He was naturally thoughtful and
reserved, and greatly sustained in that by an innate rectitude of body and an overhanging and

forward inclination of the upper part of his face
and head. He was pale but freckled, and his dark
grey eyes were deeply set. His lightest interest was
cricket, but he did not take that lightly. His chief
holiday was to go to a cricket match, which he did
as if he was going to church, and he watched critically, applauded sparingly, and was darkly offended by any unorthodox play. His convictions
upon all subjects were taciturnly inflexible. He
was an obstinate player of draughts and chess, and
an earnest and persistent reader of the *British
Weekly*. His wife was a pink, short, wilfully smiling, managing, ingratiating, talkative woman, who
was determined to be pleasant, and take a bright
hopeful view of everything, even when it was not
really bright and hopeful. She had large blue expressive eyes and a round face, and she always
spoke of her husband as Harold. She addressed
sympathetic and considerate remarks about the deceased to Mr. Polly in notes of brisk encouragement. "He was really quite cheerful at the end,"
she said several times, with congratulatory gusto,
"quite cheerful."

She made dying seem almost agreeable.

Both these people were resolved to treat Mr.
Polly very well, and to help his exceptional incompetence in every possible way, and after a simple
supper of ham and bread and cheese and pickles
and cold apple tart and small beer had been cleared

away, they put him into the armchair almost as though he was an invalid, and sat on chairs that made them look down on him, and opened a directive discussion of the arrangements for the funeral. After all a funeral is a distinct social opportunity, and rare when you have no family and few relations, and they did not want to see it spoilt and wasted.

"You'll have a hearse of course," said Mrs. Johnson. "Not one of them combinations with the driver sitting on the coffin. Disrespectful I think they are. I can't fancy how people can bring themselves to be buried in combinations." She flattened her voice in a manner she used to intimate aesthetic feeling. "I *do* like them glass hearses," she said. "So refined and nice they are."

"Podger's hearse you'll have," said Johnson conclusively. "It's the best in Easewood."

"Everything that's right and proper," said Mr. Polly.

"Podger's ready to come and measure at any time," said Johnson.

"Then you'll want a mourner's carriage or two, according as to whom you're going to invite," said Mr. Johnson.

"Didn't think of inviting any one," said Polly.

"Oh! you'll *have* to ask a few friends," said Mr. Johnson. "You can't let your father go to his grave without asking a few friends."

"Funerial baked meats like," said Mr. Polly.

"Not baked, but of course you'll have to give them something. Ham and chicken's very suitable. You don't want a lot of cooking with the ceremony coming into the middle of it. I wonder who Alfred ought to invite, Harold. Just the immediate relations; one doesn't want a great crowd of people and one doesn't want not to show respect."

"But he hated our relations — most of them."

"He's not hating them *now*," said Mrs. Johnson, "you may be sure of that. It's just because of that I think they ought to come — all of them — even your Aunt Mildred."

"Bit vulturial, isn't it?" said Mr. Polly unheeded.

"Wouldn't be more than twelve or thirteen people if they *all* came," said Mr. Johnson.

"We could have everything put out ready in the back room and the gloves and whiskey in the front room, and while we were all at the ceremony, Bessie could bring it all into the front room on a tray and put it out nice and proper. There'd have to be whiskey and sherry or port for the ladies. . . ."

"Where'll you get your mourning?" asked Johnson abruptly.

Mr. Polly had not yet considered this by-product of sorrow. "Haven't thought of it yet, O' Man."

A disagreeable feeling spread over his body as

though he was blackening as he sat. He hated black garments.

"I suppose I must *have* mourning," he said.

"*Well!*" said Johnson with a solemn smile.

"Got to see it through," said Mr. Polly indistinctly.

"If I were you," said Johnson, "I should get ready-made trousers. That's all you really want. And a black satin tie and a top hat with a deep mourning band. And gloves."

"Jet cuff links he ought to have—as chief mourner," said Mrs. Johnson.

"Not obligatory," said Johnson.

"It shows respect," said Mrs. Johnson.

"It shows respect of course," said Johnson.

And then Mrs. Johnson went on with the utmost gusto to the details of the "casket," while Mr. Polly sat more and more deeply and droopingly into the armchair, assenting with a note of protest to all they said. After he had retired for the night he remained for a long time perched on the edge of the sofa which was his bed, staring at the prospect before him. "Chasing the O' Man about up to the last," he said.

He hated the thought and elaboration of death as a healthy animal must hate it. His mind struggled with unwonted social problems.

"Got to put 'em away somehow, I suppose," said Mr. Polly.

"Wish I'd looked him up a bit more while he was alive," said Mr. Polly.

⇥≫ II ≪⇤

BEREAVEMENT came to Mr. Polly before the realisation of opulence and its anxieties and responsibilities. That only dawned upon him on the morrow — which chanced to be Sunday — as he walked with Johnson before church time about the tangle of struggling building enterprise that constituted the rising urban district of Easewood. Johnson was off duty that morning, and devoted the time very generously to the admonitory discussion of Mr. Polly's worldly outlook.

"Don't seem to get the hang of the business somehow," said Mr. Polly. "Too much blooming humbug in it for my way of thinking."

"If I were you," said Mr. Johnson, "I should push for a first-class place in London — take almost nothing and live on my reserves. That's what I should do."

"Come the Heavy," said Mr. Polly.

"Get a better class reference."

There was a pause. "Think of investing your money?" asked Johnson.

"Hardly got used to the idea of having it yet, O' Man."

"You'll have to do something with it. Give you

nearly twenty pounds a year if you invest it properly."

"Haven't seen it yet in that light," said Mr. Polly defensively.

"There's no end of things you could put it into."

"It's getting it out again I shouldn't feel sure of. I'm no sort of Fiancianier. Sooner back horses."

"I wouldn't do that if I were you."

"Not my style, O' Man."

"It's a nest egg," said Johnson.

Mr. Polly made an indeterminate noise.

"There's building societies," Johnson threw out in a speculative tone. Mr. Polly, with detached brevity, admitted there were.

"You might lend it on mortgage," said Johnson. "Very safe form of investment."

"Shan't think anything about it—not till the O' Man's underground," said Mr. Polly with an inspiration.

They turned a corner that led towards the junction.

"Might do worse," said Johnson, "than put it into a small shop."

At the moment this remark made very little appeal to Mr. Polly. But afterwards it developed. It fell into his mind like some small obscure seed, and germinated.

"These shops aren't in a bad position," said Johnson.

The row he referred to gaped in the late painful stage in building before the healing touch of the plasterer assuages the roughness of the brickwork. The space for the shop yawned an oblong gap below, framed above by an iron girder; "windows and fittings to suit tenant," a board at the end of the row promised; and behind was the door space and a glimpse of stairs going up to the living rooms above. "Not a bad position," said Johnson, and led the way into the establishment. "Room for fixtures there," he said, pointing to the blank wall.

The two men went upstairs to the little sitting-room or best bedroom (it would have to be) above the shop. Then they descended to the kitchen below.

"Rooms in a new house always look a bit small," said Johnson.

They came out of the house again by the prospective back door, and picked their way through builder's litter across the yard space to the road again. They drew nearer the junction to where a pavement and shops already open and active formed the commercial centre of Easewood. On the opposite side of the way the side door of a flourishing little establishment opened, and a man and his wife and a little boy in a sailor suit came into the street. The wife was a pretty woman in brown with a floriferous straw hat, and the group was altogether very Sundayfied and shiny and spick and span. The shop itself had a large plate-glass window whose contents were now veiled by a buff blind on which was inscribed in scrolly letters: "Rymer, Pork Butcher and Provision Merchant," and then with voluptuous elaboration: "The World-Famed Easewood Sausage."

Greetings were exchanged between Mr. Johnson and this distinguished comestible.

"Off to church already?" said Johnson.

"Walking across the fields to Little Dorington," said Mr. Rymer.

"Very pleasant walk," said Johnson.

"Very," said Mr. Rymer.

"Hope you'll enjoy it," said Mr. Johnson.

"That chap's done well," said Johnson *sotto voce* as they went on. "Came here with nothing — practically, four years ago. And as thin as a lath. Look at him now!

"He's worked hard of course," said Johnson, improving the occasion.

Thought fell between the cousins for a space.

"Some men can do one thing," said Johnson, "and some another. . . . For a man who sticks to it there's a lot to be done in a shop."

⇒» III «⇐

ALL the preparations for the funeral ran easily and happily under Mrs. Johnson's skilful hands.

On the eve of the sad event she produced a reserve of black sateen, the kitchen steps and a box of tin-tacks, and decorated the house with festoons and bows of black in the best possible taste. She tied up the knocker with black crape, and put a large bow over the corner of the steel engraving of Garibaldi, and swathed the bust of Mr. Gladstone, that had belonged to the deceased, with inky swathings. She turned the two vases that had views of Tivoli and the Bay of Naples round, so that these rather brilliant landscapes were hidden and only the plain blue enamel showed, and she anticipated the long-contemplated purchase of a tablecloth for the front room, and substituted a violet purple cover for the now very worn and faded raptures and roses in plushette that had hitherto done duty there. Everything that loving consideration could do to impart a dignified solemnity to her little home was done.

She had released Mr. Polly from the irksome duty of issuing invitations, and as the moments of assembly drew near she sent him and Mr. Johnson out into the narrow long strip of garden at the back of the house, to be free to put a finishing touch or so to her preparations. She sent them out together because she had a queer little persuasion at the back of her mind that Mr. Polly wanted to bolt from his sacred duties, and there was no way out of the garden except through the house.

Mr. Johnson was a steady, successful gardener,

and particularly good with celery and peas. He walked slowly along the narrow path down the centre pointing out to Mr. Polly a number of interesting points in the management of peas, wrinkles neatly applied and difficulties wisely overcome, and all that he did for the comfort and propitiation of that fitful but rewarding vegetable. Presently a sound of nervous laughter and raised voices from the house proclaimed the arrival of the earlier guests, and the worst of that anticipatory tension was over.

When Mr. Polly re-entered the house he found three entirely strange young women with pink faces, demonstrative manners and emphatic mourning, engaged in an incoherent conversation with Mrs. Johnson. All three kissed him with great gusto after the ancient English fashion. "These are your cousins Larkins," said Mrs. Johnson; "that's Annie (unexpected hug and smack), that's Miriam (resolute hug and smack), and that's Minnie (prolonged hug and smack)."

"Right-O," said Mr. Polly, emerging a little crumpled and breathless from this hearty introduction. "I see."

"Here's Aunt Larkins," said Mrs. Johnson, as an elderly and stouter edition of the three young women appeared in the doorway.

Mr. Polly backed rather faint-heartedly, but Aunt Larkins was not to be denied. Having hugged and kissed her nephew resoundingly she gripped him by the wrists and scanned his features. She had a round, sentimental, freckled face. "I should 'ave known 'im anywhere," she said with fervour.

"Hark at mother!" said the cousin called Annie. "Why, she's never set eyes on him before!"

"I should 'ave known 'im anywhere," said Mrs. Larkins, "for Lizzie's child. You've got her eyes! It's a Resemblance! And as for never seeing 'im — I've *dandled* him, Miss Imperence. I've dandled him."

"You couldn't dandle him now, Ma!" Miss Annie remarked with a shriek of laughter.

All the sisters laughed at that. "The things you say, Annie!" said Miriam, and for a time the room was full of mirth.

Mr. Polly felt it incumbent upon him to say something. "*My* dandling days are over," he said.

The reception of this remark would have convinced a far more modest character than Mr. Polly that it was extremely witty.

Mr. Polly followed it up by another one almost equally good. "My turn to dandle," he said, with a sly look at his aunt, and convulsed everyone.

"Not me," said Mrs. Larkins, taking his point, "*thank* you," and achieved a climax.

It was queer, but they seemed to be easy people to get on with anyhow. They were still picking little ripples and giggles of mirth from the idea of

83

Mr. Polly dandling Aunt Larkins when Mr. Johnson, who had answered the door, ushered in a stooping figure, who was at once hailed by Mrs. Johnson as "Why! Uncle Pentstemon!" Uncle Pentstemon was rather a shock. His was an aged rather than venerable figure; Time had removed the hair from the top of his head and distributed a small dividend of the plunder in little bunches carelessly and impartially over the rest of his features; he was dressed in a very big old frock coat and a long cylindrical top hat, which he had kept on; he was very much bent, and he carried a rush basket from which protruded coy intimations of the lettuces and onions he had brought to grace the occasion. He hobbled into the room, resisting the efforts of Johnson to divest him of his various encumbrances, halted and surveyed the company with an expression of profound hostility, breathing hard. Recognition quickened in his eyes.

"*You* here," he said to Aunt Larkins and then; "You *would* be. . . . These your gals?"

"They are," said Aunt Larkins, "and better gals——"

"That Annie?" asked Uncle Pentstemon, pointing a horny thumb-nail.

"Fancy your remembering her name!"

"She mucked up my mushroom bed, the baggage!" said Uncle Pentstemon ungenially, "and I give it to her to rights. Trounced her I did —

fairly. *I* remember her. Here's some green stuff for you, Grace. Fresh it is and wholesome. I shall be wanting the basket back and mind you let me have it. . . . Have you nailed him down yet? You always was a bit in front of what was needful."

His attention was drawn inward by a troublesome tooth, and he sucked at it spitefully. There was something potent about this old man that silenced everyone for a moment or so. He seemed a fragment from the ruder agricultural past of our race, like a lump of soil among things of paper. He put his basket of vegetables very deliberately on the new violet tablecloth, removed his hat carefully and dabbled his brow, and wiped out his hat brim with a crimson and yellow pocket handkerchief.

"I'm glad you were able to come, Uncle," said Mrs. Johnson.

"Oh, I *came*," said Uncle Pentstemon. "I *came*."

He turned on Mrs. Larkins. "Gals in service?" he asked.

"They aren't and they won't be," said Mrs. Larkins.

"No," he said with infinite meaning, and turned his eye on Mr. Polly.

"You Lizzie's boy?" he said.

Mr. Polly was spared much self-exposition by the tumult occasioned by further arrivals.

"Ah! here's May Punt!" said Mrs. Johnson, and a small woman dressed in the borrowed mourn-

ing of a large woman and leading a very small
long-haired observant little boy — it was his first
funeral — appeared, closely followed by several
friends of Mrs. Johnson who had come to swell the
display of respect and made only vague, confused
impressions upon Mr. Polly's mind. (Aunt Mildred, who was an unexplained family scandal, had
declined Mrs. Johnson's hospitality.)

Everybody was in profound mourning, of course,
mourning in the modern English style, with the
dyer's handiwork only too apparent, and hats and
jackets of the current cut. There was very little
crape, and the costumes had none of the goodness and specialisation and genuine enjoyment of
mourning for mourning's sake that a similar con-
tinental gathering would have displayed. Still that
congestion of strangers in black sufficed to stun
and confuse Mr. Polly's impressionable mind. It
seemed to him much more extraordinary than anything he had expected.

"Now, gals," said Mrs. Larkins, "see if you can
help," and the three daughters became confusingly
active between the front room and the back.

"I hope everyone'll take a glass of sherry and a
biscuit," said Mrs. Johnson. "We don't stand on
ceremony," and a decanter appeared in the place
of Uncle Pentstemon's vegetables.

Uncle Pentstemon had refused to be relieved of
his hat; he sat stiffly down on a chair against the

wall with that venerable headdress between his feet, watching the approach of anyone jealously. "Don't you go squashing my hat," he said. Conversation became confused and general. Uncle Pentstemon addressed himself to Mr. Polly. "You're a little chap," he said, "a puny little chap. I never did agree to Lizzie marrying him, but I suppose bygones must be bygones now. I suppose they made you a clerk or something."

"Outfitter," said Mr. Polly.

"I remember. Them girls pretend to be dressmakers."

"They *are* dressmakers," said Mrs. Larkins across the room.

"I *will* take a glass of sherry. They 'old to it, you see."

He took the glass Mrs. Johnson handed him, and poised it critically between a horny finger and thumb. "You'll be paying for this," he said to Mr. Polly. "Here's *to* you. . . . Don't you go treading on my hat, young woman. You brush your skirts against it and you take a shillin' off its value. It ain't the sort of 'at you see nowadays."

He drank noisily.

The sherry presently loosened everybody's tongue, and the early coldness passed.

"There ought to have been a *post-mortem*," Polly heard Mrs. Punt remarking to one of Mrs. Johnson's friends, and Miriam and another were

87

lost in admiration of Mrs. Johnson's decorations. "So very nice and refined," they were both repeating at intervals.

The sherry and biscuits were still being discussed when Mr. Podger, the undertaker, arrived, a broad, cheerfully sorrowful, clean-shaven little man, accompanied by a melancholy-faced assistant. He conversed for a time with Johnson in the passage outside; the sense of his business stilled the rising waves of chatter and carried off everyone's attention in the wake of his heavy footsteps to the room above.

⇶ IV ⬱

THINGS crowded upon Mr. Polly. Everyone, he noticed, took sherry with a solemn avidity, and a small portion even was administered sacramentally to the Punt boy. There followed a distribution of black kid gloves, and much trying on and humouring of fingers. "*Good* gloves," said one of Mrs. Johnson's friends. "There's a little pair there for Willie," said Mrs. Johnson triumphantly. Everyone seemed gravely content with the amazing procedure of the occasion. Presently Mr. Podger was picking Mr. Polly out as Chief Mourner to go with Mrs. Johnson, Mrs. Larkins and Annie in the first mourning carriage.

"Right O," said Mr. Polly, and repented instantly of the alacrity of the phrase.

"There'll have to be a walking party," said Mrs. Johnson cheerfully. "There's only two coaches. I daresay we can put in six in each, but that leaves three over."

There was a generous struggle to be pedestrian, and the two other Larkins girls, confessing coyly to tight new boots and displaying a certain eagerness, were added to the contents of the first carriage.

"It'll be a squeeze," said Annie.

"*I* don't mind a squeeze," said Mr. Polly.

He decided privately that the proper phrase for the result of that remark was "Hysterial catechunations."

Mr. Podger re-entered the room from a momentary supervision of the bumping business that was now proceeding down the staircase.

"Bearing up," he said cheerfully, rubbing his hands together. "Bearing up!"

That stuck very vividly in Mr. Polly's mind, and so did the close-wedged drive to the churchyard, bunched in between two young women in confused dull and shiny black, and the fact that the wind was bleak and that the officiating clergyman had a cold, and sniffed between his sentences. The wonder of life! The wonder of everything! What had he expected that this should all be so astoundingly different.

He found his attention converging more and

more upon the Larkins cousins. The interest was
reciprocal. They watched him with a kind of suppressed excitement and became risible with his every word and gesture. He was more and more
aware of their personal quality. Annie had blue
eyes and a red, attractive mouth, a harsh voice and
a habit of extreme liveliness that even this occasion
could not suppress; Minnie was fond, extremely
free about the touching of hands and suchlike en-
dearments; Miriam was quieter and regarded him
earnestly. Mrs. Larkins was very happy in her
daughters, and they had the naïve affectionateness
of those who see few people and find a strange
cousin a wonderful outlet. Mr. Polly had never
been very much kissed, and it made his mind swim.
He did not know for the life of him whether he
liked or disliked all or any of the Larkins cousins.
It was rather attractive to make them laugh; they
laughed at anything.

There they were tugging at his mind, and the
funeral tugging at his mind, too, and the sense of
himself as Chief Mourner in a brand new silk hat
with a broad mourning band. He watched the ceremony and missed his responses, and strange feelings twisted at his heartstrings.

→» V «←

Mr. Polly walked back to the house because he
wanted to be alone. Miriam and Minnie would have

accompanied him, but finding Uncle Pentstemon beside the Chief Mourner they went on in front.

"You're wise," said Uncle Pentstemon.

"Glad you think so," said Mr. Polly, rousing himself to talk.

"I likes a bit of walking before a meal," said Uncle Pentstemon, and made a kind of large hiccup. "That sherry rises," he remarked. "Grocer's stuff, I expect."

He went on to ask how much the funeral might be costing, and seemed pleased to find Mr. Polly didn't know.

"In that case," he said impressively, "it's pretty certain to cost more'n you expect, my boy."

He meditated for a time. "I've seen a mort of undertakers," he declared; "a mort of undertakers."

The Larkins girls attracted his attention.

"Let's lodgin's and chars," he commented. "Leastways she goes out to cook dinners. And look at 'em!

"Dressed up to the nines. If it ain't borryd clothes, that is. And they goes out to work at a factory!"

"Did you know my father much, Uncle Pentstemon?" asked Mr. Polly.

"Couldn't stand Lizzie throwin' herself away like that," said Uncle Pentstemon, and repeated his hiccup on a larger scale.

"That *weren't* good sherry," said Uncle Pent-

stemon with the first note of pathos Mr. Polly had
detected in his quavering voice.

The funeral in the rather cold wind had proved
wonderfully appetising, and every eye brightened
at the sight of the cold collation that was now
spread in the front room. Mrs. Johnson was very
brisk, and Mr. Polly, when he re-entered the house
found everybody sitting down. "Come along, Alfred," cried the hostess cheerfully. "We can't very
well begin without you. Have you got the bottled
beer ready to open, Betsy? Uncle, you'll have a
drop of whiskey, I expect."

"Put it where I can mix for myself," said Uncle
Pentstemon, placing his hat very carefully out of
harm's way on the bookcase.

There were two cold boiled chickens, which Johnson carved with great care and justice, and a nice
piece of ham, some brawn and a steak and kidney
pie, a large bowl of salad and several sorts of pickles, and afterwards came cold apple tart, jam roll
and a good piece of Stilton cheese, lots of bottled
beer, some lemonade for the ladies and milk for
Master Punt; a very bright and satisfying meal.
Mr. Polly found himself seated between Mrs.
Punt, who was much preoccupied with Master
Punt's table manners, and one of Mrs. Johnson's
school friends, who was exchanging reminiscences
of school days and news of how various common
friends had changed and married with Mrs. John-

son. Opposite him was Miriam and another of the
Johnson circle, and also he had brawn to carve and
there was hardly room for the helpful Betsy to
pass behind his chair, so that altogether his mind
would have been amply distracted from any mortu-
ary broodings, even if a wordy warfare about the
education of the modern young woman had not
sprung up between Uncle Pentstemon and Mrs.
Larkins and threatened for a time, in spite of a
word or so in season from Johnson, to wreck all the
harmony of the sad occasion.

The general effect was after this fashion:

First an impression of Mrs. Punt on the right
speaking in a refined undertone: "You didn't, I
suppose, Mr. Polly, think to 'ave your poor dear
father post-mortemed——"

Lady on the left side breaking in: "I was just reminding Grace of the dear dead days beyond recall——"

Attempted reply to Mrs. Punt: "Didn't think of
it for a moment. Can't give you a piece of this
brawn, can I?"

Fragment from the left: "Grace and Beauty
they used to call us and we used to sit at the same
desk——"

Mrs. Punt, breaking out suddenly: "Don't *swal-
ler* your fork, Willy. You see, Mr. Polly, I used to
'ave a young gentleman, a medical student, lodging with me——"

Voice from down the table: "'Am, Alfred? I didn't give you very much."

Bessie became evident at the back of Mr. Polly's chair, struggling wildly to get past. Mr. Polly did his best to be helpful. "Can you get past? Lemme sit forward a bit. Urr-oo! Right O."

Lady to the left going on valiantly and speaking to everyone who cares to listen, while Mrs. Johnson beams beside her: "There she used to sit as bold as brass, and the fun she used to make of things no one *could* believe — knowing her now. She used to make faces at the mistress through the——"

Mrs. Punt keeping steadily on: "The contents of the stummik at any rate *ought* to be examined."

Voice of Mr. Johnson. "Elfrid, pass the mustid down."

Miriam leaning across the table: "Elfrid!"

"Once she got us all kept in. The whole school!"

Miriam, more insistently: "Elfrid!"

Uncle Pentstemon, raising his voice defiantly: "Trounce 'er again I would if she did as much now. That I would! Dratted mischief!"

Miriam, catching Mr. Polly's eye: "Elfrid! This lady knows Canterbury. I been telling her you been there."

Mr. Polly: "Glad you know it."

The lady shouting: "I like it."

Mrs. Larkins, raising her voice: "I won't 'ave

94

my girls spoken of, not by nobody, old *or* young."

Pop! imperfectly located.

Mr. Johnson at large: "*Ain't* the beer up! It's the 'eated room."

Bessie: "Scuse me, sir, passing so soon again, but——" Rest inaudible. Mr. Polly, accommodating himself: "Urr-oo! Right? Right O."

The knives and forks, probably by some secret common agreement, clash and clatter together and drown every other sound.

"Nobody 'ad the least idea 'ow 'E died, — nobody. . . . Willie, don't *golp* so. You ain't in a 'urry, are you? You don't want to ketch a train or anything, — golping like that!"

"D'you remember, Grace, 'ow one day we 'ad writing lesson. . . ."

"Nicer girls no one ever 'ad — though I say it who shouldn't."

Mrs. Johnson in a shrill clear hospitable voice: "Harold, won't Mrs. Larkins 'ave a teeny bit more fowl?"

Mr. Polly rising to the situation. "Or some brawn, Mrs. Larkins?" Catching Uncle Pentstemon's eye: "Can't send *you* some brawn, sir?"

"Elfrid!"

Loud hiccup from Uncle Pentstemon, momentary consternation followed by giggle from Annie.

The narration at Mr. Polly's elbow pursued a quiet but relentless course. "Directly the new doctor came in he said: 'Everything must be took out and put in spirits—everything.'"

Willie,—audible ingurgitation.

The narration on the left was flourishing up to a climax. "Ladies," she sez, "dip their pens *in* their ink and keep their noses out of it!"

"Elfrid!"—persuasively.

"Certain people may cast snacks at other people's daughters, never having had any of their own, though two poor souls of wives dead and buried through their goings on——"

Johnson ruling the storm: "We don't want old scores dug up on such a day as this——"

"Old scores you may call them, but worth a dozen of them that put them to their rest, poor dears."

"Elfrid!"—with a note of remonstrance.

"If you choke yourself, my lord, not another mouthful do you 'ave. No nice puddin'! Nothing!"

"And kept us in, she did, every afternoon for a week!"

It seemed to be the end, and Mr. Polly replied with an air of being profoundly impressed: "Really!"

"Elfrid!"—a little disheartened.

"And then they 'ad it! They found he'd swallowed the very key to unlock the drawer——"

"Then don't let people go casting snacks!"

"*Who's* casting snacks!"

"Elfrid! This lady wants to know, 'ave the Prossers left Canterbury?"

"No wish to make myself disagreeable, not to God's 'umblest worm——"

"Alf, you aren't very busy with that brawn up there!"

And so on for the hour.

The general effect upon Mr. Polly at the time was at once confusing and exhilarating; but it led him to eat copiously and carelessly, and long before the end, when after an hour and a quarter a movement took the party, and it pushed away its cheese plates and rose sighing and stretching from the remains of the repast, little streaks and bands of dyspeptic irritation and melancholy were darkening the serenity of his mind.

He stood between the mantel shelf and the window — the blinds were up now — and the Larkins sisters clustered about him. He battled with the oncoming depression and forced himself to be extremely facetious about two noticeable rings on Annie's hand. "They ain't real," said Annie coquettishly. "Got 'em out of a prize packet."

"Prize packet in trousers, I expect," said Mr. Polly, and awakened inextinguishable laughter.

"Oh! the things you say!" said Minnie, slapping his shoulder.

Suddenly something he had quite extraordinarily forgotten came into his head.

"Bless my heart!" he cried, suddenly serious.

"What's the matter?" asked Johnson.

"Ought to have gone back to shop—three days ago. They'll make no end of a row!"

"Lor, you *are* a Treat!" said cousin Annie, and screamed with laughter at a delicious idea. "You'll get the Chuck," she said.

Mr. Polly made a convulsing grimace at her.

"I'll die!" she said. "I don't believe you care a bit!"

Feeling a little disorganized by her hilarity and a shocked expression that had come to the face of cousin Miriam, he made some indistinct excuse and went out through the back room and scullery into the little garden. The cool air and a very slight drizzle of rain was a relief—anyhow. But the black mood of the replete dyspeptic had come upon him. His soul darkened hopelessly. He walked with his hands in his pockets down the path between the rows of exceptionally cultured peas and unreasonably, overwhelmingly, he was smitten by sorrow for his father. The heady noise and muddle and confused excitement of the feast passed from him like a curtain drawn away. He thought of that hot and angry and struggling creature who had tugged and sworn so foolishly at the sofa upon the twisted staircase, and who was now lying still and hidden, at the bottom of a wall-sided oblong pit beside the heaped gravel that would presently cover him. The

stillness of it! the wonder of it! the infinite re-
proach! Hatred for all these people — all of them
— possessed Mr. Polly's soul.

"Hen-witted gigglers," said Mr. Polly.

He went down to the fence, and stood with his
hands on it staring away at nothing. He stayed
there for what seemed a long time. From the house
came a sound of raised voices that subsided, and
then Mrs. Johnson calling for Bessie.

"Gowlish gusto," said Mr. Polly. "Jumping it
in. Funererial Games. Don't hurt *him* of course.
Doesn't matter to *him*. . . ."

Nobody missed Mr. Polly for a long time.

When at last he reappeared among them his eye
was almost grim, but nobody noticed his eye. They
were looking at watches, and Johnson was being
omniscient about trains. They seemed to discover
Mr. Polly afresh just at the moment of parting,
and said a number of more or less appropriate
things. But Uncle Pentstemon was far too worried
about his rush basket, which had been carelessly
mislaid, he seemed to think with larcenous inten-
tions, to remember Mr. Polly at all. Mrs. Johnson
had tried to fob him off with a similar but inferior
basket, — his own had one handle mended with
string according to a method of peculiar virtue and
inimitable distinction known only to himself — and
the old gentleman had taken her attempt as the
gravest reflection upon his years and intelligence.

Mr. Polly was left very largely to the Larkins trio. Cousin Minnie became shameless and kept kissing him good-by — and then finding out it wasn't time to go. Cousin Miriam seemed to think her silly, and caught Mr. Polly's eye sympathetically. Cousin Annie ceased to giggle and lapsed into a nearly sentimental state. She said with real feeling that she had enjoyed the funeral more than words could tell.

CHAPTER
THE FIFTH

MR. POLLY

TAKES A VACATION

MR. POLLY

TAKES A VACATION

⤜ I ⤛

Mr. Polly returned to Clapham from the funeral celebration prepared for trouble, and took his dismissal in a manly spirit.

"You've merely anti-*separated* me by a hair," he said politely.

And he told them in the dormitory that he meant to take a little holiday before his next crib, though a certain inherited reticence suppressed the fact of the legacy.

"You'll do that all right," said Ascough, the head of the boot shop. "It's quite the fashion just at present. Six Weeks in Wonderful Wood Street. They're running excursions. . . ."

"A little holiday"; that was the form his sense of wealth took first, that it made a little holiday possible. Holidays were his life, and the rest merely adulterated living. And now he might take a little holiday and have money for railway fares and money for meals and money for inns. But—he wanted someone to take the holiday with.

For a time he cherished a design of hunting up Parsons, getting him to throw up his situation, and going with him to Stratford-on-Avon and Shrewsbury and the Welsh mountains and the Wye and a lot of places like that, for a really gorgeous, careless, illimitable old holiday of a month. But alas! Parsons had gone from the St. Paul's Churchyard outfitter's long ago, and left no address.

Mr. Polly tried to think he would be almost as happy wandering alone, but he knew better. He had dreamt of casual encounters with delightfully interesting people by the wayside—even romantic encounters. Such things happened in Chaucer and "Bocashiew," they happened with extreme facility in Mr. Richard Le Gallienne's very detrimental book, *The Quest of the Golden Girl*, which he had read at Canterbury, but he had no confidence they would happen in England—to him.

When, a month later, he came out of the Clapham side door at last into the bright sunshine of a fine London day, with a dazzling sense of limitless freedom upon him, he did nothing more adventurous than order the cabman to drive to Waterloo, and there take a ticket for Easewood.

He wanted—what *did* he want most in life? I think his distinctive craving is best expressed as

fun — fun in companionship. He had already
spent a pound or two upon three select feasts to his
fellow assistants, sprat suppers they were, and
there had been a great and very successful Sunday pilgrimage to Richmond, by Wandsworth and
Wimbledon's open common, a trailing garrulous
company walking about a solemnly happy host, to
wonderful cold meat and salad at the Roebuck, a
bowl of punch, punch! and a bill to correspond;
but now it was a weekday, and he went down to
Easewood with his bag and portmanteau in a solitary compartment, and looked out of the window
upon a world in which every possible congenial
seemed either toiling in a situation or else looking
for one with a gnawing and hopelessly preoccupy-
ing anxiety. He stared out of the window at the ex-
ploitation roads of suburbs, and rows of houses all
very much alike, either emphatically and impa-
tiently TO LET or full of rather busy unsocial people. Near Wimbledon he had a glimpse of golf
links, and saw two elderly gentlemen who, had they
chosen, might have been gentlemen of grace and
leisure, addressing themselves to smite little hunted
white balls great distances with the utmost bitterness and dexterity. Mr. Polly could not understand
them.

Every road he remarked, as freshly as though
he had never observed it before, was bordered by
inflexible palings or iron fences or severely dis-

ciplined hedges. He wondered if perhaps abroad there might be beautifully careless, unenclosed high roads. Perhaps after all the best way of taking a holiday is to go abroad.

He was haunted by the memory of what was either a half-forgotten picture or a dream; a carriage was drawn up by the wayside and four beautiful people, two men and two women graciously dressed, were dancing a formal ceremonious dance full of bows and curtseys, to the music of a wandering fiddler they had encountered. They had been driving one way and he walking another — a happy encounter with this obvious result. They might have come straight out of happy Theleme, whose motto is: "Do what thou wilt." The driver had taken his two sleek horses out; they grazed unchallenged; and he sat on a stone clapping time with his hands while the fiddler played. The shade of the trees did not altogether shut out the sunshine, the grass in the wood was lush and full of still daffodils, the turf they danced on was starred with daisies.

Mr. Polly, dear heart! firmly believed that things like that could and did happen — somewhere. Only it puzzled him that morning that he never saw them happening. Perhaps they happened south of Guilford. Perhaps they happened in Italy. Perhaps they ceased to happen a hundred years ago. Perhaps they happened just round the corner —

on weekdays when all good Mr. Pollys are safely shut up in shops. And so dreaming of delightful impossibilities until his heart ached for them, he was rattled along in the suburban train to Johnson's discreet home and the briskly stimulating welcome of Mrs. Johnson.

→» II «←

MR. POLLY translated his restless craving for joy and leisure into Harold-Johnsonese by saying that he meant to look about him for a bit before going into another situation. It was a decision Johnson very warmly approved. It was arranged that Mr. Polly should occupy his former room and board with the Johnsons in consideration of a weekly payment of eighteen shillings. And the next morning Mr. Polly went out early and reappeared with a purchase, a safety bicycle, which he proposed to study and master in the sandy lane below the Johnsons' house. But over the struggles that preceded his mastery it is humane to draw a veil.

And also Mr. Polly bought a number of books, Rabelais for his own, and "The Arabian Nights," the works of Sterne, a pile of "Tales from Blackwood," cheap in a second-hand bookshop, the plays of William Shakespeare, a second-hand copy of Belloc's "Road to Rome," an odd volume of "Purchas his Pilgrimes" and "The Life and Death of Jason."

"Better get yourself a good book on bookkeeping," said Johnson, turning over perplexing pages.

A belated spring was now advancing with great strides to make up for lost time. Sunshine and a stirring wind were poured out over the land, fleets of towering clouds sailed upon urgent tremendous missions across the blue seas of heaven, and presently Mr. Polly was riding a little unstably along unfamiliar Surrey roads, wondering always what was round the next corner, and marking the blackthorn and looking out for the first white flowerbuds of the may. He was perplexed and distressed, as indeed are all right thinking souls, that there is no may in early May.

He did not ride at the even pace sensible people use who have marked out a journey from one place to another, and settled what time it will take them. He rode at variable speeds, and always as though he was looking for something that, missing, left life attractive still, but a little wanting in significance. And sometimes he was so unreasonably happy he had to whistle and sing, and sometimes he was incredibly, but not at all painfully, sad. His indigestion vanished with air and exercise, and it was quite pleasant in the evening to stroll about the garden with Johnson and discuss plans for the future. Johnson was full of ideas. Moreover, Mr.

Polly had marked the road that led to Stamton, that rising populous suburb; and as his bicycle legs grew strong his wheel with a sort of inevitableness carried him towards the row of houses in a back street in which his Larkins cousins made their home together.

He was received with great enthusiasm.

The street was a dingy little street, a *cul-de-sac* of very small houses in a row, each with an almost flattened bow window and a blistered brown door with a black knocker. He poised his bright new bicycle against the window, and knocked and stood waiting, and felt himself in his straw hat and black serge suit a very pleasant and prosperous-looking figure. The door was opened by cousin Miriam. She was wearing a bluish print dress that brought out a kind of sallow warmth in her skin, and although it was nearly four o'clock in the afternoon, her sleeves were tucked up, as if for some domestic work, above the elbows, showing her rather slender but very shapely yellowish arms. The loosely pinned bodice confessed a delicately rounded neck.

For a moment she regarded him with suspicion and a faint hostility, and then recognition dawned in her eyes.

"Why!" she said, "it's cousin Elfrid!"

"Thought I'd look you up," he said.

"Fancy! you coming to see us like this!" she answered.

They stood confronting one another for a moment, while Miriam collected herself for the unexpected emergency.

"Exploratious menanderings," said Mr. Polly, indicating the bicycle.

Miriam's face betrayed no appreciation of the remark.

"Wait a moment," she said, coming to a rapid decision, "and I'll tell Ma."

She closed the door on him abruptly, leaving him a little surprised in the street. "Ma!" he heard her calling, and swift speech followed, the import of which he didn't catch. Then she reappeared. It seemed but an instant, but she was changed; the arms had vanished into sleeves, the apron had gone, a certain pleasing disorder of the hair had been at least reproved.

"I didn't mean to shut you out," she said, coming out upon the step. "I just told Ma. How are you, Elfrid? You *are* looking well. I didn't know you rode a bicycle. Is it a new one?"

She leaned upon his bicycle. "Bright it is!" she said. "What a trouble you must have to keep it clean!"

Mr. Polly was aware of a rustling transit along the passage, and of the house suddenly full of hushed but strenuous movement.

"It's plated mostly," said Mr. Polly.

"What do you carry in that little bag thing?"

she asked, and then branched off to: "We're all in a mess to-day you know. It's my cleaning up day to-day. I'm not a bit tidy I know, but I *do* like to 'ave a go in at things now and then. You got to take us as you find us, Elfrid. Mercy we wasn't all out." She paused. She was talking against time. "I *am* glad to see you again," she repeated.

"Couldn't keep away," said Mr. Polly gallantly. "Had to come over and see my pretty cousins again."

Miriam did not answer for a moment. She coloured deeply. "You *do say* things!" she said.

She stared at Mr. Polly, and his unfortunate sense of fitness made him nod his head towards her, regard her firmly with a round brown eye, and add impressively: "I don't say *which* of them."

Her answering expression made him realise for an instant the terrible dangers he trifled with. Avidity flared up in her eyes. Minnie's voice came happily to dissolve the situation.

"'Ello, Elfrid!" she said from the doorstep.

Her hair was just passably tidy, and she was a little effaced by a red blouse, but there was no mistaking the genuine brightness of her welcome.

He was to come in to tea, and Mrs. Larkins, exuberantly genial in a floriferous but dingy flannel dressing gown, appeared to confirm that. He brought in his bicycle and put it in the narrow, empty passage, and everyone crowded into a small untidy kitchen, whose table had been hastily cleared of the débris of the midday repast.

"You must come in 'ere," said Mrs. Larkins, "for Miriam's turning out the front room. I never did see such a girl for cleanin' up. Miriam's 'oliday's a scrub. You've caught us on the 'Op as the sayin' is, but Welcome all the same. Pity Annie's at work to-day; she won't be 'ome till seven."

Miriam put chairs and attended to the fire, Minnie edged up to Mr. Polly and said: "I *am* glad to see you again, Elfrid," with a warm contiguous intimacy that betrayed a broken tooth. Mrs. Larkins got out tea things, and descanted on the noble simplicity of their lives, and how he "mustn't mind our simple ways." They enveloped Mr. Polly with a geniality that intoxicated his amiable nature; he insisted upon helping lay the things, and created enormous laughter by pretending not to know where plates and knives and cups ought to go. "Who'm I going to sit next?" he said, and developed voluminous amusement by attempts to arrange the plates so that he could rub elbows with all three. Mrs. Larkins had to sit down in the windsor chair by the grandfather clock (which was dark with dirt and not going) to laugh at her ease at his well-acted perplexity.

They got seated at last, and Mr. Polly struck a vein of humour in telling them how he learnt to ride the bicycle. He found the mere repetition of the word "wabble" sufficient to produce almost inextinguishable mirth.

"No foreseeing little accidentulous misadventures," he said, "none whatever."

(Giggle from Minnie.)

"Stout elderly gentleman — shirt sleeves — large straw wastepaper basket sort of hat — starts to cross the road — going to the oil shop — prodic refreshment of oil can ———"

"Don't say you run 'im down," said Mrs. Larkins, gasping. "Don't say you run 'im down, Elfrid!"

"Run 'im down! Not me, Madam. I never run anything down. Wabble. Ring the bell. Wabble, wabble ———"

(Laughter and tears.)

"No one's going to run him down. Hears the bell! Wabble. Gust of wind. Off comes the hat smack into the wheel. Wabble. *Lord! what's* going to happen? Hat across the road, old gentleman after it, bell, shriek. He ran into me. Didn't ring his bell, hadn't *got* a bell — just ran into me. Over I went clinging to his venerable head. Down he went with me clinging to him. Oil can blump, blump into the road."

(Interlude while Minnie is attended to for crumb in the windpipe.)

"Well, what happened to the old man with the oil can?" said Mrs. Larkins.

113

"We sat about among the debreece and had a bit of an argument. I told him he oughtn't to come out wearing such a dangerous hat — flying at things. Said if he couldn't control his hat he ought to leave it at home. High old jawbacious argument we had, I tell you. 'I tell you, sir —' 'I tell *you*, sir.' Waw-waw-waw. Infuriacious. But that's the sort of thing that's constantly happening you know — on a bicycle. People run into you, hens and cats and dogs and things. Everything seems to have its mark on you; everything."

"*You* never run into anything."

"Never. Swelpme," said Mr. Polly very solemnly.

"Never, 'E say!" squealed Minnie. "Hark at 'im!" and relapsed into a condition that urgently demanded back thumping. "Don't be so silly," said Miriam, thumping hard.

Mr. Polly had never been such a social success before. They hung upon his every word — and laughed. What a family they were for laughter! And he loved laughter. The background he apprehended dimly; it was very much the sort of background his life had always had. There was a threadbare tablecloth on the table, and the slop basin and teapot did not go with the cups and saucers, the plates were different again, the knives worn down, the butter lived in a greenish glass dish of its own. Behind was a dresser hung with spare and miscellaneous crockery, with a workbox and an

114

untidy work-basket, there was an ailing musk plant in the window, and the tattered and blotched wall-paper was covered by bright-coloured grocers' almanacs. Feminine wrappings hung from pegs upon the door, and the floor was covered with a varied collection of fragments of oilcloth. The windsor chair he sat in was unstable — which presently afforded material for humour. "Steady, old nag," he said; "whoa, my friskiacious palfry!"

"The things he says! You never know what he won't say next!"

→»   III   «←

"You ain't talkin' of goin'!" cried Mrs. Larkins.

"Supper at eight."

"Stay to supper with *us*, now you *'ave* come over," said Mrs. Larkins, with corroborating cries from Minnie. "'Ave a bit of a walk with the gals, and then come back to supper. You might all go and meet Annie while I straighten up, and lay things out."

"You're not to go touching the front room mind," said Miriam.

"*Who's* going to touch yer front room?" said Mrs. Larkins, apparently forgetful for a moment of Mr. Polly.

Both girls dressed with some care while Mrs. Larkins sketched the better side of their charac-

ters, and then the three young people went out to
see something of Stamton. In the streets their risible mood gave way to a self-conscious propriety
that was particularly evident in Miriam's bearing.
They took Mr. Polly to the Stamton Wreckery-
ation ground — that at least was what they called
it — with its handsome custodian's cottage, its as-
phalt paths, its Jubilee drinking fountain, its
clumps of wallflower and daffodils, and so to the
new cemetery and a distant view of the Surrey
hills, and round by the gasworks to the canal to the
factory, that presently disgorged a surprised and
radiant Annie.

"El-*lo!*" said Annie.

It is very pleasant to every properly constituted
mind to be a centre of amiable interest for one's
fellow creatures, and when one is a young man
conscious of becoming mourning and a certain wit,
and the fellow creatures are three young and ar-
dent and sufficiently expressive young women who
dispute for the honour of walking by one's side,
one may be excused a secret exaltation. They did
dispute.

"I'm going to 'ave 'im now," said Annie. "You
two've been 'aving 'im all the afternoon. Besides,
I've got something to say to him."

She had something to say to him. It came presently. "I say," she said abruptly. "I *did* get them
rings out of a prize packet."

116

"What rings?" asked Mr. Polly.

"What you saw at your poor father's funeral. You made out they meant something. They didn't —straight."

"Then some people have been very remiss about their chances," said Mr. Polly, understanding.

"They haven't had any chances," said Annie. "I don't believe in making oneself too free with people."

"Nor me," said Mr. Polly.

"I may be a bit larky and cheerful in my manner," Annie admitted. "But it don't *mean* anything. I ain't that sort."

"Right O," said Mr. Polly.

→» IV «←

IT WAS past ten when Mr. Polly found himself riding back towards Easewood in a broad moonlight with a little Japanese lantern dangling from his handle bar and making a fiery circle of pinkish light on and round about his front wheel. He was mightily pleased with himself and the day. There had been four-ale to drink at supper mixed with gingerbeer, very free and jolly in a jug. No shadow fell upon the agreeable excitement of his mind until he faced the anxious and reproachful face of Johnson, who had been sitting up for him, smoking and trying to read the odd volume of "Purchas

117

his Pilgrimes,"—about the monk who went into
Sarmatia and saw the Tartar carts.

"Not had an accident, Elfrid?" said Johnson.

The weakness of Mr. Polly's character came out
in his reply. "Not much," he said. "Pedal got a bit
loose in Stamton, O' Man. Couldn't ride it. So I
looked up the cousins while I waited."

"Not the Larkins lot?"

"Yes."

Johnson yawned hugely and asked for and was
given friendly particulars. "Well," he said, "better
get to bed. I have been reading that book of yours
—rum stuff. Can't make it out quite. Quite out of
date I should say if you asked me."

"That's all right, O' Man," said Mr. Polly.

"Not a bit of use for anything I can see."

"Not a bit."

"See any shops in Stamton?"

"Nothing to speak of," said Mr. Polly. "Goo-
night, O' Man."

Before and after this brief conversation his mind
ran on his cousins very warmly and prettily in the
vein of high spring. Mr. Polly had been drinking
at the poisoned fountains of English literature,
fountains so unsuited to the needs of a decent clerk
or shopman, fountains charged with the dangerous
suggestion that it becomes a man of gaiety and
spirit to make love, gallantly and rather carelessly.
It seemed to him that evening to be handsome and

humorous and practicable to make love to all his cousins. It wasn't that he liked any of them particularly, but he liked something about them. He liked their youth and femininity, their resolute high spirits and their interest in him.

They laughed at nothing and knew nothing, and Minnie had lost a tooth and Annie screamed and shouted, but they were interesting, intensely interesting.

And Miriam wasn't so bad as the others. He had kissed them all and had been kissed in addition several times by Minnie,—"oscoolatory exercise."

He buried his nose in his pillow and went to sleep —to dream of anything rather than getting on in the world, as a sensible young man in his position ought to have done.

⇢⟫ V ⟪⇠

And now Mr. Polly began to lead a divided life. With the Johnsons he professed to be inclined, but not so conclusively inclined as to be inconvenient, to get a shop for himself, to be, to use the phrase he preferred, "looking for an opening." He would ride off in the afternoon upon that research, remarking that he was going to "cast a strategetical eye" on Chertsey or Weybridge. But if not all roads, still a great majority of them, led by however devious ways to Stamton, and to laughter and

increasing familiarity. Relations developed with
Annie and Minnie and Miriam. Their various characters were increasingly interesting. The laughter
became perceptibly less abundant, something of
the fizz had gone from the first opening, still these
visits remained wonderfully friendly and uphold-
ing. Then back he would come to grave but evasive
discussions with Johnson.

Johnson was really anxious to get Mr. Polly
"into something." His was a reserved honest character, and he would really have preferred to see his
lodger doing things for himself than receive his
money for housekeeping. He hated waste, any-
body's waste, much more than he desired profit.
But Mrs. Johnson was all for Mr. Polly's loiter-
ing. She seemed much the more human and likeable
of the two to Mr. Polly.

He tried at times to work up enthusiasm for the
various avenues to well-being his discussion with
Johnson opened. But they remained dishearten-
ing prospects. He imagined himself wonderfully
smartened up, acquiring style and value in a London shop, but the picture was stiff and unconvinc-
ing. He tried to rouse himself to enthusiasm by
the idea of his property increasing by leaps and
bounds, by twenty pounds a year or so, let us say,
each year, in a well-placed little shop, the corner
shop Johnson favoured. There was a certain pic-

turesque interest in imagining cut-throat econo-
mies, but his heart told him there would be little in
practising them.

And then it happened to Mr. Polly that real Romance came out of dreamland into life, and intoxicated and gladdened him with sweetly beautiful
suggestions — and left him. She came and left him
as that dear lady leaves so many of us, alas! not
sparing him one jot or one tittle of the hollowness
of her retreating aspect.

It was all the more to Mr. Polly's taste that the
thing should happen as things happen in books.

In a resolute attempt not to get to Stamton
that day, he had turned due southward from Easewood towards a country where the abundance of
bracken jungles, lady's smock, stitchwork, bluebells
and grassy stretches by the wayside under shady
trees does much to compensate the lighter type of
mind for the absence of promising "openings." He
turned aside from the road, wheeled his machine
along a faintly marked attractive trail through
bracken until he came to a heap of logs against a
high old stone wall with a damaged coping and
wallflower plants already gone to seed. He sat
down, balanced the straw hat on a convenient lump
of wood, lit a cigarette, and abandoned himself to
agreeable musings and the friendly observation of
a cheerful little brown and grey bird his stillness

presently encouraged to approach him. "This is All Right," said Mr. Polly softly to the little brown and grey bird. "Business—later."

He reflected that he might go on this way for four or five years, and then be scarcely worse off than he had been in his father's lifetime.

"Vile Business," said Mr. Polly.

Then Romance appeared. Or to be exact, Romance became audible.

Romance began as a series of small but increasingly vigorous movements on the other side of the wall, then as a voice murmuring, then as a falling of little fragments on the hither side and as ten pink finger tips, scarcely apprehended before Romance became startling and emphatically a leg, remained for a time a fine, slender, actively struggling limb, brown stockinged and wearing a brown toe-worn shoe, and then—. A handsome red-haired girl wearing a short dress of blue linen was sitting astride the wall, panting, considerably disarranged by her climbing, and as yet unaware of Mr. Polly. . . .

His fine instincts made him turn his head away and assume an attitude of negligent contemplation, with his ears and mind alive to every sound behind him.

"Goodness!" said a voice with a sharp note of surprise.

Mr. Polly was on his feet in an instant. "Dear me! Can I be of any assistance?" he said with deferential gallantry.

"I don't know," said the young lady, and regarded him calmly with clear blue eyes.

"I didn't know there was anyone here," she added.

"Sorry," said Mr. Polly, "if I am intrudaceous. I didn't know you didn't want me to be here."

She reflected for a moment on the word.

"It isn't that," she said, surveying him.

"I oughtn't to get over the wall," she explained. "It's out of bounds. At least in term time. But this being holidays——"

Her manner placed the matter before him.

"Holidays is different," said Mr. Polly.

"I don't want to actually *break* the rules," she said.

"Leave them behind you," said Mr. Polly with a catch of the breath, "where they are safe"; and marvelling at his own wit and daring, and indeed trembling within himself, he held out a hand for her.

She brought another brown leg from the unknown, and arranged her skirt with a dexterity altogether feminine. "I think I'll stay on the wall," she decided. "So long as some of me's in bounds——"

She continued to regard him with eyes that presently joined dancing in an irresistible smile of satisfaction. Mr. Polly smiled in return.

"You bicycle?" she said.

Mr. Polly admitted the fact, and she said she did too.

"All my people are in India," she explained. "It's beastly rot — I mean it's frightfully dull being left here alone."

"All *my* people," said Mr. Polly, "are in Heaven!"

"I say!"

"Fact!" said Mr. Polly. "Got nobody."

"And that's why —" she checked her artless comment on his mourning. "I say," she said in a sympathetic voice, "I *am* sorry. I really am. Was it a fire or a ship — or something?"

Her sympathy was very delightful. He shook his head. "The ordinary table of mortality," he said. "First one and then another."

Behind his outward melancholy, delight was dancing wildly. "Are *you* lonely?" asked the girl.

Mr. Polly nodded.

"I was just sitting there in melancholy rectrospectatiousness," he said, indicating the logs, and again a swift thoughtfulness swept across her face.

"There's no harm in our talking," she reflected.

"It's a kindness. Won't you get down?"

124

She reflected, and surveyed the turf below and the scene around and him.

"I'll stay on the wall," she said. "If only for bounds' sake."

She certainly looked quite adorable on the wall. She had a fine neck and pointed chin that was particularly admirable from below, and pretty eyes and fine eyebrows are never so pretty as when they look down upon one. But no calculation of that sort, thank Heaven, was going on beneath her ruddy shock of hair.

⇾≫ VI ≪⇽

"LET's talk," she said, and for a time they were both tongue-tied.

Mr. Polly's literary proclivities had taught him that under such circumstances a strain of gallantry was demanded. And something in his blood repeated that lesson.

"You make me feel like one of those old knights," he said, "who rode about the country looking for dragons and beautiful maidens and chivalresque adventures."

"Oh!" she said. "Why?"

"Beautiful maiden," he said.

She flushed under her freckles with the quick bright flush those pretty red-haired people have. "Nonsense!" she said.

"You are. I'm not the first to tell you that. A beautiful maiden imprisoned in an enchanted school."

"*You* wouldn't think it enchanted!"

"And here am I — clad in steel. Well, not exactly, but my fiery war horse is anyhow. Ready to absquatulate all the dragons and rescue you."

She laughed, a jolly laugh that showed delightfully gleaming teeth. "I wish you could *see* the dragons," she said with great enjoyment. Mr. Polly felt they were a sun's distance from the world of everyday.

"Fly with me!" he dared.

She stared for a moment, and then went off into peals of laughter. "You *are* funny!" she said. "Why, I haven't known you five minutes."

"One doesn't — in this medevial world. My mind is made up, anyhow."

He was proud and pleased with his joke, and quick to change his key neatly. "I wish one could," he said.

"I wonder if people ever did!"

"If there were people like you."

"We don't even know each other's names," she remarked with a descent to matters of fact.

"Yours is the prettiest name in the world."

"How do you know?"

"It must be — anyhow."

"It *is* rather pretty you know — it's Christabel."

126

"What did I tell you?"

"And yours?"

"Poorer than I deserve. It's Alfred."

"*I* can't call you Alfred."

"Well, Polly."

"It's a girl's name!"

For a moment he was out of tune. "I wish it was!" he said, and could have bitten out his tongue at the Larkins sound of it.

"I shan't forget it," she remarked consolingly.

"I say," she said in the pause that followed. "Why are you riding about the country on a bicycle?"

"I'm doing it because I like it."

She sought to estimate his social status on her limited basis of experience. He stood leaning with one hand against the wall, looking up at her and tingling with daring thoughts. He was a littleish man, you must remember, but neither mean-looking nor unhandsome in those days, sunburnt by his holiday and now warmly flushed. He had an inspiration to simple speech that no practised trifler with love could have bettered. "There *is* love at first sight," he said, and said it sincerely.

She stared at him with eyes round and big with excitement.

"I think," she said slowly, and without any signs of fear or retreat, "I ought to get back over the wall."

127

"It needn't matter to you," he said. "I'm just a nobody. But I know you are the best and most beautiful thing I've ever spoken to." His breath caught against something. "No harm in telling you that," he said.

"I should have to go back if I thought you were serious," she said after a pause, and they both smiled together.

After that they talked in a fragmentary way for some time. The blue eyes surveyed Mr. Polly with kindly curiosity from under a broad, finely modelled brow, much as an exceptionally intelligent cat might survey a new sort of dog. She meant to find out all about him. She asked questions that riddled the honest knight in armour below, and probed ever nearer to the hateful secret of the shop and his normal servitude. And when he made a flourish and mispronounced a word a thoughtful shade passed like the shadow of a cloud across her face.

"Boom!" came the sound of a gong.

"Lordy!" cried the girl and flashed a pair of brown legs at him and was gone.

Then her pink finger tips reappeared, and the top of her red hair. "Knight!" she cried from the other side of the wall. "Knight there!"

"Lady!" he answered.

"Come again to-morrow!"

"At your command. But——"

"Yes?"

"Just one finger."

"What do you mean?"

"To kiss."

The rustle of retreating footsteps and silence. . . .

But after he had waited next day for twenty minutes she reappeared, a little out of breath with the effort to surmount the wall — and head first this time. And it seemed to him she was lighter and more daring and altogether prettier than the dreams and enchanted memories that had filled the interval.

⇒≫ VII ≪⇐

FROM first to last their acquaintance lasted ten days, but into that time Mr. Polly packed ten years of dreams.

"He don't seem," said Johnson, "to take a serious interest in anything. That shop at the corner's bound to be snapped up if he don't look out."

The girl and Mr. Polly did not meet on every one of those ten days; one was Sunday and she could not come, and on the eighth the school reassembled and she made vague excuses. All their meetings amounted to this, that she sat on the wall, more or less in bounds as she expressed it, and let Mr. Polly fall in love with her and try to express it below. She sat in a state of irresponsible exaltation, watching him and at intervals prodding a vivisecting point of encouragement into him — with that strange passive cruelty which is natural to her sex and age.

And Mr. Polly fell in love, as though the world had given way beneath him and he had dropped through into another, into a world of luminous clouds and of desolate hopeless wildernesses of desiring and of wild valleys of unreasonable ecstasies, a world whose infinite miseries were finer and in some inexplicable way sweeter than the purest gold of the daily life, whose joys — they were indeed but the merest remote glimpses of joy — were brighter than a dying martyr's vision of heaven. Her smiling face looked down upon him out of heaven, her careless pose was the living body of life. It was senseless, it was utterly foolish, but all that was best and richest in Mr. Polly's nature broke like a wave and foamed up at that girl's feet, and died, and never touched her. And she sat on the wall and marvelled at him and was amused, and once, suddenly moved and wrung by his pleading, she bent down rather shamefacedly and gave him a freckled, tennis-blistered little paw to kiss. And she looked into his eyes and suddenly felt a perplexity, a curious swimming of the mind that made her recoil and stiffen, and wonder afterwards and dream. . . .

And then with some dim instinct of self-protection, she went and told her three best friends, great students of character all, of this remarkable phenomenon she had discovered on the other side of the wall.

"Look here," said Mr. Polly, "I'm wild for the love of you! I can't keep up this gesticulatious game any more! I'm not a Knight. Treat me as a human man. You may sit up there smiling, but I'd die in torments to have you mine for an hour. I'm nobody and nothing. But look here! Will you wait for me for five years? You're just a girl yet, and it wouldn't be hard."

"Shut up!" said Christabel in an aside he did not hear, and something he did not see touched her hand.

"I've always been just dilletentytating about till now, but I could work. I've just woke up. Wait till I've got a chance with the money I've got."

"But you haven't got much money!"

"I've got enough to take a chance with, some sort of a chance. I'd find a chance. I'll do that anyhow. I'll go away. I mean what I say — I'll stop trifling and shirking. If I don't come back it won't matter. If I do ——"

Her expression had become uneasy. Suddenly she bent down towards him.

"Don't!" she said in an undertone.

"Don't — what?"

"Don't go on like this! You're different! Go on being the knight who wants to kiss my hand as his —what did you call it?" The ghost of a smile curved her face. "Gurdrum!"

"But—— !"

Then through a pause they both stared at each other, listening.

A muffled tumult on the other side of the wall asserted itself.

"Shut *up*, Rosie!" said a voice.

"I tell you I will see! I can't half hear. Give me a leg up!"

"You Idiot! He'll see you. You're spoiling everything."

The bottom dropped out of Mr. Polly's world. He felt as people must feel who are going to faint.

"You've got someone——" he said aghast.

She found life inexpressible to Mr. Polly. She addressed some unseen hearers. "You filthy little Beasts!" she cried with a sharp note of agony in her voice, and swung herself back over the wall and vanished. There was a squeal of pain and fear, and a swift, fierce altercation.

For a couple of seconds he stood agape.

Then a wild resolve to confirm his worst sense of what was on the other side of the wall made him seize a log, put it against the stones, clutch the parapet with insecure fingers, and lug himself to a momentary balance on the wall.

Romance and his goddess had vanished.

A red-haired girl with a pigtail was wringing the wrist of a schoolfellow who shrieked with pain and cried: "Mercy! mercy! Ooo! Christabel!"

"You idiot!" cried Christabel. "You giggling Idiot!"

Two other young ladies made off through the beech trees from this outburst of savagery.

Then the grip of Mr. Polly's fingers gave, and he hit his chin against the stones and slipped clumsily to the ground again, scraping his cheek against the wall and hurting his shin against the log by which he had reached the top. Just for a moment he crouched against the wall.

He swore, staggered to the pile of logs and sat down.

He remained very still for some time, with his lips pressed together.

"Fool," he said at last; "you Blithering Fool!" and began to rub his shin as though he had just discovered its bruises.

Afterwards he found his face was wet with blood —which was none the less red stuff from the heart because it came from slight abrasions.

CHAPTER
THE SIXTH

MIRIAM

MIRIAM

I T is an illogical consequence of one human being's ill-treatment that we should fly immediately to another, but that is the way with us. It seemed to Mr. Polly that only a human touch could assuage the smart of his humiliation. Moreover it had for some undefined reason to be a feminine touch, and the number of women in his world was limited.

He thought of the Larkins family — the Larkins whom he had not been near now for ten long days. Healing people they seemed to him now — healing, simple people. They had good hearts, and he had neglected them for a mirage. If he rode over to them he would be able to talk nonsense and laugh and forget the whirl of memories and thoughts that was spinning round and round so unendurably in his brain.

"Law!" said Mrs. Larkins, "come in! You're quite a stranger, Elfrid!"

"Been seeing to business," said the unveracious Polly.

"None of 'em ain't at 'ome, but Miriam's just out to do a bit of shopping. Won't let me shop, she won't, because I'm so keerless. She's a wonderful manager, that girl. Minnie's got some work at the carpet place. 'Ope it won't make 'er ill again. She's a loving deliket sort, is Minnie. . . . Come into the front parlour. It's a bit untidy, but you got to take us as you find us. Wot you been doing to your face?"

"Bit of a scrase with the bicycle," said Mr. Polly.

" 'Ow?"

"Trying to pass a carriage on the on side, and he drew up and ran me against a wall."

Mrs. Larkins scrutinised it. "You ought to 'ave someone look after your scrases," she said. "That's all red and rough. It ought to be cold-creamed. Bring your bicycle into the passage and come in."

She "straightened up a bit," that is to say she increased the dislocation of a number of scattered articles, put a workbasket on the top of several books, swept two or three dogs'-eared numbers of the *Lady's Own Novelist* from the table into the broken armchair, and proceeded to sketch together

the tea-things with various such interpolations as:
"Law, if I ain't forgot the butter!" All the while
she talked of Annie's good spirits and cleverness
with her millinery, and of Minnie's affection and
Miriam's relative love of order and management.
Mr. Polly stood by the window uneasily and
thought how good and sincere was the Larkins
tone. It was well to be back again.

"You're a long time finding that shop of yours,"
said Mrs. Larkins.

"Don't do to be precipitous," said Mr. Polly.

"No," said Mrs. Larkins, "once you got it you
got it. Like choosing a 'usband. You better see you
got it good. I kept Larkins 'esitating two years I
did, until I felt sure of him. A 'ansom man 'e was
as you can see by the looks of the girls, but 'ansom
is as 'ansom does. You'd like a bit of jam to your
tea, I expect? I 'ope they'll keep *their* men waiting
when the time comes. I tell them if they think of
marrying it only shows they don't know when
they're well off. Here's Miriam!"

Miriam entered with several parcels in a net, and
a peevish expression. "Mother," she said, "you
might 'ave prevented my going out with the net
with the broken handle. I've been cutting my fingers with the string all the way 'ome." Then she
discovered Mr. Polly and her face brightened.

"Ello, Elfrid!" she said. "Where you been all
this time?"

"Looking round," said Mr. Polly.

"Found a shop?"

"One or two likely ones. But it takes time."

"You've got the wrong cups, Mother."

She went into the kitchen, disposed of her purchases, and returned with the right cups. "What you done to your face, Elfrid?" she asked, and came and scrutinised his scratches. "All rough it is."

He repeated his story of the accident, and she was sympathetic in a pleasant homely way.

"You *are* quiet to-day," she said as they sat down to tea.

"Meditatious," said Mr. Polly.

Quite by accident he touched her hand on the table, and she answered his touch.

"Why not?" thought Mr. Polly, and looking up, caught Mrs. Larkins' eye and flushed guiltily. But Mrs. Larkins, with unusual restraint, said nothing. She merely made a grimace, enigmatical, but in its essence friendly.

Presently Minnie came in with some vague grievance against the manager of the carpet-making place about his method of estimating piece work. Her account was redundant, defective and highly technical, but redeemed by a certain earnestness. "I'm never within sixpence of what I reckon to be," she said. "It's a bit too 'ot." Then Mr. Polly, feeling that he was being conspicuously dull, launched into a description of the shop he was looking for and the shops he had seen. His mind warmed up as he talked.

"Found your tongue again," said Mrs. Larkins.

He had. He began to embroider the subject and work upon it. For the first time it assumed picturesque and desirable qualities in his mind. It stimulated him to see how readily and willingly they accepted his sketches. Bright ideas appeared in his mind from nowhere. He was suddenly enthusiastic.

"When I get this shop of mine I shall have a cat. Must make a home for a cat, you know."

"What, to catch the mice?" said Mrs. Larkins.

"No — sleep in the window. A venerable signor of a cat. Tabby. Cat's no good if it isn't tabby. Cat I'm going to have, and a canary! Didn't think of that before, but a cat and a canary seem to go, you know. Summer weather I shall sit at breakfast in the little room behind the shop, sun streaming in the window to rights, cat on a chair, canary singing and — Mrs. Polly. . . ."

"Ello!" said Mrs. Larkins.

"Mrs. Polly frying an extra bit of bacon. Bacon singing, cat singing, canary singing. Kettle singing. Mrs. Polly ——"

"But who's Mrs. Polly going to be?" said Mrs. Larkins.

"Figment of the imagination, ma'am," said Mr.

Polly. "Put in to fill up picture. No face to figure as yet. Still, that's how it will be, I can assure you. I think I must have a bit of garden. Johnson's the man for a garden of course," he said, going off at a tangent, "but I don't mean a fierce sort of garden. Earnest industry. Anxious moments. Fervous digging. Shan't go in for that sort of garden, ma'am. No! Too much backache for me. My garden will be just a patch of 'sturtiums and sweet pea. Red brick yard, clothes' line. Trellis put up in odd time. Humorous wind vane. Creeper up the back of the house."

"Virginia creeper?" asked Miriam.

"Canary creeper," said Mr. Polly.

"You *will* 'ave it nice," said Miriam, desirously.

"Rather," said Mr. Polly. "Ting-a-ling-a-ling. *Shop!*"

He straightened himself up and then they all laughed.

"Smart little shop," he said. "Counter. Desk. All complete. Umbrella stand. Carpet on the floor. Cat asleep on the counter. Ties and hose on a rail over the counter. All right."

"I wonder you don't set about it right off," said Miriam.

"Mean to get it exactly right, m'am," said Mr. Polly.

"Have to have a tomcat," said Mr. Polly, and paused for an expectant moment. "Wouldn't do to

142

open shop one morning, you know, and find the window full of kittens. Can't sell kittens. . . ."

When tea was over he was left alone with Minnie for a few minutes, and an odd intimation of an incident occurred that left Mr. Polly rather scared and shaken. A silence fell between them — an uneasy silence. He sat with his elbows on the table looking at her. All the way from Easewood to Stamton his erratic imagination had been running upon neat ways of proposing marriage. I don't know why it should have done, but it had. It was a kind of secret exercise that had not had any definite aim at the time, but which now recurred to him with extraordinary force. He couldn't think of anything in the world that wasn't the gambit to a proposal. It was almost irresistibly fascinating to think how immensely a few words from him would excite and revolutionise Minnie. She was sitting at the table with a workbasket among the tea things, mending a glove in order to avoid her share of clearing away.

"I like cats," said Minnie after a thoughtful pause. "I'm always saying to mother, 'I wish we 'ad a cat.' But we couldn't 'ave a cat 'ere — not with no yard."

"Never had a cat myself," said Mr. Polly. "No!"

"I'm fond of them," said Minnie.

"I like the look of them," said Mr. Polly. "Can't exactly call myself fond."

"I expect I shall get one some day. When about you get your shop."

"I shall have my shop all right before long," said Mr. Polly. "Trust me. Canary bird and all."

She shook her head. "I shall get a cat first," she said. "You never mean anything you say."

"Might get 'em together," said Mr. Polly, with his sense of a neat thing outrunning his discretion.

"Why! 'ow d'you mean?" said Minnie, suddenly alert.

"Shop and cat thrown in," said Mr. Polly in spite of himself, and his head swam and he broke out into a cold sweat as he said it.

He found her eyes fixed on him with an eager expression. "Mean to say——" she began as if for verification. He sprang to his feet, and turned to the window. "Little dog!" he said, and moved door-ward hastily. "Eating my bicycle tire, I believe," he explained. And so escaped.

He saw his bicycle in the hall and cut it dead.

He heard Mrs. Larkins in the passage behind him as he opened the front door.

He turned to her. "Thought my bicycle was on fire," he said. "Outside. Funny fancy! All right, reely. Little dog outside. . . . Miriam ready?"

"What for?"

"To go and meet Annie."

Mrs. Larkins stared at him. "You're stopping for a bit of supper?"

144

"If I may," said Mr. Polly.

"You're a rum un," said Mrs. Larkins, and called: "Miriam!"

Minnie appeared at the door of the room looking infinitely perplexed. "There ain't a little dog anywhere, Elfrid," she said.

Mr. Polly passed his hand over his brow. "I had a most curious sensation. Felt exactly as though something was up somewhere. That's why I said Little Dog. All right now."

He bent down and pinched his bicycle tire.

"You was saying something about a cat, Elfrid," said Minnie.

"Give you one," he answered without looking up. "The very day my shop is opened."

He straightened himself up and smiled reassuringly. "Trust me," he said.

⋙ II ⋘

WHEN, after imperceptible manœuvres by Mrs. Larkins, he found himself starting circuitously through the inevitable recreation ground with Miriam to meet Annie, he found himself quite unable to avoid the topic of the shop that had now taken such a grip upon him. A sense of danger only increased the attraction. Minnie's persistent disposition to accompany them had been crushed by a novel and violent and urgently expressed desire on

145

the part of Mrs. Larkins to see her do something in the house sometimes. . . .

"You really think you'll open a shop?" asked Miriam.

"I hate cribs," said Mr. Polly, adopting a moderate tone. "In a shop there's this drawback and that, but one *is* one's own master."

"That wasn't all talk?"

"Not a bit of it."

"After all," he went on, "a little shop needn't be so bad."

"It's a 'ome," said Miriam.

"It's a home."

Pause.

"There's no need to keep accounts and that sort of thing if there's no assistant. I daresay I could run a shop all right if I wasn't interfered with."

"I should like to see you in your shop," said Miriam. "I expect you'd keep everything tremendously neat."

The conversation flagged.

"Let's sit down on one of those seats over there," said Miriam. "Where we can see those blue flowers."

They did as she suggested, and sat down in a corner where a triangular bed of stock and delphinium brightened the asphalted traceries of the Recreation Ground.

"I wonder what they call those flowers," she said. "I always like them. They're handsome."

"Delphicums and larkspurs," said Mr. Polly. "They used to be in the park at Port Burdock.

"Floriferous corner," he added approvingly.

He put an arm over the back of the seat, and assumed a more comfortable attitude. He glanced at Miriam, who was sitting in a lax, thoughtful pose with her eyes on the flowers. She was wearing her old dress, she had not had time to change, and the blue tones of her old dress brought out a certain warmth in her skin, and her pose exaggerated whatever was feminine in her rather lean and insufficient body, and rounded her flat chest delusively. A little line of light lay along her profile. The afternoon was full of transfiguring sunshine, children were playing noisily in the adjacent sand-pit, some Judas trees were brightly abloom in the villa gardens that bordered the Recreation Ground, and all the place was bright with touches of young summer colour. It all merged with the effect of Miriam in Mr. Polly's mind.

Her thoughts found speech. "One did ought to be happy in a shop," she said with a note of unusual softness in her voice.

It seemed to him that she was right. One did ought to be happy in a shop. Folly not to banish dreams that made one ache of townless woods and bracken tangles and red-haired linen-clad figures sitting in dappled sunshine upon grey and crumbling walls and looking queenly down on one with clear blue eyes. Cruel and foolish dreams they were, that ended in one's being laughed at and made a mock of. There was no mockery here.

"A shop's such a respectable thing to be," said Miriam thoughtfully.

"*I* could be happy in a shop," he said.

His sense of effect made him pause.

"If I had the right company," he added.

She became very still.

Mr. Polly swerved a little from the conversational ice-run upon which he had embarked.

"I'm not such a blooming Geezer," he said, "as not to be able to sell goods a bit. One has to be nosy over one's buying of course. But I shall do all right."

He stopped, and felt falling, falling through the aching silence that followed.

"If you get the right company," said Miriam.

"I shall get that all right."

"You don't mean you've got someone——"

He found himself plunging.

"I've got someone in my eye, this minute," he said.

"Elfrid!" she said, turning on him. "You don't mean——"

Well, *did* he mean? "I do!" he said.

"Not reely!" She clenched her hands to keep still.

He took the conclusive step.

148

"Well, you and me, Miriam, in a little shop—with a cat and a canary—." He tried too late to get back to a hypothetical note. "Just suppose it!"

"You mean," said Miriam, "you're in love with me, Elfrid?"

What possible answer can a man give to such a question but "Yes!"

Regardless of the public park, the children in the sandpit and everyone, she bent forward and seized his shoulder and kissed him on the lips. Something lit up in Mr. Polly at the touch. He put an arm about her and kissed her back, and felt an irrevocable act was sealed. He had a curious feeling that it would be very satisfying to marry and have a wife—only somehow he wished it wasn't Miriam. Her lips were very pleasant to him, and the feel of her in his arm.

They recoiled a little from each other and sat for a moment, flushed and awkwardly silent. His mind was altogether incapable of controlling its confusion.

"I didn't dream," said Miriam, "you cared—. Sometimes I thought it was Annie, sometimes Minnie——"

"Always liked you better than them," said Mr. Polly.

"I loved you, Elfrid," said Miriam, "since ever we met at your poor father's funeral. Leastways I

would have done, if I had thought. You didn't seem
to mean anything you said.

"I *can't* believe it!" she added.

"Nor I," said Mr. Polly.

"You mean to marry me and start that little
shop ——"

"Soon as ever I find it," said Mr. Polly.

"I had no more idea when I came out with
you ——"

"Nor me!"

"It's like a dream."

They said no more for a little while.

"I got to pinch myself to think it's real," said
Miriam. "What they'll do without me at 'ome I
can't imagine. When I tell them ——"

For the life of him Mr. Polly could not tell
whether he was fullest of tender anticipations or
regretful panic.

"Mother's no good at managing — not a bit.
Annie don't care for 'ouse work and Minnie's got
no 'ed for it. What they'll do without me I can't
imagine."

"They'll have to do without you," said Mr.
Polly, sticking to his guns.

A clock in the town began striking.

"Lor'!" said Miriam, "we shall miss Annie —
sitting 'ere and love-making!"

She rose and made as if to take Mr. Polly's arm.
But Mr. Polly felt that their condition must be

nakedly exposed to the ridicule of the world by such a linking, and evaded her movement.

Annie was already in sight before a flood of hesitation and terrors assailed Mr. Polly.

"Don't tell anyone yet a bit," he said.

"Only mother," said Miriam firmly.

⇛ III ⇚

Figures are the most shocking things in the world. The prettiest little squiggles of black — looked at in the right light, and yet consider the blow they can give you upon the heart. You return from a little careless holiday abroad, and turn over the page of a newspaper, and against the name of that distant, vague-conceived railway in mortgages upon which you have embarked the bulk of your capital, you see instead of the familiar, persistent 95–6 (varying at most to 93 *ex. div.*) this slightly richer arrangement of marks: $76\frac{1}{2}$–$78\frac{1}{2}$.

It is like the opening of a pit just under your feet!

So, too, Mr. Polly's happy sense of limitless resources was obliterated suddenly by a vision of this tracery: "298"

instead of the   "350"

he had come to regard as the fixed symbol of his affluence.

It gave him a disagreeable feeling about the diaphragm, akin in a remote degree to the sensation he had when the perfidy of the red-haired schoolgirl became plain to him. It made his brow moist.

"Going down a vortex!" he whispered.

By a characteristic feat of subtraction he decided that he must have spent sixty-two pounds.

"Funererial baked meats," he said, recalling possible items.

The happy dream in which he had been living of long warm days, of open roads, of limitless unchecked hours, of infinite time to look about him, vanished like a thing enchanted. He was suddenly back in the hard old economic world, that exacts work, that limits range, that discourages phrasing and dispels laughter. He saw Wood Street and its fearful suspenses yawning beneath his feet.

And also he had promised to marry Miriam, and on the whole rather wanted to.

He was distraught at supper. Afterwards, when Mrs. Johnson had gone to bed with a slight headache, he opened a conversation with Johnson.

"It's about time, O' Man, I saw about doing something," he said. "Riding about and looking at shops, all very debonnairious, O' Man, but it's time I took one for keeps."

"What did I tell you?" said Johnson.

"How do you think that corner shop of yours will figure out?" Mr. Polly asked.

"You're really meaning it?"

"If it's a practable proposition, O' Man. Assuming it's practable. What's your idea of the figures?"

Johnson went to the chiffonier, got out a letter and tore off the back sheet. "Let's figure it out," he said with solemn satisfaction. "Let's see the lowest you could do it on."

He squared himself to the task, and Mr. Polly sat beside him like a pupil, watching the evolution of the grey, distasteful figures that were to dispose of his little hoard.

"What running expenses have we got to provide for?" said Johnson, wetting his pencil. "Let's have them first. Rent? . . ."

At the end of an hour of hideous speculations, Johnson decided: "It's close. But you'll have a chance."

"M'm," said Mr. Polly. "What more does a brave man want?"

"One thing you can do quite easily. I've asked about it."

"What's that, O' Man?" said Mr. Polly.

"Take the shop without the house above it."

"I suppose I might put my head in to mind it," said Mr. Polly, "and get a job with my body."

"Not exactly that. But I thought you'd save a lot if you stayed on here — being all alone as you are."

"Never thought of that, O' Man," said Mr. Polly, and reflected silently upon the needlessness of Miriam.

"We were talking of eighty pounds for stock," said Johnson. "Of course seventy-five is five pounds less, isn't it? Not much else we can cut."

"No," said Mr. Polly.

"It's very interesting, all this," said Johnson, folding up the half sheet of paper and unfolding it. "I wish sometimes I had a business of my own instead of a fixed salary. You'll have to keep books of course."

"One wants to know where one is."

"I should do it all by double entry," said Johnson. "A little troublesome at first, but far the best in the end."

"Lemme see that paper," said Mr. Polly, and took it with the feeling of a man who takes a nauseating medicine, and scrutinised his cousin's neat figures with listless eyes.

"Well," said Johnson, rising and stretching. "Bed! Better sleep on it, O' Man."

"Right O," said Mr. Polly without moving, but indeed he could as well have slept upon a bed of thorns.

He had a dreadful night. It was like the end of the annual holiday, only infinitely worse. It was like a newly arrived prisoner's backward glance at the trees and heather through the prison gates.

154

He had to go back to harness, and he was as fitted
to go in harness as the ordinary domestic cat. All
night, Fate, with the quiet complacency, and indeed at times the very face and gestures of Johnson, guided him towards that undesired establishment at the corner near the station. "Oh Lord!" he
cried, "I'd rather go back to cribs. I *should* keep
my money anyhow." Fate never winced.

"Run away to sea," whispered Mr. Polly, but he
knew he wasn't man enough.

"Cut my blooming throat."

Some braver strain urged him to think of Miriam, and for a little while he lay still. . . .

"Well, O' Man?" said Johnson, when Mr. Polly
came down to breakfast, and Mrs. Johnson looked
up brightly. Mr. Polly had never felt breakfast so
unattractive before.

"Just a day or so more, O' Man — to turn it
over in my mind," he said.

"You'll get the place snapped up," said Johnson.

There were times in those last few days of coy-
ness with his destiny when his engagement seemed
the most negligible of circumstances, and times —
and these happened for the most part at nights
after Mrs. Johnson had indulged everybody in a
Welsh rarebit — when it assumed so sinister and
portentous an appearance as to make him think of
suicide. And there were times too when he very dis-

tinctly desired to be married, now that the idea had got into his head, at any cost. Also he tried to recall all the circumstances of his proposal, time after time, and never quite succeeded in recalling what had brought the thing off. He went over to Stamton with a becoming frequency, and kissed all his cousins, and Miriam especially, a great deal, and found it very stirring and refreshing. They all appeared to know; and Minnie was tearful, but resigned. Mrs. Larkins met him, and indeed enveloped him, with unwonted warmth, and there was a big pot of household jam for tea. And he could not make up his mind to sign his name to anything about the shop, though it crawled nearer and nearer to him, though the project had materialised now to the extent of a draft agreement with the place for his signature indicated in pencil.

One morning, just after Mr. Johnson had gone to the station, Mr. Polly wheeled his bicycle out into the road, went up to his bedroom, packed his long white nightdress, a comb, and a toothbrush in a manner that was as offhand as he could make it, informed Mrs. Johnson, who was manifestly curious, that he was "off for a day or two to clear his head," and fled forthright into the road, and mounting turned his wheel towards the tropics and the equator and the south coast of England, and indeed more particularly to where the little village of Fishbourne slumbers and sleeps.

When he returned four days later, he astonished Johnson beyond measure by remarking so soon as the shop project was reopened:

"I've took a little contraption at Fishbourne, O' Man, that I fancy suits me better."

He paused, and then added in a manner, if possible, even more offhand:

"Oh! and I'm going to have a bit of a nuptial over at Stamton with one of the Larkins cousins."

"Nuptial!" said Johnson.

"Wedding bells, O' Man. Benedictine collapse."

On the whole Johnson showed great self-control. "It's your own affair, O' Man," he said, when things had been more clearly explained, "and I hope you won't feel sorry when it's too late."

But Mrs. Johnson was first of all angrily silent, and then reproachful. "I don't see what we've done to be made fools of like this," she said. "After all the trouble we've 'ad to make you comfortable and see after you. Out late and sitting up and everything. And then you go off as sly as sly without a word, and get a shop behind our backs as though you thought we meant to steal your money. I 'aven't patience with such deceitfulness, and I didn't think it of you, Elfrid. And now the letting season's 'arf gone by, and what I shall do with that room of yours I've no idea. Frank is frank, and fair play fair play; so *I* was told any'ow when I was a girl. Just as long as it suits you to stay 'ere you stay 'ere, and then it's off and no thank you whether we like it or not. Johnson's too easy with you. 'E sits there and doesn't say a word, and night after night 'e's been addin' and thinkin' for you, instead of seeing to his own affairs——"

She paused for breath.

"Unfortunate amoor," said Mr. Polly, apologetically and indistinctly. "Didn't expect it myself."

→» IV «←

Mr. Polly's marriage followed with a certain inevitableness.

He tried to assure himself that he was acting upon his own forceful initiative, but at the back of his mind was the completest realisation of his powerlessness to resist the gigantic social forces he had set in motion. He had got to marry under the will of society, even as in times past it has been appointed for other sunny souls under the will of society that they should be led out by serious and unavoidable fellow-creatures and ceremoniously drowned or burnt or hung. He would have preferred infinitely a more observant and less conspicuous rôle, but the choice was no longer open to him. He did his best to play his part, and he procured some particularly neat check trousers to do it in. The rest of his costume, except for some bright yellow gloves, a grey and blue mixture tie, and that the broad crape hat-band was changed for a livelier piece of silk, were the things he had worn at the funeral of his father. So nearly akin are human joy and sorrow.

The Larkins sisters had done wonders with grey sateen. The idea of orange blossom and white veils had been abandoned reluctantly on account of the expense of cabs. A novelette in which the heroine had stood at the altar in "a modest going-away dress" had materially assisted this decision. Miriam was frankly tearful, and so indeed was Annie, but with laughter as well to carry it off. Mr. Polly heard Annie say something vague about never getting a chance because of Miriam always sticking about at home like a cat at a mouse-hole, that became, as people say, food for thought. Mrs. Larkins was from the first flushed, garrulous, and wet and smeared by copious weeping; an incredibly soaked and crumpled and used-up pocket handkerchief never left the clutch of her plump red hand. "Goo' girls, all of them," she kept on saying in a tremulous voice; "such-goo-goo-goo-girls!" She wetted Mr. Polly dreadfully when she kissed him. Her emotion affected the buttons down the back of her bodice, and almost the last filial duty Miriam did before entering on her new life was to close that gaping orifice for the eleventh time. Her bonnet was small and ill-balanced, black adorned with red roses, and first it got over her right eye until Annie

told her of it, and then she pushed it over her left
eye and looked ferocious for a space, and after that
baptismal kissing of Mr. Polly the delicate millinery took fright and climbed right up to the back
part of her head and hung on there by a pin, and
flapped piteously at all the larger waves of emotion
that filled the gathering. Mr. Polly became more
and more aware of that bonnet as time went on, until he felt for it like a thing alive. Towards the end
it had yawning fits.

The company did not include Mrs. Johnson, but
Johnson came with a manifest surreptitiousness
and backed against walls and watched Mr. Polly
with doubt and speculation in his large grey eyes
and whistled noiselessly and doubtful on the edge
of things. He was, so to speak, to be best man, *sotto
voce*. A sprinkling of girls in gay hats from Miriam's place of business appeared in church, great
nudgers all of them, but only two came on afterwards to the house. Mrs. Punt brought her son
with his ever-widening mind, it was his first wedding, and a Larkins uncle, a Mr. Voules, a licenced
victualler, very kindly drove over in a gig from
Sommershill with a plump, well-dressed wife to give
the bride away. One or two total strangers drifted
into the church and sat down observantly far away.

This sprinkling of people seemed only to enhance the cool brown emptiness of the church, the
rows and rows of empty pews, disengaged prayer-

books and abandoned hassocks. It had the effect of a preposterous misfit. Johnson consulted with a thin-legged, short-skirted verger about the disposition of the party. The officiating clergy appeared distantly in the doorway of the vestry, putting on his surplice, and relapsed into a contemplative cheek-scratching that was manifestly habitual. Before the bride arrived Mr. Polly's sense of the church found an outlet in whispered criticisms of ecclesiastical architecture with Johnson. "Early Norman arches, eh?" he said, "or Perpendicular."

"Can't say," said Johnson.

"Telessated pavements, all right."

"It's well laid anyhow."

"Can't say I admire the altar. Scrappy rather with those flowers."

He coughed behind his hand and cleared his throat. At the back of his mind he was speculating whether flight at this eleventh hour would be criminal or merely reprehensible bad taste. A murmur from the nudgers announced the arrival of the bridal party.

The little procession from a remote door became one of the enduring memories of Mr. Polly's life. The little verger had bustled to meet it, and arrange it according to tradition and morality. In spite of Mrs. Larkins' "Don't take her from me yet!" he made Miriam go first with Mr. Voules, the bridesmaids followed and then himself hopelessly

unable to disentangle himself from the whispering
maternal anguish of Mrs. Larkins. Mrs. Voules, a
compact, rounded woman with a square, expressionless face, imperturbable dignity, and a dress of
considerable fashion, completed the procession.

Mr. Polly's eye fell first upon the bride; the
sight of her filled him with a curious stir of emotion. Alarm, desire, affection, respect — and a
queer element of reluctant dislike all played their
part in that complex eddy. The grey dress made
her a stranger to him, made her stiff and common-
place, she was not even the rather drooping form
that had caught his facile sense of beauty when he
had proposed to her in the Recreation Ground.
There was something too that did not please him
in the angle of her hat, it was indeed an ill-conceived hat with large aimless rosettes of pink and
grey. Then his mind passed to Mrs. Larkins and
the bonnet that was to gain such a hold upon him;
it seemed to be flag-signalling as she advanced, and
to the two eager, unrefined sisters he was acquiring.

A freak of fancy set him wondering where and
when in the future a beautiful girl with red hair
might march along some splendid aisle. Never
mind! He became aware of Mr. Voules.

He became aware of Mr. Voules as a watchful,
blue eye of intense forcefulness. It was the eye of a
man who has got hold of a situation. He was a fat,

short, red-faced man clad in a tight-fitting tail
coat of black and white check with a coquettish bow
tie under the lowest of a number of crisp little red
chins. He held the bride under his arm with an air
of invincible championship, and his free arm flour-
ished a grey top hat of an equestrian type. Mr.
Polly instantly learnt from the eye that Mr. Voules
knew all about his longing for flight. Its azure pupil glowed with disciplined resolution. It said: "I've
come to give this girl away, and give her away I
will. I'm here now and things have to go on all
right. So don't think of it any more"—and Mr.
Polly didn't. A faint phantom of a certain "lill'
dog" that had hovered just beneath the threshold
of consciousness vanished into black impossibility.
Until the conclusive moment of the service was at-
tained the eye of Mr. Voules watched Mr. Polly
relentlessly, and then instantly he relieved guard,
and blew his nose into a voluminous and richly patterned handkerchief, and sighed and looked round
for the approval and sympathy of Mrs. Voules,
and nodded to her brightly like one who has always
foretold a successful issue to things. Mr. Polly felt
then like a marionette that has just dropped off
its wire. But it was long before that release arrived.

He became aware of Miriam breathing close to
him.

"Hullo!" he said, and feeling that was clumsy

and would meet the eye's disapproval: "Grey dress
—suits you no end."

Miriam's eyes shone under her hat-brim.

"Not reely!" she whispered.

"You're all right," he said with the feeling of
observation and criticism stiffening his lips. He
cleared his throat.

The verger's hand pushed at him from behind.
Someone was driving Miriam towards the altar
rail and the clergyman. "We're in for it," said Mr.
Polly to her sympathetically. "Where? Here?
Right O."

He was interested for a moment or so in something indescribably habitual in the clergyman's
pose. What a lot of weddings he must have seen!
Sick he must be of them!

"Don't let your attention wander," said the eye.

"Got the ring?" whispered Johnson.

"Pawned it yesterday," answered Mr. Polly and
then had a dreadful moment under that pitiless
scrutiny while he felt in the wrong waistcoat
pocket. . . .

The officiating clergy sighed deeply, began, and
married them wearily and without any hitch.

*"D'b'loved, we gath'd 'gether sight o' Gard 'n
face this con'gation join 'gather Man, Wom'
Holy Mat'my which is on'bl state stooted by Gard
in times man's innocency. . . ."*

Mr. Polly's thoughts wandered wide and far,

and once again something like a cold hand touched his heart, and he saw a sweet face in sunshine under the shadow of trees.

Someone was nudging him. It was Johnson's finger diverted his eyes to the crucial place in the prayer-book to which they had come.

"Wiltou lover, cumfer, oner, keeper sickness and health . . ."

"Say 'I will.'"

Mr. Polly moistened his lips. "I will," he said hoarsely.

Miriam, nearly inaudible, answered some similar demand.

Then the clergyman said: "Who gifs Wom married to this man?"

"Well, *I'm* doing that," said Mr. Voules in a refreshingly full voice and looking round the church. "You see, me and Martha Larkins being cousins——"

He was silenced by the clergyman's rapid grip directing the exchange of hands.

"Pete arf me," said the clergyman to Mr. Polly. "Take thee Mirum wed wife——"

"Take thee Mirum wed' wife," said Mr. Polly.

"Have hold this day ford."

"Have hold this day ford."

"Betworse, richpoo'——"

"Bet worsh, richpoo'. . . ."

Then came Miriam's turn.

"Lego hands," said the clergyman; "got the ring? No! On the book. So! Here! Pete arf me, 'withis ring Ivy wed.'"

"Withis ring Ivy wed———"

So it went on, blurred and hurried, like the momentary vision of an utterly beautiful thing seen through the smoke of a passing train. . . .

"Now, my boy," said Mr. Voules at last, gripping Mr. Polly's elbow tightly, "you've got to sign the registry, and there you are! Done!"

Before him stood Miriam, a little stiffly, the hat with a slight rake across her forehead, and a kind of questioning hesitation in her face. Mr. Voules urged him past her.

It was astounding. She was his wife!

And for some reason Miriam and Mrs. Larkins were sobbing, and Annie was looking grave. Hadn't they after all wanted him to marry her? Because if that was the case——— !

He became aware for the first time of the presence of Uncle Pentstemon in the background, but approaching, wearing a tie of a light mineral blue colour, and grinning and sucking enigmatically and judiciously round his principal tooth.

⇉ V ⇇

IT WAS in the vestry that the force of Mr. Voules' personality began to show at its true value. He seemed to open out and spread over things directly the restraints of the ceremony were at an end.

"Everything," he said to the clergyman, "excellent." He also shook hands with Mrs. Larkins, who clung to him for a space, and kissed Miriam on the cheek. "First kiss for me," he said, "anyhow."

He led Mr. Polly to the register by the arm, and then got chairs for Mrs. Larkins and his wife. He then turned on Miriam. "Now, young people," he said. "One! or *I* shall again."

"That's right!" said Mr. Voules. "Same again, Miss."

Mr. Polly was overcome with modest confusion, and turning, found a refuge from this publicity in the arms of Mrs. Larkins. Then in a state of profuse moisture he was assaulted and kissed by Annie and Minnie, who were immediately kissed upon some indistinctly stated grounds by Mr. Voules, who then kissed the entirely impassive Mrs. Voules and smacked his lips and remarked: "Home again safe and sound!" Then with a strange harrowing cry Mrs. Larkins seized upon and bedewed Miriam with kisses, Annie and Minnie kissed each other, and Johnson went abruptly to the door of the vestry and stared into the church — no doubt with ideas of sanctuary in his mind. "Like a bit of a kiss round sometimes," said Mr. Voules, and made a kind of hissing noise with his teeth, and suddenly smacked his hands together with great *éclat* several times. Meanwhile the clergyman scratched his cheek with one hand and fiddled the pen with the other and the verger coughed protestingly.

"The dog cart's just outside," said Mr. Voules. "No walking home to-day for the bride, Mam."

"Not going to drive us?" cried Annie.

"The happy pair, Miss. *Your* turn soon."

"Get out!" said Annie. "I shan't marry — ever."

"You won't be able to help it. You'll have to do it — just to disperse the crowd." Mr. Voules laid his hand on Mr. Polly's shoulder. "The bridegroom gives his arm to the bride. Hands across and down the middle. Prump. Prump, Perump-pump-pump-pump."

Mr. Polly found himself and the bride leading the way towards the western door.

Mrs. Larkins passed close to Uncle Pentstemon, sobbing too earnestly to be aware of him. "Such a goo-goo-goo-girl!" she sobbed.

"Didn't think *I'd* come, did you?" said Uncle Pentstemon, but she swept past him, too busy with the expression of her feelings to observe him.

"She didn't think I'd come, I lay," said Uncle Pentstemon, a little foiled, but effecting an auditory lodgment upon Johnson.

"I don't know," said Johnson uncomfortably. "I suppose you were asked. How are you getting on?"

168

"I was *arst*," said Uncle Pentstemon, and brooded for a moment.

"I goes about seeing wonders," he added, and then in a sort of enhanced undertone: "One of 'er girls gettin' married. That's what I mean by wonders. Lord's goodness! Wow!"

"Nothing the matter?" asked Johnson.

"Got it in the back for a moment. Going to be a change of weather I suppose," said Uncle Pentstemon. "I brought 'er a nice present, too, what I got in this passel. Vallyble old tea caddy that uset' be my mother's. What I kep' my baccy in for years and years—till the hinge at the back got broke. It ain't been no use to me particular since, so thinks I, drat it! I may as well give it 'er as not. . . ."

Mr. Polly found himself emerging from the western door.

Outside, a crowd of half-a-dozen adults and about fifty children had collected, and hailed the approach of the newly wedded couple with a faint, indeterminate cheer. All the children were holding something in little bags, and his attention was caught by the expression of vindictive concentration upon the face of a small big-eared boy in the foreground. He didn't for the moment realise what these things might import. Then he received a stinging handful of rice in the ear, and a great light shone.

"Not yet, you young fool!" he heard Mr. Voules saying behind him, and then a second handful spoke against his hat.

"Not yet," said Mr. Voules with increasing emphasis, and Mr. Polly became aware that he and Miriam were the focus of two crescents of small boys, each with the light of massacre in his eyes and a grubby fist clutching into a paper bag for rice; and that Mr. Voules was warding off probable discharges with a large red hand.

The dog cart was in charge of a loafer, and the horse and the whip were adorned with white favours, and the back seat was confused but not untenable with hampers. "Up we go," said Mr. Voules, "old birds in front and young ones behind." An ominous group of ill-restrained rice-throwers followed them up as they mounted.

"Get your handkerchief for your face," said Mr. Polly to his bride, and took the place next the pavement with considerable heroism, held on, gripped his hat, shut his eyes and prepared for the worst. "Off!" said Mr. Voules, and a concentrated fire came stinging Mr. Polly's face.

The horse shied, and when the bridegroom could look at the world again it was manifest the dog cart had just missed an electric tram by a hairsbreadth, and far away outside the church railings the verger and Johnson were battling with an active crowd of small boys for the life of the rest of the Larkins family. Mrs. Punt and her son had escaped across the road, the son trailing and stumbling at the end of a remorseless arm, but Uncle Pentstemon, encumbered by the tea-caddy, was the centre of a little circle of his own, and appeared to be dratting them all very heartily. Remoter, a policeman approached with an air of tranquil unconsciousness.

"Steady, you idiot. Stead-y!" cried Mr. Voules, and then over his shoulder: "I brought that rice! I like old customs! Whoa! Stead-y."

The dog cart swerved violently, and then, evoking a shout of groundless alarm from a cyclist, took a corner, and the rest of the wedding party was hidden from Mr. Polly's eyes.

→» VI «←

"WE'LL get the stuff into the house before the old gal comes along," said Mr. Voules, "if you'll hold the hoss."

"How about the key?" asked Mr. Polly.

"I got the key, coming."

And while Mr. Polly held the sweating horse and dodged the foam that dripped from its bit, the house absorbed Miriam and Mr. Voules altogether. Mr. Voules carried in the various hampers he had brought with him, and finally closed the door behind him.

For some time Mr. Polly remained alone with his charge in the little blind alley outside the Larkins' house, while the neighbours scrutinised him from behind their blinds. He reflected that he was a married man, that he must look very like a fool, that the head of a horse is a silly shape and its eye a bulger; he wondered what the horse thought of him, and whether it really liked being held and patted on the neck or whether it only submitted out of contempt. Did it know he was married? Then he wondered if the clergyman had thought him much of an ass, and then whether the individual lurking behind the lace curtains of the front room next door was a man or a woman. A door opened over the way, and an elderly gentleman in a kind of embroidered fez appeared smoking a pipe with a quiet satisfied expression. He regarded Mr. Polly for some time with mild but sustained curiosity. Finally he called: "Hi!"

"Hullo!" said Mr. Polly.

"You needn't 'old that 'orse," said the old gentleman.

"Spirited beast," said Mr. Polly. "And," — with some faint analogy to ginger beer in his mind — "he's up to-day."

" 'E won't turn 'isself round," said the old gentleman, "anyow. And there ain't no way through for 'im to go."

"Verbum sap," said Mr. Polly, and abandoned

172

the horse and turned to the door. It opened to him just as Mrs. Larkins on the arm of Johnson, followed by Annie, Minnie, two friends, Mrs. Punt and her son and at a slight distance Uncle Pentstemon, appeared round the corner.

"They're coming," he said to Miriam, and put an arm about her and gave her a kiss.

She was kissing him back when they were startled violently by the shying of two empty hampers into the passage. Then Mr. Voules appeared holding a third.

"Here! you'll 'ave plenty of time for that presently," he said, "get these hampers away before the old girl comes. I got a cold collation here to make her sit up. My eye!"

Miriam took the hampers, and Mr. Polly under compulsion from Mr. Voules went into the little front room. A profuse pie and a large ham had been added to the modest provision of Mrs. Larkins, and a number of select-looking bottles shouldered the bottle of sherry and the bottle of port she had got to grace the feast. They certainly went better with the iced wedding cake in the middle. Mrs. Voules, still impassive, stood by the window regarding these things with a faint approval.

"Makes it look a bit thicker, eh?" said Mr. Voules, and blew out both his cheeks and smacked his hands together violently several times. "Surprise the old girl no end."

He stood back and smiled and bowed with arms extended as the others came clustering at the door.

"Why, Un-cle Voules!" cried Annie, with a rising note.

It was his reward.

And then came a great wedging and squeezing and crowding into the little room. Nearly everyone was hungry, and eyes brightened at the sight of the pie and the ham and the convivial array of bottles. "Sit down everyone," cried Mr. Voules, "leaning against anything counts as sitting, and makes it easier to shake down the grub!"

The two friends from Miriam's place of business came into the room among the first, and then wedged themselves so hopelessly against Johnson in an attempt to get out again and take off their things upstairs that they abandoned the attempt. Amid the struggle Mr. Polly saw Uncle Pentstemon relieve himself of his parcel by giving it to the bride. "Here!" he said and handed it to her. "Weddin' present," he explained, and added with a confidential chuckle, "*I* never thought I'd 'ave to give you one — ever."

"Who says steak and kidney pie?" bawled Mr. Voules. "Who says steak and kidney pie? You 'ave a drop of old Tommy, Martha. That's what you want to steady you. . . . Sit down everyone and don't all speak at once. Who says steak and kidney pie? . . ."

"Vocificeratious," whispered Mr. Polly. "Convivial vocificerations."

"Bit of 'am with it," shouted Mr. Voules, poising a slice of ham on his knife. "Anyone 'ave a bit of 'am with it? Won't that little man of yours, Mrs. Punt — won't 'e 'ave a bit of 'am? . . ."

"And now ladies and gentlemen," said Mr. Voules, still standing and dominating the crammed roomful, "now you got your plates filled and something I can warrant you good in your glasses, wot about drinking the 'ealth of the bride?"

"Eat a bit fust," said Uncle Pentstemon, speaking with his mouth full, amidst murmurs of applause. "Eat a bit fust."

So they did, and the plates clattered and the glasses chinked.

Mr. Polly stood shoulder to shoulder with Johnson for a moment.

"In for it," said Mr. Polly cheeringly. "Cheer up, O' Man, and peck a bit. No reason why *you* shouldn't eat, you know."

The Punt boy stood on Mr. Polly's boots for a minute, struggling violently against the compunction of Mrs. Punt's grip.

"Pie," said the Punt boy, "Pie!"

"You sit 'ere and 'ave 'am, my lord!" said Mrs. Punt, prevailing. "Pie you can't 'ave and you won't."

"Lor bless my heart, Mrs. Punt!" protested Mr.

Voules, "let the boy 'ave a bit if he wants it — wedding and all!"

"You 'aven't 'ad 'im sick on your 'ands, Uncle Voules," said Mrs. Punt. "Else you wouldn't want to humour his fancies as you do. . . ."

"I can't help feeling it's a mistake, O' Man," said Johnson, in a confidential undertone. "I can't help feeling you've been Rash. Let's hope for the best."

"Always glad of good wishes, O' Man," said Mr. Polly. "You'd better have a drink of something. Anyhow, sit down to it."

Johnson subsided gloomily, and Mr. Polly secured some ham and carried it off and sat himself down on the sewing machine on the floor in the corner to devour it. He was hungry, and a little cut off from the rest of the company by Mrs. Voules' hat and back, and he occupied himself for a time with ham and his own thoughts. He became aware of a series of jangling concussions on the table. He craned his neck and discovered that Mr. Voules was standing up and leaning forward over the table in the manner distinctive of after-dinner speeches, tapping upon the table with a black bottle. "Ladies and gentlemen," said Mr. Voules, raising his glass solemnly in the empty desert of sound he had made, and paused for a second or so. "Ladies and gentlemen, — The Bride." He searched his mind for some suitable wreath of speech, and brightened at last with discovery. "Here's Luck to her!" he said at last.

"Here's Luck!" said Johnson hopelessly but resolutely, and raised his glass. Everybody murmured: "Here's luck."

"Luck!" said Mr. Polly, unseen in his corner, lifting a forkful of ham.

"That's all right," said Mr. Voules with a sigh of relief at having brought off a difficult operation. "And now, who's for a bit more pie?"

For a time conversation was fragmentary again. But presently Mr. Voules rose from his chair again; he had subsided with a contented smile after his first oratorical effort, and produced a silence by renewed hammering. "Ladies and gents," he said, "fill up for the second toast:—the happy Bridegroom!" He stood for half a minute searching his mind for the apt phrase that came at last in a rush. "Here's (hic) luck to *him*," said Mr. Voules.

"Luck to him!" said everyone, and Mr. Polly, standing up behind Mrs. Voules, bowed amiably, amidst enthusiasm.

"He may say what he likes," said Mrs. Larkins, "he's *got* luck. That girl's a treasure of treasures, and always has been ever since she tried to nurse her own little sister, being but three at the time, and fell the full flight of stairs from top to bottom, no hurt that any outward eye 'as even seen, but always ready and helpful, always tidying and busy. A treasure, I must say, and a treasure I will say, giving no more than her due. . . ."

She was silenced altogether by a rapping sound that would not be denied. Mr. Voules had been struck by a fresh idea and was standing up and hammering with the bottle again.

"The third Toast, ladies and gentlemen," he said; "fill up, please. The Mother of the bride. I —er. . . . Uoo. . . . Ere! . . . Ladies and gem, 'Ere's Luck to 'er! . . ."

⇉ VII ⇇

THE dingy little room was stuffy and crowded to its utmost limit, and Mr. Polly's skies were dark with the sense of irreparable acts. Everybody seemed noisy and greedy and doing foolish things. Miriam, still in that unbecoming hat — for presently they had to start off to the station together — sat just beyond Mrs. Punt and her son, doing her share in the hospitalities, and ever and again glancing at him with a deliberately encouraging smile. Once she leant over the back of the chair to him and whispered cheeringly: "Soon be together now." Next to her sat Johnson, profoundly silent, and then Annie, talking vigorously to a friend. Uncle Pentstemon was eating voraciously opposite, but with a kindling eye for Annie. Mrs. Larkins sat next to Mr. Voules. She was unable to eat a mouthful, she declared, it would choke her, but ever and again Mr. Voules wooed her to swallow a little drop of liquid refreshment.

There seemed a lot of rice upon everybody, in their hats and hair and the folds of their garments.

Presently Mr. Voules was hammering the table for the fourth time in the interests of the Best Man. . . .

All feasts come to an end at last, and the break-up of things was precipitated by alarming symptoms on the part of Master Punt. He was taken out hastily after a whispered consultation, and since he had got into the corner between the fire-place and the cupboard, that meant everyone moving to make way for him. Johnson took the opportunity to say, "Well—so long," to anyone who might be listening, and disappear. Mr. Polly found himself smoking a cigarette and walking up and down outside in the company of Uncle Pentstemon, while Mr. Voules replaced bottles in hampers and prepared for departure, and the womenkind of the party crowded upstairs with the bride. Mr. Polly felt taciturn, but the events of the day had stirred the mind of Uncle Pentstemon to speech. And so he spoke, discursively and disconnectedly, a little heedless of his listener as wise old men will.

"They do say," said Uncle Pentstemon, "one funeral makes many. This time it's a wedding. But it's all very much of a muchness," said Uncle Pentstemon. . . .

" 'Am *do* get in my teeth nowadays," said Uncle Pentstemon, "I can't understand it. 'Tisn't like there was nubbicks or strings or such in 'am. It's a plain food.

"That's better," he said at last.

"You *got* to get married," said Uncle Pentstemon. "Some has. Some hain't. I done it long before I was your age. It hain't for me to blame you. You can't 'elp being the marrying sort any more than me. It's nat'ral — like poaching or drinking or wind on the stummik. You can't 'elp it and there you are! As for the good of it, there ain't no particular good in it as I can see. It's a toss up. The hotter come, the sooner cold, but they all gets tired of it sooner or later. . . . I hain't no grounds to complain. Two I've 'ad and berried, and might 'ave 'ad a third, and never no worrit with kids — never. . . .

"You done well not to 'ave the big gal. I will say that for ye. She's a gad-about grinny, she is, if ever was. A gad-about grinny. Mucked up my mushroom bed to rights, she did, and I 'aven't forgot it. Got the feet of a centipede, she 'as — all over everything and neither with your leave nor by your leave. Like a stray 'en in a pea patch. Cluck! cluck! Trying to laugh it off. *I* laughed 'er off, I did. Dratted lumpin baggage! . . ."

180

For a while he mused malevolently upon Annie, and routed out a reluctant crumb from some coy sitting-out place in his tooth.

"Wimmin's a toss up," said Uncle Pentstemon. "Prize packets they are, and you can't tell what's in 'em till you took 'em 'ome and undone 'em. Never was a bachelor married yet that didn't buy a pig in a poke. Never. Marriage seems to change the very natures in 'em through and through. You can't tell what they won't turn into — nohow.

"I seen the nicest girls go wrong," said Uncle Pentstemon, and added with unusual thoughtfulness, "Not that I mean *you* got one of that sort."

He sent another crumb on to its long home with a sucking, encouraging noise.

"The wust sort's the grizzler," Uncle Pentstemon resumed. "If ever I'd 'ad a grizzler I'd up and 'it 'er on the 'ed with sumpthin' pretty quick. I don't think I *could* abide a grizzler," said Uncle Pentstemon. "I'd liefer 'ave a lump-about like that other gal. I would indeed. I lay I'd make 'er stop laughing after a bit for all 'er airs. And mind where her clumsy great feet went. . . .

"A man's got to tackle 'em, whatever they be," said Uncle Pentstemon, summing up the shrewd observation of an old-world life time. "Good or bad," said Uncle Pentstemon raising his voice fearlessly, "a man's got to tackle 'em."

→»» VIII «««←

AT LAST it was time for the two young people to catch the train for Waterloo *en route* for Fishbourne. They had to hurry, and as a concluding glory of matrimony they travelled second-class, and were seen off by all the rest of the party except the Punts, Master Punt being now beyond any question unwell.

"Off!" The train moved out of the station.

Mr. Polly remained waving his hat and Mrs. Polly her handkerchief until they were hidden under the bridge. The dominating figure to the last was Mr. Voules. He had followed them along the platform waving the equestrian grey hat and kissing his hand to the bride.

They subsided into their seats.

"Got a compartment to ourselves anyhow," said Mrs. Polly after a pause.

Silence for a moment.

"The rice 'e must 'ave bought. Pounds and pounds!"

Mr. Polly felt round his collar at the thought.

"Ain't you going to kiss me, Elfrid, now we're alone together?"

He roused himself to sit forward hands on knees, cocked his hat over one eye, and assumed an expression of avidity becoming to the occasion.

"Never!" he said. "Ever!" and feigned to be selecting a place to kiss with great discrimination.

"Come here," he said, and drew her to him.

"Be careful of my 'at," said Mrs. Polly, yielding awkwardly.

CHAPTER
THE SEVENTH

THE LITTLE SHOP AT

FISHBOURNE

THE LITTLE SHOP AT

FISHBOURNE

⇒⇒⇒ I ⇐⇐⇐

For fifteen years Mr. Polly was a respectable
shopkeeper in Fishbourne.

Years they were in which every day was tedious,
and when they were gone it was as if they had gone
in a flash. But now Mr. Polly had good looks no
more, he was as I have described him in the beginning of this story, thirty-seven and fattish in a
not very healthy way, dull and yellowish about the
complexion, and with discontented wrinklings
round his eyes. He sat on the stile above Fishbourne and cried to the Heavens above him: "Oh!
Roo-o-o-tten Be-e-astly Silly Hole!" And he wore
a rather shabby black morning coat and vest, and
his tie was richly splendid, being from stock, and
his golf cap aslant over one eye.

Fifteen years ago, and it might have seemed to
you that the queer little flower of Mr. Polly's im-

agination must be altogether withered and dead,
and with no living seed left in any part of him. But
indeed it still lived as an insatiable hunger for
bright and delightful experiences, for the gracious
aspects of things, for beauty. He still read books
when he had a chance, books that told of glorious
places abroad and glorious times, that wrung a
rich humour from life and contained the delight
of words freshly and expressively grouped. But
alas! there are not many such books, and for the
newspapers and the cheap fiction that abounded
more and more in the world Mr. Polly had little
taste. There was no epithet in them. And there was
no one to talk to, as he loved to talk. And he had
to mind his shop.

It was a reluctant little shop from the beginning.

He had taken it to escape the doom of Johnson's
choice and because Fishbourne had a hold upon
his imagination. He had disregarded the ill-built
cramped rooms behind it in which he would have
to lurk and live, the relentless limitations of its
dimensions, the inconvenience of an underground
kitchen that must necessarily be the living-room in
winter, the narrow yard behind giving upon the
yard of the Royal Fishbourne Hotel, the tiresome
sitting and waiting for custom, the restricted prospects of trade. He had visualised himself and Miriam first as at breakfast on a clear bright winter

morning amidst a tremendous smell of bacon, and
then as having muffins for tea. He had also thought
of sitting on the beach on Sunday afternoons and
of going for a walk in the country behind the town
and picking marguerites and poppies. But, in fact,
Miriam and he were extremely cross at breakfast,
and it didn't run to muffins at tea. And she didn't
think it looked well, she said, to go trapesing about
the country on Sundays.

It was unfortunate that Miriam never took to
the house from the first. She did not like it when
she saw it, and liked it less as she explored it.
"There's too many stairs," she said, "and the coal
being indoors will make a lot of work."

"Didn't think of that," said Mr. Polly, following her round.

"It'll be a hard house to keep clean," said
Miriam.

"White paint's all very well in its way," said
Miriam, "but it shows the dirt something fearful.
Better 'ave 'ad it nicely grained."

"There's a kind of place here," said Mr. Polly,
"where we might have some flowers in pots."

"Not me," said Miriam. "I've 'ad trouble enough
with Minnie and 'er musk. . . ."

They stayed for a week in a cheap boarding
house before they moved in. They had bought some
furniture in Stamton, mostly second-hand, but
with new cheap cutlery and china and linen, and

189

they had supplemented this from the Fishbourne shops. Miriam, relieved from the hilarious associations of home, developed a meagre and serious quality of her own, and went about with knitted brows pursuing some ideal of "'aving everything right." Mr. Polly gave himself to the arrangement of the shop with a certain zest, and whistled a good deal until Miriam appeared and said that it went through her head. So soon as he had taken the shop he had filled the window with aggressive posters announcing in no measured terms that he was going to open, and now he was getting his stuff put out he was resolved to show Fishbourne what window dressing could do. He meant to give them boater straws, imitation Panamas, bathing dresses with novelties in stripes, light flannel shirts, summer ties, and ready-made flannel trousers for men, youths and boys. Incidentally he watched the small fishmonger over the way, and had a glimpse of the china dealer next door, and wondered if a friendly nod would be out of place. And on the first Sunday in this new life he and Miriam arrayed themselves with great care, he in his wedding-funeral hat and coat and she in her going-away dress, and went processionally to church, a more respectable looking couple you could hardly imagine, and looked about them.

Things began to settle down next week into their places. A few customers came, chiefly for bathing suits and hat guards, and on Saturday night the cheapest straw hats and ties, and Mr. Polly found himself more and more drawn towards the shop door and the social charm of the street. He found the china dealer unpacking a crate at the edge of the pavement, and remarked that it was a fine day. The china dealer gave a reluctant assent, and plunged into the crate in a manner that presented no encouragement to a loquacious neighbour.

"Zealacious commerciality," whispered Mr. Polly to that unfriendly back view. . . .

⇒⇒ II ⇐⇐

MIRIAM combined earnestness of spirit with great practical incapacity. The house was never clean nor tidy, but always being frightfully disarranged for cleaning or tidying up, and she cooked because food had to be cooked and with a sound moralist's entire disregard of the quality of the consequences. The food came from her hands done rather than improved, and looking as uncomfortable as savages clothed under duress by a missionary with a stock of out-sizes. Such food is too apt to behave resentfully, rebel and work Obi. She ceased to listen to her husband's talk from the day she married him, and ceased to unwrinkle the kink in her brow at his presence, giving herself up to mental states that had a quality of secret preoccupation. And

191

she developed an idea for which perhaps there was legitimate excuse, that he was lazy. He seemed to stand about in the shop a great deal, to read — an indolent habit — and presently to seek company for talking. He began to attend the bar parlour of the God's Providence Inn with some frequency, and would have done so regularly in the evening if cards, which bored him to death, had not arrested conversation. But the perpetual foolish variation of the permutations and combinations of two and fifty cards taken five at a time, and the meagre surprises and excitements that ensue had no charms for Mr. Polly's mind, which was at once too vivid in its impressions and too easily fatigued.

It was soon manifest the shop paid only in the least exacting sense, and Miriam did not conceal her opinion that he ought to bestir himself and "do things," though what he was to do was hard to say. You see, when you have once sunken your capital in a shop you do not very easily get it out again. If customers will not come to you cheerfully and freely the law sets limits upon the compulsion you may exercise. You cannot pursue people about the streets of a watering place, compelling them either by threats or importunity to buy flannel trousers. Additional sources of income for a tradesman are not always easy to find. Wintershed at the bicycle and gramaphone shop to the right, played the organ in the church, and Clamp of the toy shop was

pew opener and so forth, Gambell, the greengrocer, waited at table and his wife cooked, and Carter, the watchmaker, left things to his wife while
he went about the world winding clocks, but Mr.
Polly had none of these arts, and wouldn't, in spite
of Miriam's quietly persistent protests, get any
other. And on summer evenings he would ride his
bicycle about the country, and if he discovered a
sale where there were books he would as often as
not waste half the next day in going again to acquire a job lot of them haphazard, and bring them
home tied about with a string, and hide them from
Miriam under the counter in the shop. That is a
heartbreaking thing for any wife with a serious in-
vestigatory turn of mind to discover. She was always thinking of burning these finds, but her natural turn for economy prevailed with her.

The books he read during those fifteen years!
He read everything he got except theology, and
as he read his little unsuccessful circumstances
vanished and the wonder of life returned to him,
the routine of reluctant getting up, opening shop,
pretending to dust it with zest, breakfasting with
a shop egg underdone or overdone or a herring raw
or charred, and coffee made Miriam's way and full
of little particles, the return to the shop, the morning paper, the standing, standing at the door saying "How do!" to passers-by, or getting a bit of
gossip or watching unusual visitors, all these

things vanished as the auditorium of a theatre vanishes when the stage is lit. He acquired hundreds of books at last, old dusty books, books with torn covers and broken covers, fat books whose backs were naked string and glue, an inimical litter to Miriam.

There was, for example, the voyages of La Perouse, with many careful, explicit woodcuts and the frankest revelations of the ways of the eighteenth century sailorman, homely, adventurous, drunken, incontinent and delightful, until he floated, smooth and slow, with all sails set and mirrored in the glassy water, until his head was full of the thought of shining kindly brown-skinned women, who smiled at him and wreathed his head with unfamiliar flowers. He had, too, a piece of a book about the lost palaces of Yucatan, those vast terraces buried in primordial forest, of whose makers there is now no human memory. With La Perouse he linked "The Island Nights Entertainments," and it never palled upon him that in the dusky stabbing of the "Island of Voices" something poured over the stabber's hands "like warm tea." Queer incommunicable joy it is, the joy of the vivid phrase that turns the statement of the horridest fact to beauty!

And another book which had no beginning for him was the second volume of the Travels of the Abbés Huc and Gabet. He followed those two sweet

194

souls from their lessons in Thibetan under San-
dura the Bearded (who called them donkeys to
their infinite benefit and stole their store of butter)
through a hundred misadventures to the very heart
of Lhassa, and it was a thirst in him that was never
quenched to find the other volume and whence they
came, and who in fact they were. He read Fenimore
Cooper and "Tom Cringle's Log" side by side with
Joseph Conrad, and dreamt of the many-hued humanity of the East and West Indies until his heart
ached to see those sun-soaked lands before he died.
Conrad's prose had a pleasure for him that he was
never able to define, a peculiar deep coloured effect. He found too one day among a pile of soiled
sixpenny books at Port Burdock, to which place
he sometimes rode on his ageing bicycle, Bart Ken-
nedy's "A Sailor Tramp," all written in livid jerks,
and had forever after a kindlier and more understanding eye for every burly rough who slouched
through Fishbourne High Street. Sterne he read
with a wavering appreciation and some perplexity,
but except for the Pickwick Papers, for some reason that I do not understand he never took at all
kindly to Dickens. Yet he liked Lever and Thack-
eray's "Catherine," and all Dumas until he got to
the Vicomte de Bragelonne. I am puzzled by his in-
sensibility to Dickens, and I record it as a good
historian should, with an admission of my perplexity. It is much more understandable that he had no

love for Scott. And I suppose it was because of his ignorance of the proper pronunciation of words that he infinitely preferred any prose to any metrical writing.

A book he browsed over with a recurrent pleasure was Waterton's Wanderings in South America. He would even amuse himself by inventing descriptions of other birds in the Watertonian manner, new birds that he invented, birds with peculiarities that made him chuckle when they occurred to him. He tried to make Rusper, the ironmonger, share this joy with him. He read Bates, too, about the Amazon, but when he discovered that you could not see one bank from the other, he lost, through some mysterious action of the soul that again I cannot understand, at least a tithe of the pleasure he had taken in that river. But he read all sorts of things; a book of old Keltic stories collected by Joyce charmed him, and Mitford's Tales of Old Japan, and a number of paper-covered volumes, *Tales from Blackwood*, he had acquired at Easewood, remained a stand-by. He developed a quite considerable acquaintance with the plays of William Shakespeare, and in his dreams he wore cinque cento or Elizabethan clothes, and walked about a stormy, ruffling, taverning, teeming world. Great land of sublimated things, thou World of Books, happy asylum, refreshment and refuge from the world of everyday! . . .

The essential thing of those fifteen long years of shopkeeping is Mr. Polly, well athwart the counter of his rather ill-lit shop, lost in a book, or rousing himself with a sigh to attend to business.

Meanwhile he got little exercise, indigestion grew with him until it ruled all his moods, he fattened and deteriorated physically, moods of distress invaded and darkened his skies, little things irritated him more and more, and casual laughter ceased in him. His hair began to come off until he had a large bald space at the back of his head. Suddenly one day it came to him — forgetful of those books and all he had lived and seen through them — that he had been in his shop for exactly fifteen years, that he would soon be forty, and that his life during that time had not been worth living, that it had been in apathetic and feebly hostile and critical company, ugly in detail and mean in scope — and that it had brought him at last to an outlook utterly hopeless and grey.

→» III «←

I HAVE already had occasion to mention, indeed I have quoted, a certain high-browed gentleman living at Highbury, wearing a golden pince-nez and writing for the most part in that beautiful room, the library of the Reform Club. There he wrestles with what he calls "social problems" in a bloodless but at times, I think one must admit, an extremely illuminating manner. He has a fixed idea that something called a "collective intelligence" is wanted in the world, which means in practice that you and I and everyone have to think about things frightfully hard and pool the results, and oblige ourselves to be shamelessly and persistently clear and truthful and support and respect (I suppose) a perfect horde of professors and writers and artists and ill-groomed difficult people, instead of using our brains in a moderate, sensible manner to play golf and bridge (pretending a sense of humour prevents our doing anything else with them) and generally taking life in a nice, easy, gentlemanly way, confound him! Well, this dome-headed monster of intellect alleges that Mr. Polly was unhappy entirely through that.

"A rapidly complicating society," he writes, "which as a whole declines to contemplate its future or face the intricate problems of its organisation, is in exactly the position of a man who takes no thought of dietary or regimen, who abstains from baths and exercise and gives his appetites free play. It accumulates useless and aimless lives as a man accumulates fat and morbid products in his blood, it declines in its collective efficiency and vigour and secretes discomfort and misery. Every phase of its evolution is accompanied by a maximum of avoidable distress and inconvenience and human waste. . . .

"Nothing can better demonstrate the collective dulness of our community, the crying need for a strenuous intellectual renewal than the consideration of that vast mass of useless, uncomfortable, under-educated, under-trained and altogether pitiable people we contemplate when we use that inaccurate and misleading term, the Lower Middle Class. A great proportion of the lower middle class should properly be assigned to the unemployed and the unemployable. They are only not that, because the possession of some small hoard of money, savings during a period of wage earning, an insurance policy or suchlike capital, prevents a direct appeal to the rates. But they are doing little or nothing for the community in return for what they consume; they have no understanding of any relation of service to the community, they have never been trained nor their imaginations touched to any social purpose. A great proportion of small shopkeepers, for example, are people who have, through the inefficiency that comes from inadequate training and sheer aimlessness, or improvements in machinery or the drift of trade, been thrown out of employment, and who set up in needless shops as a method of eking out the savings upon which they count. They contrive to make sixty or seventy per cent. of their expenditure, the rest is drawn from the shrinking capital. Essentially their lives are failures, not the sharp and tragic failure of the

199

labourer who gets out of work and starves, but a slow, chronic process of consecutive small losses which may end if the individual is exceptionally fortunate in an impoverished death bed before actual bankruptcy or destitution supervenes. Their chances of ascendant means are less in their shops than in any lottery that was ever planned. The secular development of transit and communications has made the organisation of distributing businesses upon large and economical lines, inevitable; except in the chaotic confusions of newly opened countries, the day when a man might earn an independent living by unskilled or practically unskilled retailing has gone for ever. Yet every year sees the melancholy procession towards petty bankruptcy and imprisonment for debt go on, and there is no statesmanship in us to avert it. Every issue of every trade journal has its four or five columns of abridged bankruptcy proceedings, nearly every item in which means the final collapse of another struggling family upon the resources of the community, and continually a fresh supply of superfluous artisans and shop assistants, coming out of employment with savings or 'help' from relations, of widows with a husband's insurance money, of the ill-trained sons of parsimonious fathers, replaces the fallen in the ill-equipped, jerry-built shops that everywhere abound. . . ."

I quote these fragments from a gifted, if unpleasant, contemporary for what they are worth. I feel this has come in here as the broad aspect of this History. I come back to Mr. Polly sitting upon his gate and swearing in the east wind, and I so returning have a sense of floating across unbridged abysses between the General and the Particular. There, on the one hand, is the man of understanding, seeing clearly — I suppose he sees clearly — the big process that dooms millions of lives to thwarting and discomfort and unhappy circumstances, and giving us no help, no hint, by which we may get that better "collective will and intelligence" which would dam the stream of human failure, and, on the other hand, Mr. Polly sitting on his gate, untrained, unwarned, confused, distressed, angry, seeing nothing except that he is, as it were, nettled in greyness and discomfort — with life dancing all about him; Mr. Polly with a capacity for joy and beauty at least as keen and subtle as yours or mine.

⋙ IV ⋘

I HAVE hinted that our Mother England had equipped Mr. Polly for the management of his internal concerns no whit better than she had for the direction of his external affairs. With a careless generosity she affords her children a variety of foods unparalleled in the world's history, and including many condiments and preserved preparations novel to the human economy. And Miriam did the cooking. Mr. Polly's system, like a confused and ill-governed democracy, had been brought to a state of perpetual clamour and disorder, demanding now evil and unsuitable internal satisfactions, such as pickles and vinegar and the crackling on pork, and now vindictive external expression, war and bloodshed throughout the world. So that Mr. Polly had been led into hatred and a series of disagreeable quarrels with his landlord, his wholesalers, and most of his neighbours.

Rumbold, the china dealer next door, seemed hostile from the first for no apparent reason, and always unpacked his crates with a full back to his new neighbour, and from the first Mr. Polly resented and hated that uncivil breadth of expressionless humanity, wanted to prod it, kick it, satirise it. But you cannot satirise a back, if you have no friend to nudge while you do it.

At last Mr. Polly could stand it no longer. He approached and prodded Rumbold.

"Ello!" said Rumbold, suddenly erect and turned about.

"Can't we have some other point of view?" said Mr. Polly. "I'm tired of the end elevation."

"Eh?" said Mr. Rumbold, frankly puzzled.

"Of all the vertebracious animals man alone raises his face to the sky, O' Man. Well,—why invert it?"

Rumbold shook his head with a helpless expression.

"Don't like so much Arreary Pensy."

Rumbold distressed in utter obscurity.

"In fact, I'm sick of your turning your back on me, see?"

A great light shone on Rumbold. "*That's* what you're talking about!" he said.

"That's it," said Polly.

Rumbold scratched his ear with the three strawy jampots he held in his hand. "Way the wind blows, I expect," he said. "But what's the fuss?"

"No fuss!" said Mr. Polly. "Passing Remark. I don't like it, O' Man, that's all."

"Can't help it, if the wind blows my stror," said Mr. Rumbold, still far from clear about it. . . .

"It isn't ordinary civility," said Mr. Polly.

"Got to unpack 'ow it suits me. Can't unpack with the stror blowing into one's eyes."

"Needn't unpack like a pig rooting for truffles, need you?"

"Truffles?"

"Needn't unpack like a pig."

Mr. Rumbold apprehended something.

"Pig!" he said, impressed. "You calling me a pig?"

"It's the side I seem to get of you."

" 'Ere," said Mr. Rumbold, suddenly fierce and shouting and marking his point with gesticulated jampots, "you go indoors. I don't want no row with you, and I don't want you to row with me. I don't know what you're after, but I'm a peaceable man — teetotaller, too, and a good thing if *you* was. See? You go indoors!"

"You mean to say — I'm asking you civilly to stop unpacking — with your back to me."

"Pig ain't civil, and you ain't sober. You go indoors and lemme go on unpacking. You — you're excited."

"D'you mean — !" Mr. Polly was foiled.

He perceived an immense solidity about Rumbold.

"Get back to your shop and lemme get on with my business," said Mr. Rumbold. "Stop calling me pigs. See? Sweep your pavemint."

"I came here to make a civil request."

"You came 'ere to make a row. I don't want no truck with you. See? I don't like the looks of you. See? And I can't stand 'ere all day arguing. See?"

Pause of mutual inspection.

It occurred to Mr. Polly that probably he was to some extent in the wrong.

Mr. Rumbold, blowing heavily, walked past him, deposited the jampots in his shop with an immense affectation that there was no Mr. Polly in the world, returned, turned a scornful back on Mr. Polly and dived to the interior of the crate. Mr. Polly stood baffled. Should he kick this solid mass before him? Should he administer a resounding kick?

No!

He plunged his hands deeply into his trowser pockets, began to whistle and returned to his own doorstep with an air of profound unconcern. There for a time, to the tune of "Men of Harlech," he contemplated the receding possibility of kicking Mr. Rumbold hard. It would be splendid — and for the moment satisfying. But he decided not to do it. For indefinable reasons he could not do it. He went indoors and straightened up his dress ties very slowly and thoughtfully. Presently he went to the window and regarded Mr. Rumbold obliquely. Mr. Rumbold was still unpacking. . . .

Mr. Polly had no human intercourse thereafter with Rumbold for fifteen years. He kept up a Hate.

There was a time when it seemed as if Rumbold might go, but he had a meeting of his creditors and then went on unpacking as obtusely as ever.

⇉ V ⇇

HINKS, the saddler, two shops further down the street, was a different case. Hinks was the aggressor — practically.

Hinks was a sporting man in his way, with that taste for checks in costume and tight trousers which is, under Providence, so mysteriously and invariably associated with equestrian proclivities. At first Mr. Polly took to him as a character, became frequent in the God's Providence Inn under his guidance, stood and was stood drinks and concealed a great ignorance of horses until Hinks became urgent for him to play billiards or bet.

Then Mr. Polly took to evading him, and Hinks ceased to conceal his opinion that Mr. Polly was in reality a softish sort of flat.

He did not, however, discontinue conversation with Mr. Polly; he would come along to him whenever he appeared at his door, and converse about sport and women and fisticuffs and the pride of life with an air of extreme initiation, until Mr. Polly felt himself the faintest underdeveloped intimation of a man that had ever hovered on the verge of non-existence.

So he invented phrases for Hinks' clothes and took Rusper, the ironmonger, into his confidence upon the weaknesses of Hinks. He called him the "Chequered Careerist," and spoke of his patterned legs as "shivery shakys." Good things of this sort are apt to get round to people.

He was standing at his door one day, feeling bored, when Hinks appeared down the street, stood still and regarded him with a strange malignant expression for a space.

Mr. Polly waved a hand in a rather belated salutation.

Mr. Hinks spat on the pavement and appeared to reflect. Then he came towards Mr. Polly portentously and paused, and spoke between his teeth in an earnest confidential tone.

"You been flapping your mouth about me, I'm told," he said.

Mr. Polly felt suddenly spiritless. "Not that I know of," he answered.

"Not that you know of, be blowed! You been flapping your mouth."

"Don't see it," said Mr. Polly.

"Don't see it, be blowed! You go flapping your silly mouth about me and I'll give you a poke in the eye. See?"

Mr. Hinks regarded the effect of this coldly but firmly, and spat again.

"Understand me?" he enquired.

"Don't recollect," began Mr. Polly.

"Don't recollect, be blowed! You flap your mouth a dam sight too much. This place gets more of your mouth than it wants. . . . Seen this?"

And Mr. Hinks, having displayed a freckled fist of extraordinary size and pugginess in an ostentatiously familiar manner to Mr. Polly's close inspection by sight and smell, turned it about this way and that and shaken it gently for a moment or so, replaced it carefully in his pocket as if for future use, receded slowly and watchfully for a pace, and then turned away as if to other matters,

207

and ceased to be even in outward seeming a
friend. . . .

⇒≫ VI ≪⇐

Mr. Polly's intercourse with all his fellow tradesmen was tarnished sooner or later by some such ad-
verse incident, until not a friend remained to him,
and loneliness made even the shop door terrible.
Shops bankrupted all about him and fresh people
came and new acquaintances sprang up, but sooner
or later a discord was inevitable, the tension under
which these badly fed, poorly housed, bored and
bothered neighbours lived, made it inevitable. The
mere fact that Mr. Polly had to see them every
day, that there was no getting away from them,
was in itself sufficient to make them almost unen-
durable to his frettingly active mind.

Among other shopkeepers in the High Street
there was Chuffles, the grocer, a small, hairy, silently intent polygamist, who was given rough music by the youth of the neighbourhood because of
a scandal about his wife's sister, and who was nevertheless totally uninteresting, and Tonks, the second grocer, an old man with an older, very en-
feebled wife, both submerged by piety. Tonks went
bankrupt, and was succeeded by a branch of the
National Provision Company, with a young manager exactly like a fox, except that he barked. The

toy and sweetstuff shop was kept by an old woman of repellent manners, and so was the little fish shop at the end of the street. The Berlin-wool shop having gone bankrupt, became a newspaper shop, then fell to a haberdasher in consumption, and finally to a stationer; the three shops at the end of the street wallowed in and out of insolvency in the hands of a bicycle repairer and dealer, a gramaphone dealer, a tobacconist, a sixpenny-halfpenny bazaar-keeper, a shoemaker, a greengrocer, and the exploiter of a cinematograph peep-show — but none of them supplied friendship to Mr. Polly. These adventurers in commerce were all more or less distraught souls, driving without intelligible comment before the gale of fate. The two milkmen of Fishbourne were brothers who had quarrelled about their father's will, and started in opposition to each other; one was stone deaf and no use to Mr. Polly, and the other was a sporting man with a natural dread of epithet who sided with Hinks. So it was all about him, on every hand it seemed were uncongenial people, uninteresting people, or people who conceived the deepest distrust and hostility towards him, a magic circle of suspicious, preoccupied and dehumanised humanity. So the poison in his system poisoned the world without.

(But Boomer, the wine merchant, and Tashingford, the chemist, be it noted, were fraught with pride, and held themselves to be a cut above Mr.

Polly. They never quarrelled with him, preferring to bear themselves from the outset as though they had already done so.)

As his internal malady grew upon Mr. Polly and he became more and more a battle-ground of fermenting foods and warring juices, he came to hate the very sight, as people say, of every one of these neighbours. There they were, every day and all the days, just the same, echoing his own stagnation. They pained him all round the top and back of his head; they made his legs and arms weary and spiritless. The air was tasteless by reason of them. He lost his human kindliness.

In the afternoons he would hover in the shop bored to death with his business and his home and Miriam, and yet afraid to go out because of his inflamed and magnified dislike and dread of these neighbours. He could not bring himself to go out and run the gauntlet of the observant windows and the cold estranged eyes.

One of his last friendships was with Rusper, the ironmonger. Rusper took over Worthington's shop about three years after Mr. Polly opened. He was a tall, lean, nervous, convulsive man with an up-turned, back-thrown, oval head, who read news-papers and the *Review of Reviews* assiduously, had belonged to a Literary Society somewhere once, and had some defect of the palate that at first gave his lightest word a charm and interest for Mr. Polly. It caused a peculiar clicking sound, as though he had something between a giggle and a gas-meter at work in his neck.

His literary admirations were not precisely Mr. Polly's literary admirations; he thought books were written to enshrine Great Thoughts, and that art was pedagogy in fancy dress, he had no sense of phrase or epithet or richness of texture, but still he knew there were books, he did know there were books and he was full of large windy ideas of the sort he called "Modern (kik) Thought," and seemed needlessly and helplessly concerned about "(kik) the Welfare of the Race."

Mr. Polly would dream about that (kik) at nights.

It seemed to that undesirable mind of his that Rusper's head was the most egg-shaped head he had ever seen; the similarity weighed upon him; and when he found an argument growing warm with Rusper he would say: "Boil it some more, O' Man; boil it harder!" or "Six minutes at least," allusions Rusper could never make head or tail of, and got at last to disregard as a part of Mr. Polly's general eccentricity. For a long time that little tendency threw no shadow over their intercourse, but it contained within it the seeds of an ultimate disruption.

Often during the days of this friendship Mr. Polly would leave his shop and walk over to Mr.

Rusper's establishment, and stand in his doorway and enquire: "Well, O' Man, how's the Mind of the Age working?" and get quite an hour of it, and sometimes Mr. Rusper would come into the outfitter's shop with "Heard the (kik) latest?" and spend the rest of the morning.

Then Mr. Rusper married, and he married very inconsiderately a woman who was totally uninteresting to Mr. Polly. A coolness grew between them from the first intimation of her advent. Mr. Polly couldn't help thinking when he saw her that she drew her hair back from her forehead a great deal too tightly, and that her elbows were angular. His desire not to mention these things in the apt terms that welled up so richly in his mind, made him awkward in her presence, and that gave her an impression that he was hiding some guilty secret from her. She decided he must have a bad influence upon her husband, and she made it a point to appear whenever she heard him talking to Rusper.

One day they became a little heated about the German peril.

"I lay (kik) they'll invade us," said Rusper.

"Not a bit of it. William's not the Zerxiacious sort."

"You'll see, O' Man."

"Just what I shan't do."

"Before (kik) five years are out."

"Not it."

"Yes."

"No."

"Yes."

"Oh! *Boil* it hard!" said Mr. Polly.

Then he looked up and saw Mrs. Rusper standing behind the counter half hidden by a trophy of spades and garden shears and a knife-cleaning machine, and by her expression he knew instantly that she understood.

The conversation paled and presently Mr. Polly withdrew.

After that, estrangement increased steadily.

Mr. Rusper ceased altogether to come over to the outfitter's, and Mr. Polly called upon the ironmonger only with the completest air of casuality. And everything they said to each other led now to flat contradiction and raised voices. Rusper had been warned in vague and alarming terms that Mr. Polly insulted and made game of him; he couldn't discover exactly where; and so it appeared to him now that every word of Mr. Polly's might be an insult meriting his resentment, meriting it none the less because it was masked and cloaked.

Soon Mr. Polly's calls upon Mr. Rusper ceased also, and then Mr. Rusper, pursuing incomprehensible lines of thought, became afflicted with a specialised shortsightedness that applied only to Mr. Polly. He would look in other directions when

Mr. Polly appeared, and his large oval face assumed an expression of conscious serenity and deliberate happy unawareness that would have maddened a far less irritable person than Mr. Polly. It evoked a strong desire to mock and ape, and produced in his throat a cough of singular scornfulness, more particularly when Mr. Rusper also assisted, with an assumed unconsciousness that was all his own.

Then one day Mr. Polly had a bicycle accident.

His bicycle was now very old, and it is one of the concomitants of a bicycle's senility that its free wheel should one day obstinately cease to be free. It corresponds to that epoch in human decay when an old gentleman loses an incisor tooth. It happened just as Mr. Polly was approaching Mr. Rusper's shop, and the untoward chance of a motor car trying to pass a waggon on the wrong side gave Mr. Polly no choice but to get on to the pavement and dismount. He was always accustomed to take his time and step off his left pedal at its lowest point, but the jamming of the free wheel gear made that lowest moment a transitory one, and the pedal was lifting his foot for another revolution before he realised what had happened. Before he could dismount according to his habit the pedal had to make a revolution, and before it could make a revolution Mr. Polly found himself among the

various sonorous things with which **Mr. Rusper**
adorned the front of his shop, zinc dustbins, household pails, lawn mowers, rakes, spades and all manner of clattering things. Before he got among
them he had one of those agonising moments of
helpless wrath and suspense that seem to last ages,
in which one seems to perceive everything and
think of nothing but words that are better forgotten. He sent a column of pails thundering across
the doorway and dismounted with one foot in a
sanitary dustbin amidst an enormous uproar of
falling ironmongery.

"Put all over the place!" he cried, and found
Mr. Rusper emerging from his shop with the large
tranquillities of his countenance puckered to an-
ger, like the frowns in the brow of a reefing sail.
He gesticulated speechlessly for a moment.

"Kik—jer doing?" he said at last.

"Tin mantraps!" said Mr. Polly.

"Jer (kik) doing?"

"Dressing all over the pavement as though the
blessed town belonged to you! Ugh!"

And Mr. Polly in attempting a dignified movement realised his entanglement with the dustbin
for the first time. With a low embittering expression he kicked his foot about in it for a moment
very noisily, and finally sent it thundering to the
curb. On its way it struck a pail or so. Then Mr.
Polly picked up his bicycle and proposed to re-

sume his homeward way. But the hand of Mr. Rusper arrested him.

"Put it (kik) all (kik kik) back (kik)."

"Put it (kik) back yourself."

"You got (kik) put it back."

"Get out of the (kik) way."

Mr. Rusper laid one hand on the bicycle handle, and the other gripped Mr. Polly's collar urgently. Whereupon Mr. Polly said: "Leggo!" and again, "D'you *hear!* Leggo!" and then drove his elbow with considerable force into the region of Mr. Rusper's midriff. Whereupon Mr. Rusper, with a loud impassioned cry, resembling "Woo kik" more than any other combination of letters, released the bicycle handle, seized Mr. Polly by the cap and hair and bore his head and shoulders downward. Thereat Mr. Polly, emitting such words as everyone knows and nobody prints, butted his utmost into the concavity of Mr. Rusper, entwined a leg about him and after terrific moments of swaying instability, fell headlong beneath him amidst the bicycles and pails. There on the pavement these inexpert children of a pacific age, untrained in arms and uninured to violence, abandoned themselves to amateurish and absurd efforts to hurt and injure one another — of which the most palpable consequences were dusty backs, ruffled hair and torn and twisted collars. Mr. Polly, by accident, got his finger into Mr. Rusper's mouth, and strove earnestly for some time to prolong that aperture in the direction of Mr. Rusper's ear before it occurred to Mr. Rusper to bite him (and even then he didn't bite very hard), while Mr. Rusper concentrated his mind almost entirely on an effort to rub Mr. Polly's face on the pavement. (And their positions bristled with chances of the deadliest sort!) They didn't from first to last draw blood.

Then it seemed to each of them that the other had become endowed with many hands and several voices and great accessions of strength. They submitted to fate and ceased to struggle. They found themselves torn apart and held up by outwardly scandalised and inwardly delighted neighbours, and invited to explain what it was all about.

"Got to (kik) puttem all back!" panted Mr. Rusper in the expert grasp of Hinks. "Merely asked him to (kik) puttem all back."

Mr. Polly was under restraint of little Clamp, of the toy shop, who was holding his hands in a complex and uncomfortable manner that he afterwards explained to Wintershed was a combination of something romantic called "Ju-jitsu" and something else still more romantic called the "Police Grip."

"Pails," explained Mr. Polly in breathless fragments. "All over the road. Pails. Bungs up the street with his pails. Look at them!"

"Deliber (kik) lib (kik) liberately rode into my

goods (kik). Constantly (kik) annoying me (kik) !" said Mr. Rusper. . . .

They were both tremendously earnest and reasonable in their manner. They wished everyone to regard them as responsible and intellectual men acting for the love of right and the enduring good of the world. They felt they must treat this business as a profound and publicly significant affair. They wanted to explain and orate and show the entire necessity of everything they had done. Mr. Polly was convinced he had never been so absolutely correct in all his life as when he planted his foot in the sanitary dustbin, and Mr. Rusper considered his clutch at Mr. Polly's hair as the one faultless impulse in an otherwise undistinguished career. But it was clear in their minds they might easily become ridiculous if they were not careful, if for a second they stepped over the edge of the high spirit and pitiless dignity they had hitherto maintained. At any cost they perceived they must not become ridiculous.

Mr. Chuffles, the scandalous grocer, joined the throng about the principal combatants, mutely as became an outcast, and with a sad, distressed helpful expression picked up Mr. Polly's bicycle. Gambell's summer errand boy, moved by example, restored the dustbin and pails to their self-respect.

" 'E ought—'e ought (kik) pick them up," protested Mr. Rusper.

"What's it all about?" said Mr. Hinks for the third time, shaking Mr. Rusper gently. "'As 'e been calling you names?"

"Simply ran into his pails — as anyone might," said Mr. Polly, "and out he comes and scrags me!"

"(Kik) Assault!" said Mr. Rusper.

"He assaulted *me*," said Mr. Polly.

"Jumped (kik) into my dus'bin!" said Mr. Rusper. "That assault? Or isn't it?"

"You better drop it," said Mr. Hinks.

"Great pity they can't be'ave better, both of 'em," said Mr. Chuffles, glad for once to find himself morally unassailable.

"Anyone see it begin?" said Mr. Wintershed.

"*I* was in the shop," said Mrs. Rusper suddenly from the doorstep, piercing the little group of men and boys with the sharp horror of an unexpected woman's voice. "If a witness is wanted I suppose I've got a tongue. I suppose I got a voice in seeing my own 'usband injured. My husband went out and spoke to Mr. Polly, who was jumping off his bicycle all among our pails and things, and immediately 'e butted him in the stomach — immediately — most savagely — butted him. Just after his dinner too and him far from strong. I could have screamed. But Rusper caught hold of him right away, I will say that for Rusper. . . ."

"I'm going," said Mr. Polly suddenly, releasing

himself from the Anglo-Japanese grip and holding out his hands for his bicycle.

"Teach you (kik) to leave things alone," said Mr. Rusper with an air of one who has given a lesson.

The testimony of Mrs. Rusper continued relentlessly in the background.

"You'll hear of me through a summons," said Mr. Polly, preparing to wheel his bicycle.

"(Kik) Me too," said Mr. Rusper.

Someone handed Mr. Polly a collar. "This yours?"

Mr. Polly investigated his neck. "I suppose it is. Anyone seen a tie?"

A small boy produced a grimy strip of spotted blue silk.

"Human life isn't safe with you," said Mr. Polly as a parting shot.

"(Kik) Yours isn't," said Mr. Rusper. . . .

And they got small satisfaction out of the Bench, which refused altogether to perceive the relentless correctitude of the behaviour of either party, and reproved the eagerness of Mrs. Rusper —speaking to her gently, firmly but exasperatingly as "My Good Woman" and telling her to "Answer the Question! Answer the Question!"

"Seems a Pity," said the chairman, when binding them over to keep the peace, "you can't behave like Respectable Tradesmen. Seems a Great Pity.

Bad Example to the Young and all that. Don't do any Good to the town, don't do any Good to yourselves, don't do any manner of Good, to have all the Tradesmen in the Place scrapping about the Pavement of an Afternoon. Think we're letting you off very easily this time, and hope it will be a Warning to you. Don't expect Men of your Position to come up before us. Very Regrettable Affair. Eh?"

He addressed the latter enquiry to his two colleagues.

"Exactly, exactly," said the colleague to the right.

"Er — (kik)," said Mr. Rusper.

⇢≫ VII ≪⇠

But the disgust that overshadowed Mr. Polly's being as he sat upon the stile, had other and profounder justification than his quarrel with Rusper and the indignity of appearing before the county bench. He was for the first time in his business career short with his rent for the approaching quarter day, and so far as he could trust his own handling of figures he was sixty or seventy pounds on the wrong side of solvency. And that was the outcome of fifteen years of passive endurance of dulness throughout the best years of his life! What would Miriam say when she learnt this, and was invited to face the prospect of exile — heaven knows what sort of exile! — from their present home? She would grumble and scold and become limply unhelpful, he knew, and none the less so because he could not help things. She would say he ought to have worked harder, and a hundred such exasperating pointless things. Such thoughts as these require no aid from undigested cold pork and cold potatoes and pickles to darken the soul, and with these aids his soul was black indeed.

"May as well have a bit of a walk," said Mr. Polly at last, after nearly intolerable meditations, and sat round and put a leg over the stile.

He remained still for some time before he brought over the other leg.

"Kill myself," he murmured at last.

It was an idea that came back to his mind nowadays with a continually increasing attractiveness — more particularly after meals. Life he felt had no further happiness to offer him. He hated Miriam, and there was no getting away from her whatever might betide. And for the rest there was toil and struggle, toil and struggle with a failing heart and dwindling courage, to sustain that dreary duologue. "Life's insured," said Mr. Polly; "place is insured. I don't see it does any harm to her or anyone."

He stuck his hands in his pockets. "Needn't hurt much," he said. He began to elaborate a plan.

He found it quite interesting elaborating his plan. His countenance became less miserable and his pace quickened.

There is nothing so good in all the world for melancholia as walking, and the exercise of the imagination in planning something presently to be done, and soon the wrathful wretchedness had vanished from Mr. Polly's face. He would have to do the thing secretly and elaborately, because otherwise there might be difficulties about the life insurance. He began to scheme how he could circumvent that difficulty. . . .

He took a long walk, for after all what is the good of hurrying back to shop when you are not only insolvent but very soon to die? His dinner and the east wind lost their sinister hold upon his soul, and when at last he came back along the Fishbourne High Street, his face was unusually bright and the craving hunger of the dyspeptic was returning. So he went into the grocer's and bought a ruddily decorated tin of a brightly pink fishlike substance known as "Deep Sea Salmon." This he was resolved to consume regardless of cost with vinegar and salt and pepper as a relish to his supper.

He did, and since he and Miriam rarely talked and Miriam thought honour and his recent behaviour demanded a hostile silence, he ate fast, and copiously and soon gloomily. He ate alone, for she refrained, to mark her sense of his extravagance. Then he prowled into the High Street for a time, thought it an infernal place, tried his pipe and found it foul and bitter, and retired wearily to bed.

He slept for an hour or so and then woke up to the contemplation of Miriam's hunched back and the riddle of life, and this bright attractive idea of ending for ever and ever and ever all the things that were locking him in, this bright idea that shone like a baleful star above all the reek and darkness of his misery. . . .

CHAPTER
THE EIGHTH

MAKING AN END

TO THINGS

MAKING AN END

TO THINGS

MR. POLLY designed his suicide with considerable
care, and a quite remarkable altruism. His passionate hatred for Miriam vanished directly the
idea of getting away from her for ever became
clear in his mind. He found himself full of solici-
tude then for her welfare. He did not want to buy
his release at her expense. He had not the remotest
intention of leaving her unprotected with a painfully dead husband and a bankrupt shop on her
hands. It seemed to him that he could contrive to
secure for her the full benefit of both his life insurance and his fire insurance if he managed things
in a tactful manner. He felt happier than he had
done for years scheming out this undertaking, albeit it was perhaps a larger and somberer kind of
happiness than had fallen to his lot before. It

227

amazed him to think he had endured his monotony of misery and failure for so long.

But there were some queer doubts and questions in the dim, half-lit background of his mind that he had very resolutely to ignore.

"Sick of it," he had to repeat to himself aloud, to keep his determination clear and firm. His life was a failure, there was nothing more to hope for but unhappiness. Why shouldn't he?

His project was to begin the fire with the stairs that led from the ground floor to the underground kitchen and scullery. This he would soak with paraffine, and assist with firewood and paper, and a brisk fire in the coal cellar underneath. He would smash a hole or so in the stairs to ventilate the blaze, and have a good pile of boxes and paper, and a convenient chair or so in the shop above. He would have the paraffine can upset and the shop lamp, as if awaiting refilling, at a convenient distance in the scullery ready to catch. Then he would smash the house lamp on the staircase, a fall with that in his hand was to be the ostensible cause of the blaze, and then he would cut his throat at the top of the kitchen stairs, which would then become his funeral pyre. He would do all this on Sunday evening while Miriam was at church, and it would appear that he had fallen downstairs with the lamp, and been burnt to death. There was really no flaw whatever that he could see in the scheme. He

228

was quite sure he knew how to cut his throat, deep
at the side and not to saw at the windpipe, and he
was reasonably sure it wouldn't hurt him very
much. And then everything would be at an end.

There was no particular hurry to get the thing
done, of course, and meanwhile he occupied his
mind with possible variations of the scheme. . . .

It needed a particularly dry and dusty east
wind, a Sunday dinner of exceptional virulence, a
conclusive letter from Konk, Maybrick, Ghool and
Gabbitas, his principal and most urgent creditors,
and a conversation with Miriam arising out of ar-
rears of rent and leading on to mutual character
sketching, before Mr. Polly could be brought to
the necessary pitch of despair to carry out his
plans. He went for an embittering walk, and came
back to find Miriam in a bad temper over the tea
things, with the brewings of three-quarters of an
hour in the pot, and hot buttered muffin gone
leathery. He sat eating in silence with his resolution made.

"Coming to church?" said Miriam after she had
cleared away.

"Rather. I got a lot to be grateful for," said
Mr. Polly.

"You got what you deserve," said Miriam.

"Suppose I have," said Mr. Polly, and went and
stared out of the back window at a despondent
horse in the hotel yard.

He was still standing there when Miriam came downstairs dressed for church. Something in his immobility struck home to her. "You'd better come to church than mope," she said.

"I shan't mope," he answered.

She remained still for a moment. Her presence irritated him. He felt that in another moment he should say something absurd to her, make some last appeal for that understanding she had never been able to give. "Oh! *go* to church!" he said.

In another moment the outer door slammed upon her. "Good riddance!" said Mr. Polly.

He turned about. "I've had my whack," he said.

He reflected. "I don't see she'll have any cause to holler," he said. "Beastly Home! Beastly Life!"

For a space he remained thoughtful. "Here goes!" he said at last.

↠ II ↞

For twenty minutes Mr. Polly busied himself about the house, making his preparations very neatly and methodically.

He opened the attic windows in order to make sure of a good draught through the house, and drew down the blinds at the back and shut the kitchen door to conceal his arrangements from casual observation. At the end he would open the door on the yard and so make a clean clear draught right through the house. He hacked at, and wedged off, the tread of a stair. He cleared out the coals from under the staircase, and built a neat fire of firewood and paper there, he splashed about paraffine and arranged the lamps and can even as he had designed, and made a fine inflammable pile of things in the little parlour behind the shop. "Looks pretty arsonical," he said as he surveyed it all. "Wouldn't do to have a caller now. Now for the stairs!"

"Plenty of time," he assured himself, and took the lamp which was to explain the whole affair, and went to the head of the staircase between the scullery and the parlour. He sat down in the twilight with the unlit lamp beside him and surveyed things. He must light the fire in the coal cellar under the stairs, open the back door, then come up them very quickly and light the paraffine puddles on each step, then sit down here again and cut his throat.

He drew his razor from his pocket and felt the edge. It wouldn't hurt much, and in ten minutes he would be indistinguishable ashes in the blaze.

And this was the end of life for him!

The end! And it seemed to him now that life had never begun for him, never! It was as if his soul had been cramped and his eyes bandaged from the hour of his birth. Why had he lived such a life? Why had he submitted to things, blundered into things? Why had he never insisted on the things he thought beautiful and the things he desired, never sought them, fought for them, taken any risk for them, died rather than abandon them? They were the things that mattered. Safety did not matter. A living did not matter unless there were things to live for. . . .

He had been a fool, a coward and a fool, he had been fooled too, for no one had ever warned him to take a firm hold upon life, no one had ever told him of the littleness of fear, or pain, or death; but what was the good of going through it now again? It was over and done with.

The clock in the back parlour pinged the half hour.

"Time!" said Mr. Polly, and stood up.

For an instant he battled with an impulse to put it all back, hastily, guiltily, and abandon this desperate plan of suicide for ever.

But Miriam would smell the paraffine!

"No way out this time, O' Man," said Mr. Polly; and he went slowly downstairs, matchbox in hand.

He paused for five seconds, perhaps, to listen to noises in the yard of the Royal Fishbourne Hotel before he struck his match. It trembled a little in his hand. The paper blackened, and an edge of blue flame ran outward and spread. The fire burnt up readily, and in an instant the wood was crackling cheerfully.

Someone might hear. He must hurry.

He lit a pool of paraffine on the scullery floor, and instantly a nest of snaky, wavering blue flame became agog for prey. He went up the stairs three steps at a time with one eager blue flicker in pursuit of him. He seized the lamp at the top. "Now!" he said and flung it smashing. The chimney broke, but the glass receiver stood the shock and rolled to the bottom, a potential bomb. Old Rumbold would hear that and wonder what it was! . . . He'd know soon enough!

Then Mr. Polly stood hesitating, razor in hand, and then sat down. He was trembling violently, but quite unafraid.

He drew the blade lightly under one ear. "Lord!" but it stung like a nettle!

Then he perceived a little blue thread of flame running up his leg. It arrested his attention, and for a moment he sat, razor in hand, staring at it. It must be paraffine on his trousers that had caught fire on the stairs. Of course his legs were wet with paraffine! He smacked the flicker with his hand to put it out, and felt his leg burn as he did so. But his trousers still charred and glowed. It seemed to him necessary that he must put this out before he cut his throat. He put down the razor beside him to smack with both hands very eagerly. And as he did so a thin tall red flame came up through the hole in the stairs he had made and stood still, quite still as it seemed, and looked at him. It was a strange-looking flame, a flattish salmon colour, redly streaked. It was so queer and quiet mannered that the sight of it held Mr. Polly agape.

"Whuff!" went the can of paraffine below, and boiled over with stinking white fire. At the outbreak the salmon-coloured flames shivered and ducked and then doubled and vanished, and instantly all the staircase was noisily ablaze.

Mr. Polly sprang up and backwards, as though the uprushing tongues of fire were a pack of eager wolves.

"Good Lord!" he cried like a man who wakes up from a dream.

He swore sharply and slapped again at a recrudescent flame upon his leg.

"What the Deuce shall I do? I'm soaked with the confounded stuff!"

He had nerved himself for throat-cutting, but this was fire!

He wanted to delay things, to put them out for a moment while he did his business. The idea of arresting all this hurry with water occurred to him.

There was no water in the little parlour and none in the shop. He hesitated for a moment whether he should not run upstairs to the bedrooms and get a ewer of water to throw on the flames. At this rate Rumbold's would be ablaze in five minutes! Things

234

were going all too fast for Mr. Polly. He ran towards the staircase door, and its hot breath pulled
him up sharply. Then he dashed out through his
shop. The catch of the front door was sometimes
obstinate; it was now, and instantly he became
frantic. He rattled and stormed and felt the parlour already ablaze behind him. In another moment he was in the High Street with the door wide
open.

The staircase behind him was crackling now like
horsewhips and pistol shots.

He had a vague sense that he wasn't doing as he
had proposed, but the chief thing was his sense of
that uncontrolled fire within. What was he going
to do? There was the fire brigade station next door
but one.

The Fishbourne High Street had never seemed
so empty.

Far off at the corner by the God's Providence
Inn a group of three stiff hobbledehoys in their
black, best clothes, conversed intermittently with
Taplow, the policeman.

"Hi!" bawled Mr. Polly to them. "Fire! Fire!"
and struck by a horrible thought, the thought of
Rumbold's deaf mother-in-law upstairs, began to
bang and kick and rattle with the utmost fury at
Rumbold's shop door.

"Hi!" he repeated, *"Fire!"*

⇻ III ⇺

THAT was the beginning of the great Fishbourne fire, which burnt its way sideways into Mr. Rusper's piles of crates and straw, and backwards to the petrol and stabling of the Royal Fishbourne Hotel, and spread from that basis until it seemed half Fishbourne would be ablaze. The east wind, which had been gathering in strength all that day, fanned the flame; everything was dry and ready, and the little shed beyond Rumbold's in which the local Fire Brigade kept its manual, was alight before the Fishbourne fire hose could be saved from disaster. In marvellously little time a great column of black smoke, shot with red streamers, rose out of the middle of the High Street, and all Fishbourne was alive with excitement.

Much of the more respectable elements of Fishbourne society was in church or chapel; many, however, had been tempted by the blue sky and the hard freshness of spring to take walks inland, and there had been the usual disappearance of loungers and conversationalists from the beach and the back streets when at the hour of six the shooting of bolts and the turning of keys had ended the British Ramadan, that weekly interlude of drought our law imposes. The youth of the place were scattered on the beach or playing in back yards, under threat

236

if their clothes were dirtied, and the adolescent were disposed in pairs among the more secluded corners to be found upon the outskirts of the place. Several godless youths, seasick but fishing steadily, were tossing upon the sea in old Tarbold's, the infidel's, boat, and the Clamps were entertaining cousins from Port Burdock. Such few visitors as Fishbourne could boast in the spring were at church or on the beach. To all these that column of smoke did in a manner address itself. "Look here!" it said, "this, within limits, is your affair; what are you going to do?"

The three hobbledehoys, had it been a weekday and they in working clothes, might have felt free to act, but the stiffness of black was upon them and they simply moved to the corner by Rusper's to take a better view of Mr. Polly beating at the door. The policeman was a young, inexpert constable with far too lively a sense of the public house. He put his head inside the Private Bar to the horror of everyone there. But there was no breach of the law, thank Heaven! "Polly's and Rumbold's on fire!" he said, and vanished again. A window in the top story over Boomer's shop opened, and Boomer, captain of the Fire Brigade, appeared, staring out with a blank expression. Still staring, he began to fumble with his collar and tie; manifestly he had to put on his uniform. Hinks' dog, which had been lying on the pavement outside Wintershed's, woke

up, and having regarded Mr. Polly suspiciously
for some time, growled nervously and went round
the corner into Granville Alley. Mr. Polly continued to beat and kick at Rumbold's door.

Then the public houses began to vomit forth the
less desirable elements of Fishbourne society, boys
and men were moved to run and shout, and more
windows went up as the stir increased. Tashingford, the chemist, appeared at his door, in shirt
sleeves and an apron, with his photographic plate
holders in his hand. And then like a vision of purpose came Mr. Gambell, the greengrocer, running
out of Clayford's Alley and buttoning on his jacket
as he ran. His great brass fireman's helmet was on
his head, hiding it all but the sharp nose, the firm
mouth, the intrepid chin. He ran straight to the
fire station and tried the door, and turned about
and met the eye of Boomer still at his upper window. "The key!" cried Mr. Gambell, "the key!"

Mr. Boomer made some inaudible explanation
about his trousers and half a minute.

"Seen old Rumbold?" cried Mr. Polly, approaching Mr. Gambell.

"Gone over Downford for a walk," said Mr.
Gambell. "He told me! But look 'ere! We 'aven't
got the key!"

"Lord!" said Mr. Polly, and regarded the china
shop with open eyes. He *knew* the old woman must
be there alone. He went back to the shop front and

stood surveying it in infinite perplexity. The other activities in the street did not interest him. A deaf old lady somewhere upstairs there! Precious moments passing! Suddenly he was struck by an idea and vanished from public vision into the open door of the Royal Fishbourne Tap.

And now the street was getting crowded and people were laying their hands to this and that.

Mr. Rusper had been at home reading a number of tracts upon Tariff Reform, during the quiet of his wife's absence in church, and trying to work out the application of the whole question to iron-mongery. He heard a clattering in the street and for a time disregarded it, until a cry of Fire! drew him to the window. He pencilled-marked the tract of Chiozza Money's that he was reading side by side with one by Mr. Holt Schooling, made a hasty note "Bal. of Trade say 12,000,000" and went to look out. Instantly he opened the window and ceased to believe the Fiscal Question the most urgent of human affairs.

"Good (kik) Gud!" said Mr. Rusper.

For now the rapidly spreading blaze had forced the partition into Mr. Rumbold's premises, swept across his cellar, clambered his garden wall by means of his well-tarred mushroom shed, and assailed the engine house. It stayed not to consume, but ran as a thing that seeks a quarry. Polly's shop and upper parts were already a furnace, and black smoke was coming out of Rumbold's cellar gratings. The fire in the engine house showed only as a sudden rush of smoke from the back, like something suddenly blown up. The fire brigade, still much under strength, were now hard at work in the front of the latter building; they had got the door open all too late, they had rescued the fire escape and some buckets, and were now lugging out their manual, with the hose already a dripping mass of molten, flaring, stinking rubber. Boomer was dancing about and swearing and shouting; this direct attack upon his apparatus outraged his sense of chivalry. The rest of the brigade hovered in a disheartened state about the rescued fire escape, and tried to piece Boomer's comments into some tangible instructions.

"Hi!" said Rusper from the window. "Kik! What's up?"

Gambell answered him out of his helmet. "Hose!" he cried. "Hose gone!"

"I (kik) got hose!" cried Rusper.

He had. He had a stock of several thousand feet of garden hose, of various qualities and calibres, and now he felt was the time to use it. In another moment his shop door was open and he was hurling pails, garden syringes, and rolls of garden hose out upon the pavement. "(Kik)," he cried, "undo it!" to the gathering crowd in the roadway.

They did. Presently a hundred ready hands were

unrolling and spreading and tangling up and twisting and hopelessly involving Mr. Rusper's stock of hose, sustained by an unquenchable assurance that presently it would in some manner contain and convey water, and Mr. Rusper, on his knees, "kik"ing violently, became incredibly busy with wire and brass junctions and all sorts of mysteries.

"Fix it to the (kik) bathroom tap!" said Mr. Rusper.

Next door to the fire station was Mantell and Throbson's, the little Fishbourne branch of that celebrated firm, and Mr. Boomer, seeking in a teeming mind for a plan of action, had determined to save this building. "Someone telephone to the Port Burdock and Hampstead-on-Sea fire brigades," he cried to the crowd and then to his fellows: "Cut away the woodwork of the fire station!" and so led the way into the blaze with a whirling hatchet that effected wonders in no time in ventilation.

But it was not, after all, such a bad idea of his. Mantell and Throbsons was separated from the fire station in front by a covered glass passage, and at the back the roof of a big outhouse sloped down to the fire station leads. The sturdy 'longshoremen, who made up the bulk of the fire brigade, assailed the glass roof of the passage with extraordinary gusto, and made a smashing of glass

241

that drowned for a time the rising uproar of the flames.

A number of willing volunteers started off to the new telephone office in obedience to Mr. Boomer's request, only to be told with cold official politeness by the young lady at the exchange that all that had been done on her own initiative ten minutes ago. She parleyed with these heated enthusiasts for a space, and then returned to the window.

And indeed the spectacle was well worth looking at. The dusk was falling, and the flames were show-ing brilliantly at half a dozen points. The Royal Fishbourne Hotel Tap, which adjoined Mr. Polly to the west, was being kept wet by the enthusiastic efforts of a string of volunteers with buckets of water, and above at a bathroom window the little German waiter was busy with the garden hose. But Mr. Polly's establishment looked more like a house afire than most houses on fire contrive to look from start to finish. Every window showed eager flick-ering flames, and flames like serpents' tongues were licking out of three large holes in the roof, which was already beginning to fall in. Behind, larger and abundantly spark-shot gusts of fire rose from the fodder that was now getting alight in the Royal Fishbourne Hotel stables. Next door to Mr. Polly, Mr. Rumbold's house was disgorging black smoke from the gratings that protected its under-ground windows, and smoke and occasional shivers of flame were also coming out of its first-floor windows. The fire station was better alight at the back than in front, and its woodwork burnt pretty briskly with peculiar greenish flickerings, and a pungent flavour. In the street an inaggressively disorderly crowd clambered over the rescued fire escape and resisted the attempts of the three local constables to get it away from the danger of Mr. Polly's tottering façade, a cluster of busy forms danced and shouted and advised on the noisy and smashing attempt to cut off Mantell and Throbson's from the fire station that was still in ineffectual progress. Further a number of people appeared to be destroying interminable red and grey snakes under the heated direction of Mr. Rusper; it was as if the High Street had a plague of worms, and beyond again the more timid and less active crowded in front of an accumulation of arrested traffic. Most of the men were in Sabbatical black, and this and the white and starched quality of the women and children in their best clothes gave a note of ceremony to the whole affair.

For a moment the attention of the telephone clerk was held by the activities of Mr. Tashingford, the chemist, who, regardless of everyone else, was rushing across the road hurling fire grenades into the fire station and running back for more, and then her eyes lifted to the slanting outhouse roof that went up to a ridge behind the parapet of

Mantell and Throbson's. An expression of incredulity came into the telephone operator's eyes and gave place to hard activity. She flung up the window and screamed out: "Two people on the roof up there! Two people on the roof!"

→→→ IV ↞↞↞

HER eyes had not deceived her. Two figures which had emerged from the upper staircase window of Mr. Rumbold's and had got after a perilous paddle in his cistern, on to the fire station, were now slowly but resolutely clambering up the outhouse roof towards the back of the main premises of Messrs. Mantell and Throbson's. They clambered slowly and one urged and helped the other, slipping and pausing ever and again, amidst a constant trickle of fragments of broken tile.

One was Mr. Polly, with his hair wildly disordered, his face covered with black smudges and streaked with perspiration, and his trouser legs scorched and blackened; the other was an elderly lady, quietly but becomingly dressed in black, with small white frills at her neck and wrists and a Sunday cap of ecru lace enlivened with a black velvet bow. Her hair was brushed back from her wrinkled brow and plastered down tightly, meeting in a small knob behind; her wrinkled mouth bore that expression of supreme resolution common with the toothless aged. She was shaky, not with fear, but with the vibrations natural to her years, and she spoke with the slow quavering firmness of the very aged.

"I don't mind scrambling," she said with piping inflexibility, "but I can't jump and I *wunt* jump."

"Scramble, old lady, then — scramble!" said Mr. Polly, pulling her arm. "It's one up and two down on these blessed tiles."

"It's not what I'm used to," she said.

"Stick to it!" said Mr. Polly, "live and learn," and got to the ridge and grasped at her arm to pull her after him.

"I can't jump, mind ye," she repeated, pressing her lips together. "And old ladies like me mustn't be hurried."

"Well, let's get as high as possible anyhow!" said Mr. Polly, urging her gently upward. "Shinning up a water-spout in your line? Near as you'll get to Heaven."

"I *can't* jump," she said. "I can do anything but jump."

"Hold on!" said Mr. Polly, "while I give you a boost. That's — wonderful."

"So long as it isn't jumping. . . ."

The old lady grasped the parapet above, and there was a moment of intense struggle.

"Urup!" said Mr. Polly. "Hold on! Gollys! where's she gone to? . . ."

Then an ill-mended, wavering, yet very reassuring spring side boot appeared for an instant.

"Thought perhaps there wasn't any roof there!" he explained, scrambling up over the parapet beside her.

"I've never been out on a roof before," said the old lady. "I'm all disconnected. It's very bumpy. Especially that last bit. Can't we sit here for a bit and rest? I'm not the girl I useto be."

"You sit here ten minutes," shouted Mr. Polly, "and you'll pop like a roast chestnut. Don't understand me? *Roast chestnut!* ROAST CHESTNUT! POP! There ought to be a limit to deafness. Come on round to the front and see if we can find an attic window. Look at this smoke!"

"Nasty!" said the old lady, her eyes following his gesture, puckering her face into an expression of great distaste.

"Come on!"

"Can't hear a word you say."

He pulled her arm. "Come on!"

She paused for a moment to relieve herself of a series of entirely unexpected chuckles. "Sich goings on!" she said, "I never did! Where's he going now?" and came along behind the parapet to the front of the drapery establishment.

Below, the street was now fully alive to their presence, and encouraged the appearance of their heads by shouts and cheers. A sort of free fight was

246

going on round the fire escape, order represented
by Mr. Boomer and the very young policeman, and
disorder by some partially intoxicated volunteers
with views of their own about the manipulation of
the apparatus. Two or three lengths of Mr. Rusper's garden hose appeared to have twined themselves round the ladder. Mr. Polly watched the
struggle with a certain impatience, and glanced
ever and again over his shoulder at the increasing
volume of smoke and steam that was pouring up
from the burning fire station. He decided to break
an attic window and get in, and so try and get
down through the shop. He found himself in a little
bedroom, and returned to fetch his charge. For
some time he could not make her understand his
purpose.

"Got to come at once!" he shouted.

"I hain't 'ad sich a time for years!" said the old
lady.

"We'll have to get down through the house!"

"Can't do no jumpin'," said the old lady. "No!"
She yielded reluctantly to his grasp.

She stared over the parapet. "Runnin' and scur-
rying about like black beetles in a kitchin," she
said.

"We've got to hurry."

"Mr. Rumbold 'E's a very Quiet man. 'E likes
everything Quiet. He'll be surprised to see me
'ere! Why!—there 'e is!" She fumbled in her gar-

ments mysteriously and at last produced a wrinkled pocket handkerchief and began to wave it.

"Oh, come on!" cried Mr. Polly, and seized her.

He got her into the attic, but the staircase, he found, was full of suffocating smoke, and he dared not venture below the next floor. He took her into a long dormitory, shut the door on those pungent and pervasive fumes, and opened the window to discover the fire escape was now against the house, and all Fishbourne boiling with excitement as an immensely helmeted and active and resolute little figure ascended. In another moment the rescuer stared over the windowsill, heroic, but just a trifle self-conscious and grotesque.

"Lawks a mussy!" said the old lady. "Wonders and Wonders! Why! it's Mr. Gambell! 'Iding 'is 'ed in that thing! I *never* did!"

"Can we get her out?" said Mr. Gambell. "There's not much time."

"He might git stuck in it."

"*You'll* get stuck in it," said Mr. Polly, "come along!"

"Not for jumpin' I don't," said the old lady, understanding his gestures rather than his words. "Not a bit of it. I bain't no good at jumping and I *wunt*."

They urged her gently but firmly towards the window.

248

"You lemme do it my own way," said the old lady at the sill. . . .

"I could do it better if 'e'd take it off."

"Oh! *carm* on!"

"It's wuss than Carter's stile," she said, "before they mended it. With a cow a-looking at you."

Mr. Gambell hovered protectingly below. Mr. Polly steered her aged limbs from above. An anxious crowd below babbled advice and did its best to upset the fire escape. Within, streamers of black smoke were pouring up through the cracks in the floor. For some seconds the world waited while the old lady gave herself up to reckless mirth again. "Sich times!" she said, and "*Poor* Rumbold!"

Slowly they descended, and Mr. Polly remained at the post of danger steadying the long ladder until the old lady was in safety below and sheltered by Mr. Rumbold (who was in tears) and the young policeman from the urgent congratulations of the crowd. The crowd was full of an impotent passion to participate. Those nearest wanted to shake her hand, those remoter cheered.

"The fust fire I was ever in and likely to be my last. It's a scurryin', 'urryin' business, but I'm real glad I haven't missed it," said the old lady as she was borne rather than led towards the refuge of the Temperance Hotel.

Also she was heard to remark: " 'E was saying

something about 'ot chestnuts. *I* 'aven't 'ad no 'ot chestnuts."

Then the crowd became aware of Mr. Polly awkwardly negotiating the top rungs of the fire escape. " 'Ere 'e comes!" cried a voice, and Mr. Polly descended into the world again out of the conflagration he had lit to be his funeral pyre, moist, excited, and tremendously alive, amidst a tempest of applause. As he got lower and lower the crowd howled like a pack of dogs at him. Impatient men unable to wait for him seized and shook his descending boots, and so brought him to earth with a run. He was rescued with difficulty from an enthusiast who wished to slake at his own expense and to his own accompaniment a thirst altogether heroic. He was hauled into the Temperance Hotel and flung like a sack, breathless and helpless, into the tear-wet embrace of Miriam.

→≫ V ≪←

WITH the dusk and the arrival of some county constabulary, and first one and presently two other fire engines from Port Burdock and Hampstead-on-Sea, the local talent of Fishbourne found itself forced back into a secondary, less responsible and more observant rôle. I will not pursue the story of the fire to its ashes, nor will I do more than glance at the unfortunate Mr. Rusper, a modern Laocoon, vainly trying to retrieve his scattered hose amidst the tramplings and rushings of the Port Burdock experts.

In a small sitting-room of the Fishbourne Temperance Hotel a little group of Fishbourne tradesmen sat and conversed in fragments and anon went to the window and looked out upon the smoking desolation of their homes across the way, and anon sat down again. They and their families were the guests of old Lady Bargrave, who had displayed the utmost sympathy and interest in their misfortunes. She had taken several people into her own house at Everdean, had engaged the Temperance Hotel as a temporary refuge, and personally superintended the housing of Mantell and Throbson's homeless assistants. The Temperance Hotel became and remained extremely noisy and congested, with people sitting about anywhere, conversing in fragments and totally unable to get themselves to bed. The manager was an old soldier, and following the best traditions of the service saw that everyone had hot cocoa. Hot cocoa seemed to be about everywhere, and it was no doubt very heartening and sustaining to everyone. When the manager detected anyone disposed to be drooping or pensive he exhorted that person at once to drink further hot cocoa and maintain a stout heart.

The hero of the occasion, the centre of interest, was Mr. Polly. For he had not only caused the fire

by upsetting a lighted lamp, scorching his trousers
and narrowly escaping death, as indeed he had now
explained in detail about twenty times, but he had
further thought at once of that amiable but helpless old lady next door, had shown the utmost decision in making his way to her over the yard wall
of the Royal Fishbourne Hotel, and had rescued
her with persistence and vigour in spite of the lev-
ity natural to her years. Everyone thought well of
him and was anxious to show it, more especially by
shaking his hand painfully and repeatedly. Mr.
Rumbold, breaking a silence of nearly fifteen years,
thanked him profusely, said he had never understood him properly and declared he ought to have
a medal. There seemed to be a widely diffused idea
that Mr. Polly ought to have a medal. Hinks
thought so. He declared, moreover, and with the
utmost emphasis, that Mr. Polly had a crowded
and richly decorated interior — or words to that
effect. There was something apologetic in this persistence; it was as if he regretted past intimations
that Mr. Polly was internally defective and hollow.
He also said that Mr. Polly was a "white man,"
albeit, as he developed it, with a liver of the deepest
chromatic satisfactions.

Mr. Polly wandered centrally through it all,
with his face washed and his hair carefully brushed
and parted, looking modest and more than a little
absent-minded, and wearing a pair of black dress

trousers belonging to the manager of the Temperance Hotel, — a larger man than himself in every way.

He drifted upstairs to his fellow-tradesmen, and stood for a time staring into the littered street, with its pools of water and extinguished gas lamps. His companions in misfortune resumed a fragmentary disconnected conversation. They touched now on one aspect of the disaster and now on another, and there were intervals of silence. More or less empty cocoa cups were distributed over the table, mantelshelf and piano, and in the middle of the table was a tin of biscuits, into which Mr. Rumbold, sitting round-shoulderedly, dipped ever and again in an absent-minded way, and munched like a distant shooting of coals. It added to the solemnity of the affair that nearly all of them were in their black Sunday clothes; little Clamp was particularly impressive and dignified in a wide open frock coat, a Gladstone-shaped paper collar, and a large white and blue tie. They felt that they were in the presence of a great disaster, the sort of disaster that gets into the papers, and is even illustrated by blurred photographs of the crumbling ruins. In the presence of that sort of disaster all honourable men are lugubrious and sententious.

And yet it is impossible to deny a certain element of elation. Not one of those excellent men but was already realising that a great door had opened, as it were, in the opaque fabric of destiny, that they were to get their money again that had seemed sunken for ever beyond any hope in the deeps of retail trade. Life was already in their imagination rising like a Phœnix from the flames.

"I suppose there'll be a public subscription," said Mr. Clamp.

"Not for those who're insured," said Mr. Wintershed.

"I was thinking of them assistants from Mantell and Throbson's. They must have lost nearly everything."

"They'll be looked after all right," said Mr. Rumbold. "Never fear."

Pause.

"*I'm* insured," said Mr. Clamp, with unconcealed satisfaction. "Royal Salamander."

"Same here," said Mr. Wintershed.

"Mine's the Glasgow Sun," Mr. Hinks remarked. "Very good company."

"You insured, Mr. Polly?"

"He deserves to be," said Rumbold.

"Ra-ther," said Hinks. "Blowed if he don't. Hard lines it *would* be — if there wasn't something for him."

"Commercial and General," answered Mr. Polly over his shoulder, still staring out of the window. "Oh! I'm all right."

The topic dropped for a time, though manifestly it continued to exercise their minds.

"It's cleared me out of a lot of old stock," said Mr. Wintershed; "that's one good thing."

The remark was felt to be in rather questionable taste, and still more so was his next comment.

"Rusper's a bit sick it didn't reach *'im.*"

Everyone looked uncomfortable, and no one was willing to point the reason why Rusper should be a bit sick.

"Rusper's been playing a game of his own," said Hinks. "Wonder what he thought he was up to! Sittin' in the middle of the road with a pair of tweezers he was, and about a yard of wire — mending somethin'. Wonder he warn't run over by the Port Burdock engine."

Presently a little chat sprang up upon the causes of fires, and Mr. Polly was moved to tell how it had happened for the one and twentieth time. His story had now become as circumstantial and exact as the evidence of a police witness. "Upset the lamp," he said. "I'd just lighted it, I was going upstairs, and my foot slipped against where one of the treads was a bit rotten, and down I went. Thing was aflare in a moment! . . ."

He yawned at the end of the discussion, and moved doorward.

"So long," said Mr. Polly.

"Good night," said Mr. Rumbold. "You played a brave man's part! If you don't get a medal——"

He left an eloquent pause.

"'Ear, 'ear!" said Mr. Wintershed and Mr.

Clamp. "Goo'night, O' Man," said Mr. Hinks.

"Goo'night All," said Mr. Polly . . .

He went slowly upstairs. The vague perplexity common to popular heroes pervaded his mind. He entered the bedroom and turned up the electric light. It was quite a pleasant room, one of the best in the Temperance Hotel, with a nice clean flowered wallpaper, and a very large looking-glass. Miriam appeared to be asleep, and her shoulders were humped up under the clothes in a shapeless, forbidding lump that Mr. Polly had found utterly loathsome for fifteen years. He went softly over to the dressing-table and surveyed himself thoughtfully. Presently he hitched up the trousers. "Miles too big for me," he remarked. "Funny not to have a pair of breeches of one's own. . . . Like being born again. Naked came I into the world. . . ."

Miriam stirred and rolled over, and stared at him.

"Hello!" she said.

"Hello."

"Come to bed?"

"It's three."

Pause, while Mr. Polly disrobed slowly.

"I been thinking," said Miriam. "It isn't going to be so bad after all. We shall get your insurance. We can easy begin all over again."

"H'm," said Mr. Polly.

She turned her face away from him and reflected.

"Get a better house," said Miriam, regarding the wallpaper pattern. "I've always 'ated them stairs."

Mr. Polly removed a boot.

"Choose a better position where there's more doing," murmured Miriam. . . .

"Not half so bad," she whispered. . . .

"You *wanted* stirring up," she said, half asleep. . . .

It dawned upon Mr. Polly for the first time that he had forgotten something.

He ought to have cut his throat!

The fact struck him as remarkable, but as now no longer of any particular urgency. It seemed a thing far off in the past, and he wondered why he had not thought of it before. Odd thing life is! If he had done it he would never have seen this clean and agreeable apartment with the electric light. . . . His thoughts wandered into a question of detail. Where could he have put the razor down? Somewhere in the little room behind the shop, he supposed, but he could not think where more precisely. Anyhow it didn't matter now.

He undressed himself calmly, got into bed, and fell asleep almost immediately.

CHAPTER
THE NINTH

THE POTWELL INN

THE POTWELL INN

⇻ I ⇺

BUT when a man has once broken through the paper walls of everyday circumstance, those unsubstantial walls that hold so many of us securely prisoned from the cradle to the grave, he has made a discovery. If the world does not please you *you can change it*. Determine to alter it at any price, and you can change it altogether. You may change it to something sinister and angry, to something appalling, but it may be you will change it to something brighter, something more agreeable, and at the worst something much more interesting. There is only one sort of man who is absolutely to blame for his own misery, and that is the man who finds life dull and dreary. There are no circumstances in the world that determined action cannot alter, unless perhaps they are the walls of a prison cell, and even those will dissolve and change, I am told,

261

into the infirmary compartment at any rate, for
the man who can fast with resolution. I give these
things as facts and information, and with no moral
intimations. And Mr. Polly lying awake at nights,
with a renewed indigestion, with Miriam sleeping
sonorously beside him and a general air of inevitableness about his situation, saw through it, understood there was no inevitable any more, and escaped his former despair.

He could, for example, "clear out."

It became a wonderful and alluring phrase to
him: "clear out!"

Why had he never thought of clearing out before?

He was amazed and a little shocked at the un-
imaginative and superfluous criminality in him
that had turned old cramped and stagnant Fishbourne into a blaze and new beginnings. (I wish
from the bottom of my heart I could add that he
was properly sorry.) But something constricting
and restrained seemed to have been destroyed by
that flare. *Fishbourne wasn't the world.* That was
the new, the essential fact of which he had lived so
lamentably in ignorance. Fishbourne as he had
known it and hated it, so that he wanted to kill
himself to get out of it, *wasn't the world.*

The insurance money he was to receive made
everything humane and kindly and practicable. He
would "clear out," with justice and humanity. He

262

would take exactly twenty-one pounds, and all the rest he would leave to Miriam. That seemed to him absolutely fair. Without him, she could do all sorts of things — all the sorts of things she was constantly urging him to do.

And he would go off along the white road that led to Garchester, and on to Crogate and so to Tunbridge Wells, where there was a Toad Rock he had heard of, but never seen. (It seemed to him this must needs be a marvel.) And so to other towns and cities. He would walk and loiter by the way, and sleep in inns at night, and get an odd job here and there and talk to strange people. Perhaps he would get quite a lot of work and prosper, and if he did not do so he would lie down in front of a train, or wait for a warm night, and then fall into some smooth, broad river. Not so bad as sitting down to a dentist, not nearly so bad. And he would never open a shop any more. Never!

So the possibilities of the future presented themselves to Mr. Polly as he lay awake at nights.

It was springtime, and in the woods so soon as one got out of reach of the sea wind there would be anemones and primroses.

➤➤ II ⬅⬅

A MONTH later a leisurely and dusty tramp, plump equatorially and slightly bald, with his hands in

his pockets and his lips puckered to a contemplative whistle, strolled along the river bank between
Uppingdon and Potwell. It was a profusely bud-
ding spring day and greens such as God had never
permitted in the world before in human memory
(though indeed they come every year), were mirrored vividly in a mirror of equally unprecedented
brown. For a time the wanderer stopped and stood
still, and even the thin whistle died away from his
lips as he watched a water vole run to and fro
upon a little headland across the stream. The vole
plopped into the water and swam and dived and
only when the last ring of its disturbance had vanished did Mr. Polly resume his thoughtful course
to nowhere in particular.

For the first time in many years he had been
leading a healthy human life, living constantly in
the open air, walking every day for eight or nine
hours, eating sparingly, accepting every conversational opportunity, not even disdaining the discussion of possible work. And beyond mending a
hole in his coat that he had made while negotiating
barbed wire, with a borrowed needle and thread in
a lodging house, he had done no work at all. Neither
had he worried about business nor about time and
seasons. And for the first time in his life he had
seen the Aurora Borealis.

So far the holiday had cost him very little. He
had arranged it on a plan that was entirely his

own. He had started with four five-pound notes
and a pound divided into silver, and he had gone
by train from Fishbourne to Ashington. At Ashington he had gone to the post-office, obtained a
registered letter, and sent his four five-pound notes
with a short brotherly note addressed to himself at
Gilhampton Post-office. He sent this letter to Gilhampton for no other reason in the world than that
he liked the name of Gilhampton and the rural suggestion of its containing county, which was Sus-
sex, and having so despatched it, he set himself to
discover, mark down and walk to Gilhampton, and
so recover his resources. And having got to Gilhampton at last, he changed his five-pound note,
bought four pound postal orders, and repeated his
manœuvre with nineteen pounds.

After a lapse of fifteen years he rediscovered
this interesting world, about which so many people go incredibly blind and bored. He went along
country roads while all the birds were piping and
chirruping and cheeping and singing, and looked
at fresh new things, and felt as happy and irresponsible as a boy with an unexpected half-holiday.
And if ever the thought of Miriam returned to him
he controlled his mind. He came to country inns
and sat for unmeasured hours talking of this and
that to those sage carters who rest for ever in the
taps of country inns, while the big sleek brass jin-
gling horses wait patiently outside with their wag-

gons; he got a job with some van people who were
wandering about the country with swings and a
steam roundabout and remained with them for
three days, until one of their dogs took a violent
dislike to him and made his duties unpleasant; he
talked to tramps and wayside labourers, he snoozed
under hedges by day and in outhouses and hay-
ricks at night, and once, but only once, he slept in
a casual ward. He felt as the etiolated grass and
daisies must do when you move the garden roller
away to a new place.

He gathered a quantity of strange and interesting memories.

He crossed some misty meadows by moonlight
and the mist lay low on the grass, so low that it
scarcely reached above his waist, and houses and
clumps of trees stood out like islands in a milky
sea, so sharply defined was the upper surface of
the mistbank. He came nearer and nearer to a
strange thing that floated like a boat upon this
magic lake, and behold! something moved at the
stern and a rope was whisked at the prow, and it
had changed into a pensive cow, drowsy-eyed, regarding him.

He saw a remarkable sunset in a new valley near
Maidstone, a very red and clear sunset, a wide red-
ness under a pale cloudless heaven, and with the
hills all round the edge of the sky a deep purple
blue and clear and flat, looking exactly as he had

seen mountains painted in pictures. He seemed
transported to some strange country, and would
have felt no surprise if the old labourer he came
upon leaning silently over a gate had addressed
him in an unfamiliar tongue. . . .

Then one night, just towards dawn, his sleep
upon a pile of brushwood was broken by the distant rattle of a racing motor car breaking all the
speed regulations, and as he could not sleep again,
he got up and walked into Maidstone as the day
came. He had never been abroad in a town at half-
past two in his life before, and the stillness of
everything in the bright sunrise impressed him profoundly. At one corner was a startling policeman,
standing in a doorway quite motionless, like a
waxen image. Mr. Polly wished him "good morning" unanswered, and went down to the bridge over
the Medway and sat on the parapet very still and
thoughtful, watching the town awaken, and wondering what he should do if it didn't, if the world
of men never woke again. . . .

One day he found himself going along a road,
with a wide space of sprouting bracken and occasional trees on either side, and suddenly this road
became strangely, perplexingly familiar. "Lord!"
he said, and turned about and stood. "It can't be."

He was incredulous, then left the road and
walked along a scarcely perceptible track to the
left, and came in half a minute to an old lichenous

267

stone wall. It seemed exactly the bit of wall he had known so well. It might have been but yesterday he was in that place; there remained even a little pile of wood. It became absurdly the same wood. The bracken perhaps was not so high, and most of its fronds still uncoiled; that was all. Here he had stood, it seemed, and there she had sat and looked down upon him. Where was she now, and what had become of her? He counted the years back and marvelled that beauty should have called to him with so imperious a voice — and signified nothing.

He hoisted himself with some little difficulty to the top of the wall, and saw off under the beech trees two schoolgirls — small, insignificant, pigtailed creatures, with heads of blond and black, with their arms twined about each other's necks, no doubt telling each other the silliest secrets.

But that girl with the red hair — was she a countess? was she a queen? Children perhaps? Had sorrow dared to touch her?

Had she forgotten altogether? . . .

A tramp sat by the roadside thinking, and it seemed to the man in the passing motor car he must needs be plotting for another pot of beer. But as a matter of fact what the tramp was saying to himself over and over again was a variant upon a well-known Hebrew word.

"Itchabod," the tramp was saying in the voice of one who reasons on the side of the inevitable.

"It's Fair Itchabod, O' Man. There's no going back to it."

»»» III «««

It was about two o'clock in the afternoon one hot day in high May when Mr. Polly, unhurrying and serene, came to that broad bend of the river to which the little lawn and garden of the Potwell Inn run down. He stopped at the sight of the place with its deep tiled roof, nestling under big trees — you never get a decently big, decently shaped tree by the seaside — its sign towards the roadway, its sun-blistered green bench and tables, its shapely white windows and its row of upshooting holly-hock plants in the garden. A hedge separated it from a buttercup-yellow meadow, and beyond stood three poplars in a group against the sky, three exceptionally tall, graceful and harmonious poplars. It is hard to say what there was about them that made them so beautiful to Mr. Polly; but they seemed to him to touch a pleasant scene to a distinction almost divine. He remained admiring them for a long time. At last the need for coarser æsthetic satisfactions arose in him.

"Provinder," he whispered, drawing near to the Inn. "Cold sirlion for choice. And nut-brown brew and wheaten bread."

The nearer he came to the place the more he

liked it. The windows on the ground floor were long and low, and they had pleasing red blinds. The green tables outside were agreeably ringed with memories of former drinks, and an extensive grape vine spread level branches across the whole front of the place. Against the wall was a broken oar, two boat-hooks and the stained and faded red cushions of a pleasure boat. One went up three steps to the glass-panelled door and peeped into a broad, low room with a bar and beer engine, behind which were many bright and helpful looking bottles against mirrors, and great and little pewter measures, and bottles fastened in brass wire upside down with their corks replaced by taps, and a white china cask labelled "Shrub," and cigar boxes and boxes of cigarettes, and a couple of Toby jugs and a beautifully coloured hunting scene framed and glazed, showing the most elegant and beautiful people taking Piper's Cherry Brandy, and cards such as the law requires about the dilution of spirits and the illegality of bringing children into bars, and satirical verses about swearing and asking for credit, and three very bright red-cheeked wax apples and a round-shaped clock.

But these were the mere background to the really pleasant thing in the spectacle, which was quite the plumpest woman Mr. Polly had ever seen, seated in an armchair in the midst of all these bottles and glasses and glittering things, peacefully and tranquilly, and without the slightest loss of dignity, asleep. Many people would have called her a fat woman, but Mr. Polly's innate sense of epithet told him from the outset that plump was the word. She had shapely brows and a straight, well-shaped nose, kind lines and contentment about her mouth, and beneath it the jolly chins clustered like chubby little cherubim about the feet of an Assumptioning-Madonna. Her plumpness was firm and pink and wholesome, and her hands, dimpled at every joint, were clasped in front of her; she seemed as it were to embrace herself with infinite confidence and kindliness as one who knew herself good in substance, good in essence, and would show her gratitude to God by that ready acceptance of all that he had given her. Her head was a little on one side, not much, but just enough to speak of trustfulness, and rob her of the stiff effect of self-reliance. And she slept.

"*My* sort," said Mr. Polly, and opened the door very softly, divided between the desire to enter and come nearer and an instinctive indisposition to break slumbers so manifestly sweet and satisfying.

She awoke with a start, and it amazed Mr. Polly to see swift terror flash into her eyes. Instantly it had gone again.

"Law!" she said, her face softening with relief, "I thought you were Jim."

"I'm never Jim," said Mr. Polly.

"You've got his sort of hat."

"Ah!" said Mr. Polly, and leant over the bar.

"It just came into my head you was Jim," said the plump lady, dismissed the topic and stood up. "I believe I was having forty winks," she said, "if all the truth was told. What can I do for you?"

"Cold meat?" said Mr. Polly.

"There *is* cold meat," the plump woman admitted.

"And room for it."

The plump woman came and leant over the bar and regarded him judicially, but kindly. "There's some cold boiled beef," she said, and added: "A bit of crisp lettuce?"

"New mustard," said Mr. Polly.

"And a tankard!"

"A tankard."

They understood each other perfectly.

"Looking for work?" asked the plump woman.

"In a way," said Mr. Polly.

They smiled like old friends.

Whatever the truth may be about love, there is certainly such a thing as friendship at first sight. They liked each other's voices, they liked each other's way of smiling and speaking.

"It's such beautiful weather this spring," said Mr. Polly, explaining everything.

"What sort of work do you want?" she asked.

"I've never properly thought that out," said Mr. Polly. "I've been looking round — for Ideas."

"Will you have your beef in the tap or outside? That's the tap."

Mr. Polly had a glimpse of an oaken settle. "In the tap will be handier for you," he said.

"Hear that?" said the plump lady.

"Hear what?"

"Listen."

Presently the silence was broken by a distant howl. "Oooooo-ver!" "Eh?" she said.

He nodded.

"That's the ferry. And there isn't a ferryman."

"Could I?"

"Can you punt?"

"Never tried."

"Well — pull the pole out before you reach the end of the punt, that's all. Try."

Mr. Polly went out again into the sunshine.

At times one can tell so much so briefly. Here are the facts then — bare. He found a punt and a pole, got across to the steps on the opposite side, picked up an elderly gentleman in an alpaca jacket and a pith helmet, cruised with him vaguely for twenty minutes, conveyed him tortuously into the midst of a thicket of forget-me-not spangled sedges, splashed some water-weed over him, hit him twice with the punt pole, and finally landed him, alarmed

273

but abusive, in treacherous soil at the edge of a hay meadow about forty yards down stream, where he immediately got into difficulties with a noisy, aggressive little white dog, which was guardian of a jacket.

Mr. Polly returned in a complicated manner to his moorings.

He found the plump woman rather flushed and tearful, and seated at one of the green tables outside.

"I been laughing at you," she said.

"What for?" asked Mr. Polly.

"I ain't 'ad such a laugh since Jim come 'ome. When you 'it 'is 'ed, it 'urt my side."

"It didn't hurt his head — not particularly."

She waved her head. "Did you charge him anything?"

"Gratis," said Mr. Polly. "I never thought of it."

The plump woman pressed her hands to her sides and laughed silently for a space. "You ought to have charged him sumpthing," she said. "You better come and have your cold meat, before you do any more puntin'. You and me'll get on together."

Presently she came and stood watching him eat. "You eat better than you punt," she said, and then, "I dessay you could learn to punt."

"Wax to receive and marble to retain," said Mr. Polly. "This beef is a Bit of All Right, Ma'm. I could have done differently if I hadn't been punting on an empty stomach. There's a lear feeling as the pole goes in——"

"I've never held with fasting," said the plump woman.

"You want a ferryman?"

"I want an odd man about the place."

"I'm odd, all right. What's your wages?"

"Not much, but you get tips and pickings. I've a sort of feeling it would suit you."

"I've a sort of feeling it would. What's the duties? Fetch and carry? Ferry? Garden? Wash bottles? *Ceteris paribus?*"

"That's about it," said the fat woman.

"Give me a trial."

"I've more than half a mind. Or I wouldn't have said anything about it. I suppose you're all right. You've got a sort of half-respectable look about you. I suppose you 'aven't *done* anything."

"Bit of Arson," said Mr. Polly, as if he jested.

"So long as you haven't the habit," said the plump woman.

"My first time, M'am," said Mr. Polly, munching his way through an excellent big leaf of lettuce. "And my last."

"It's all right if you haven't been to prison," said the plump woman. "It isn't what a man's happened to do makes 'im bad. We all happen to do things at times. It's bringing it home to him, and spoiling his self-respect does the mischief. You don't *look* a wrong 'un. 'Ave you been to prison?"

"Never."

"Nor a reformatory? Nor any institution?"

"Not me. Do I *look* reformed?"

"Can you paint and carpenter a bit?"

"Well, I'm ripe for it."

"Have a bit of cheese?"

"If I might."

And the way she brought the cheese showed Mr. Polly that the business was settled in her mind.

He spent the afternoon exploring the premises of the Potwell Inn and learning the duties that might be expected of him, such as Stockholm tarring fences, digging potatoes, swabbing out boats, helping people land, embarking, landing and time-keeping for the hirers of two rowing boats and one Canadian canoe, baling out the said vessels and concealing their leaks and defects from prospective hirers, persuading inexperienced hirers to start down stream rather than up, repairing rowlocks and taking inventories of returning boats with a view to supplementary charges, cleaning boots, sweeping chimneys, house-painting, cleaning windows, sweeping out and sanding the tap and bar, cleaning pewter, washing glasses, turpentining woodwork, whitewashing generally, plumbing and engineering, repairing locks and clocks, waiting and tapster's work generally, beating carpets

and mats, cleaning bottles and saving corks, taking
into the cellar, moving, tapping and connecting
beer casks with their engines, blocking and destroying wasps' nests, doing forestry with several trees,
drowning superfluous kittens, and dog-fancying as
required, assisting in the rearing of ducklings and
the care of various poultry, bee-keeping, stabling,
baiting and grooming horses and asses, cleaning
and "garing" motor cars and bicycles, inflating
tires and repairing punctures, recovering the bod-
ies of drowned persons from the river as required,
and assisting people in trouble in the water, first-
aid and sympathy, improvising and superintending a bathing station for visitors, attending
inquests and funerals in the interests of the establishment, scrubbing floors and all the ordinary
duties of a scullion, the ferry, chasing hens and
goats from the adjacent cottages out of the garden, making up paths and superintending drain-
age, gardening generally, delivering bottled beer
and soda water syphons in the neighbourhood, running miscellaneous errands, removing drunken and
offensive persons from the premises by tact or mus-
cle as occasion required, keeping in with the local
policemen, defending the premises in general and
the orchard in particular from depredators. . . .

"Can but try it," said Mr. Polly towards tea
time. "When there's nothing else on hand I suppose I might do a bit of fishing."

⇢≫ III ≪⇠

Mr. Polly was particularly charmed by the ducklings.

They were piping about among the vegetables
in the company of their foster mother, and as he
and the plump woman came down the garden path
the little creatures mobbed them, and ran over their
boots and in between Mr. Polly's legs, and did their
best to be trodden upon and killed after the manner of ducklings all the world over. Mr. Polly had
never been near young ducklings before, and their
extreme blondness and the delicate completeness of
their feet and beaks filled him with admiration. It
is open to question whether there is anything more
friendly in the world than a very young duckling.
It was with the utmost difficulty that he tore himself away to practise punting, with the plump
woman coaching from the bank. Punting he found
was difficult, but not impossible, and towards four
o'clock he succeeded in conveying a second pas-
senger across the sundering flood from the inn to
the unknown.

As he returned, slowly indeed, but now one might
almost say surely, to the peg to which the punt was
moored, he became aware of a singularly delightful
human being awaiting him on the bank. She stood
with her legs very wide apart, her hands behind
her back, and her head a little on one side, watch-

278

ing his gestures with an expression of disdainful interest. She had black hair and brown legs and a buff short frock and very intelligent eyes. And when he had reached a sufficient proximity she remarked: "Hello!"

"Hello," said Mr. Polly, and saved himself in the nick of time from disaster.

"Silly," said the young lady, and Mr. Polly lunged nearer.

"What are you called?"

"Polly."

"Liar!"

"Why?"

"I'm Polly."

"Then I'm Alfred. But I meant to be Polly."

"I was first."

"All right. I'm going to be the ferryman."

"I see. You'll have to punt better."

"You should have seen me early in the afternoon."

"I can imagine it. . . . I've seen the others."

"What others?" Mr. Polly had landed now and was fastening up the punt.

"What Uncle Jim has scooted."

"Scooted?"

"He comes and scoots them. He'll scoot you too, I expect."

A mysterious shadow seemed to fall athwart the sunshine and pleasantness of the Potwell Inn.

"I'm not a scooter," said Mr. Polly.

"Uncle Jim is."

She whistled a little flatly for a moment, and threw small stones at a clump of meadow-sweet that sprang from the bank. Then she remarked:

"When Uncle Jim comes back he'll cut your insides out. . . . P'raps, very likely, he'll let me see."

There was a pause.

"*Who's* Uncle Jim?" Mr. Polly asked in a faded voice.

"Don't you know who Uncle Jim is? He'll show you. He's a scorcher, is Uncle Jim. He only came back just a little time ago, and he's scooted three men. He don't like strangers about, don't Uncle Jim. He *can* swear. He's going to teach me, soon as I can whissle properly."

"Teach you to swear!" cried Mr. Polly, horrified.

"*And* spit," said the little girl proudly. "He says I'm the gamest little beast he ever came across — ever."

For the first time in his life it seemed to Mr. Polly that he had come across something sheerly dreadful. He stared at the pretty thing of flesh and spirit in front of him, lightly balanced on its stout little legs and looking at him with eyes that had still to learn the expression of either disgust or fear.

"I say," said Mr. Polly, "how old are you?"

"Nine," said the little girl.

She turned away and reflected. Truth compelled her to add one other statement.

"He's not what I should call handsome, not Uncle Jim," she said. "But he's a scorcher and no mistake. . . . Gramma don't like him."

≫ IV ≪

MR. POLLY found the plump woman in the big bricked kitchen lighting a fire for tea. He went to the root of the matter at once.

"I say," he asked, "who's Uncle Jim?"

The plump woman blanched and stood still for a moment. A stick fell out of the bundle in her hand unheeded.

"That little granddaughter of mine been saying things?" she asked faintly.

"Bits of things," said Mr. Polly.

"Well, I suppose I must tell you sooner or later. He's——. It's Jim. He's the Drorback to this place, that's what he is. The Drorback. I hoped you mightn't hear so soon. . . . Very likely he's gone."

"*She* don't seem to think so."

" 'E 'asn't been near the place these two weeks and more," said the plump woman.

"But who is he?"

"I suppose I got to tell you," said the plump woman.

"She says he scoots people," Mr. Polly remarked after a pause.

"He's my own sister's son." The plump woman watched the crackling fire for a space. "I suppose I got to tell you," she repeated.

She softened towards tears. "I try not to think of it, and night and day he's haunting me. I try not to think of it. I've been for easy-going all my life. But I'm that worried and afraid, with death and ruin threatened and evil all about me! I don't know what to do! My own sister's son, and me a widow woman and 'elpless against his doin's!"

She put down the sticks she held upon the fender, and felt for her handkerchief. She began to sob and talk quickly.

"I wouldn't mind nothing else half so much if he'd leave that child alone. But he goes talking to her — if I leave her a moment he's talking to her, teaching her words and giving her ideas!"

"That's a Bit Thick," said Mr. Polly.

"Thick!" cried the plump woman; "it's 'orrible! And what am I to do? He's been here three times now, six days and a week and a part of a week, and I pray to God night and day he may never come again. Praying! Back he's come sure as fate. He takes my money and he takes my things. He won't let no man stay here to protect me or do the boats

282

or work the ferry. The ferry's getting a scandal.
They stand and shout and scream and use language. . . . If I complain they'll say I'm helpless
to manage here, they'll take away my license, out
I shall go — and it's all the living I can get — and
he knows it, and he plays on it, and he don't care.
And here I am. I'd send the child away, but I got
nowhere to send the child. I buys him off when it
comes to that, and back he comes, worse than ever,
prowling round and doing evil. And not a soul to
help me. Not a soul! I just hoped there might be a
day or so. Before he comes back again. I was just
hoping — I'm the sort that hopes."

Mr. Polly was reflecting on the flaws and draw-
backs that seem to be inseparable from all the more
agreeable things in life.

"Biggish sort of man, I expect?" asked Mr.
Polly, trying to get the situation in all its bearings.

But the plump woman did not heed him. She was
going on with her fire-making, and retailing in disconnected fragments the fearfulness of Uncle Jim.

"There was always something a bit wrong with
him," she said, "but nothing you mightn't have
hoped for, not till they took him and carried him
off and reformed him. . . .

"He was cruel to the hens and chickings, it's
true, and stuck a knife into another boy, but then
I've seen him that nice to a cat, nobody could have
been kinder. I'm sure he didn't do no 'arm to that

cat whatever anyone tries to make out of it. I'd
never listen to that. . . . It was that reformatory
ruined him. They put him along of a lot of London
boys full of ideas of wickedness, and because he
didn't mind pain — and he don't, I *will* admit, try
as I would — they made him think himself a hero.
Them boys laughed at the teachers they set over
them, laughed and mocked at them — and I don't
suppose they *was* the best teachers in the world; I
don't suppose, and I don't suppose anyone sensible
does suppose that everyone who goes to be a teacher
or a chapl'in or a warder in a Reformatory Home
goes and changes right away into an Angel of
Grace from Heaven — and Oh, Lord! where
was I?"

"What did they send him to the Reformatory
for?"

"Playing truant and stealing. He stole right
enough — stole the money from an old woman, and
what was I to do when it came to the trial but say
what I knew. And him like a viper a-looking at me
— more like a viper than a human boy. He leans
on the bar and looks at me. 'All right, Aunt Flo,'
he says, just that and nothing more. Time after
time, I've dreamt of it, and now he's come. 'They've
Reformed me,' he says, 'and made me a devil, and
devil I mean to be to you. So out with it,' he says."

"What did you give him last time?" asked Mr.
Polly.

"Three golden pounds," said the plump woman.
" 'That won't last very long,' he says. 'But there
ain't no hurry. I'll be back in a week about.' If I
wasn't one of the hoping sort———"

She left the sentence unfinished.

Mr. Polly reflected. "What sort of a size is he?"
he asked. "I'm not one of your Herculaceous sort,
if you mean that. Nothing very wonderful bicepi-
tally."

"You'll scoot," said the plump woman with conviction rather than bitterness. "You'd better scoot
now, and I'll try and find some money for him to
go away again when he comes. It ain't reasonable
to expect you to do anything but scoot. But I suppose it's the way of a woman in trouble to try and
get help from a man, and hope and hope. I'm the
hoping sort."

"How long's he been about?" asked Mr. Polly,
ignoring his own outlook.

"Three months it is come the seventh since he
come in by that very back door—and I hadn't set
eyes on him for seven long years. He stood in the
door watchin' me, and suddenly he let off a yelp—
like a dog, and there he was grinning at the fright
he'd given me. 'Good old Aunty Flo,' he says, 'ain't
you dee-lighted to see me?' he says, 'now I'm Reformed.' "

The plump lady went to the sink and filled the
kettle.

"I never did like 'im," she said, standing at the
sink. "And seeing him there, with his teeth all black
and broken—. P'raps I didn't give him much of a
welcome at first. Not what would have been kind to
him. 'Lord!' I said, 'it's Jim.'"

"'It's Jim,' he said. 'Like a bad shillin'—like a
damned bad shilling. Jim and trouble. You all of
you wanted me Reformed and now you got me Reformed. I'm a Reformatory Reformed Character,
warranted all right and turned out as such. Ain't
you going to ask me in, Aunty dear?'

"'Come in,' I said, 'I won't have it said I wasn't
ready to be kind to you!'

"He comes in and shuts the door. Down he sits
in that chair. 'I come to torment you!' he says, 'you
Old Sumpthing!' and begins at me. . . . No human being could ever have been called such things
before. It made me cry out. 'And now,' he says,
'just to show I ain't afraid of 'urting you,' he says,
and ups and twists my wrist."

Mr. Polly gasped.

"I could stand even his vi'lence," said the plump
woman, "if it wasn't for the child."

Mr. Polly went to the kitchen window and surveyed his namesake, who was away up the garden
path with her hands behind her back, and whisps
of black hair in disorder about her little face,
thinking, thinking profoundly, about ducklings.

"You two oughtn't to be left," he said.

The plump woman stared at his back with hard hope in her eyes.

"I don't see that it's *my* affair," said Mr. Polly.

The plump woman resumed her business with the kettle.

"I'd like to have a look at him before I go," said Mr. Polly, thinking aloud. And added, "somehow. Not my business, of course."

"Lord!" he cried with a start at a noise in the bar, "who's that?"

"Only a customer," said the plump woman.

➤➤➤ V ≪≪≪

Mr. Polly made no rash promises, and thought a great deal.

"It seems a good sort of Crib," he said, and added, "for a chap who's looking for trouble."

But he stayed on and did various things out of the list I have already given, and worked the ferry, and it was four days before he saw anything of Uncle Jim. And so resistent is the human mind to things not yet experienced that he could easily have believed in that time that there was no such person in the world as Uncle Jim. The plump woman, after her one outbreak of confidence, ignored the subject, and little Polly seemed to have exhausted her impressions in her first communication, and engaged her mind now with a simple directness in the study and subjugation of the new human being Heaven had sent into her world. The first unfavourable impression of his punting was soon effaced; he could nickname ducklings very amusingly, create boats out of wooden splinters, and stalk and fly from imaginary tigers in the orchard with a convincing earnestness that was surely beyond the power of any other human being. She conceded at last that he should be called Mr. Polly, in honour of her, Miss Polly, even as he desired.

Uncle Jim turned up in the twilight.

Uncle Jim appeared with none of the disruptive violence Mr. Polly had dreaded. He came quite softly. Mr. Polly was going down the lane behind the church that led to the Potwell Inn after posting a letter to the lime-juice people at the post-office. He was walking slowly, after his habit, and thinking discursively. With a sudden tightening of the muscles he became aware of a figure walking noiselessly beside him. His first impression was of a face singularly broad above and with a wide empty grin as its chief feature below, of a slouching body and dragging feet.

"Arf a mo'," said the figure, as if in response to his start, and speaking in a hoarse whisper. "Arf a mo', mister. You the noo bloke at the Potwell Inn?"

Mr. Polly felt evasive. " 'Spose I am," he replied hoarsely, and quickened his pace.

"Arf a mo'," said Uncle Jim, taking his arm. "We ain't doing a (sanguinary) Marathon. It ain't a (decorated) cinder track. I want a word with you, mister. See?"

Mr. Polly wriggled his arm free and stopped. "What is it?" he asked, and faced the terror.

"I jest want a (decorated) word wiv you. See? — just a friendly word or two. Just to clear up any blooming errors. That's all I want. No need to be so (richly decorated) proud, if you *are* the noo bloke at Potwell Inn. Not a bit of it. See?"

Uncle Jim was certainly not a handsome person. He was short, shorter than Mr. Polly, with long arms and lean big hands, a thin and wiry neck stuck out of his grey flannel shirt and supported a big head that had something of the snake in the convergent lines of its broad knotty brow, meanly proportioned face and pointed chin. His almost toothless mouth seemed a cavern in the twilight. Some accident had left him with one small and active and one large and expressionless reddish eye, and wisps of straight hair strayed from under the blue cricket cap he wore pulled down obliquely over the latter. He spat between his teeth and wiped his mouth untidily with the soft side of his fist.

"You got to blurry well shift," he said. "See?"

"Shift!" said Mr. Polly. "How?"

" 'Cos the Potwell Inn's *my* beat. See?"

Mr. Polly had never felt less witty. "How's it your beat?" he asked.

Uncle Jim thrust his face forward and shook his open hand, bent like a claw, under Mr. Polly's nose. "Not your blooming business," he said. "You got to shift."

"S'pose I don't," said Mr. Polly.

"You got to shift."

The tone of Uncle Jim's voice became urgent and confidential.

"You don't know who you're up against," he said. "It's a kindness I'm doing to warn you. See? I'm just one of those blokes who don't stick at things, see? I don't stick at nuffin'."

Mr. Polly's manner became detached and confidential—as though the matter and the speaker interested him greatly, but didn't concern him overmuch. "What do you think you'll do?" he asked.

"If you don't clear out?"

"Yes."

"*Gaw!*" said Uncle Jim. "You'd better. '*Ere!*"

He gripped Mr. Polly's wrist with a grip of steel, and in an instant Mr. Polly understood the relative quality of their muscles. He breathed, an uninspiring breath, into Mr. Polly's face.

"What *won't* I do?" he said. "Once I start in on you."

He paused, and the night about them seemed to

be listening. "I'll make a mess of you," he said in his hoarse whisper. "I'll do you—injuries. I'll 'urt you. I'll kick you ugly, see? I'll 'urt you in 'orrible ways—'orrible, ugly ways. . . ."

He scrutinised Mr. Polly's face.

"You'll cry," he said, "to see yourself. See? Cry you will."

"You got no right," began Mr. Polly.

"Right!" His note was fierce. "Ain't the old woman me aunt?"

He spoke still closer. "I'll make a gory mess of you. I'll cut bits orf you——"

He receded a little. "I got no quarrel with *you*," he said.

"It's too late to go to-night," said Mr. Polly.

"I'll be round to-morrer—'bout eleven. See? And if I finds you——"

He produced a blood-curdling oath.

"H'm," said Mr. Polly, trying to keep things light. "We'll consider your suggestions."

"You better," said Uncle Jim, and suddenly, noiselessly, was going.

His whispering voice sank until Mr. Polly could hear only the dim fragments of sentences. "'Orrible things to you—'orrible things. . . . Kick yer ugly. . . . Cut yer—liver out . . . spread it all about, I will. . . . Outing doos. See? I don't care a dead rat one way or the uvver."

And with a curious twisting gesture of the arm

Uncle Jim receded until his face was a still, dim thing that watched, and the black shadows of the hedge seemed to have swallowed up his body altogether.

»» VI ««

Next morning about half-past ten Mr. Polly found himself seated under a clump of fir trees by the roadside and about three miles and a half from the Potwell Inn. He was by no means sure whether he was taking a walk to clear his mind or leaving that threat-marred Paradise for good and all. His reason pointed a lean, unhesitating finger along the latter course.

For after all, the thing was not *his* quarrel.

That agreeable plump woman, agreeable, motherly, comfortable as she might be, wasn't his affair; that child with the mop of black hair who combined so magically the charm of mouse and butterfly and flitting bird, who was daintier than a flower and softer than a peach, was no concern of his. Good heavens! what were they to him? Nothing! . . .

Uncle Jim, of course, *had* a claim, a sort of claim.

If it came to duty and chucking up this attractive, indolent, observant, humorous, tramping life, there were those who had a right to him, a legitimate right, a prior claim on his protection and chivalry.

Why not listen to the call of duty and go back to Miriam now? . . .

He had had a very agreeable holiday. . . .

And while Mr. Polly sat thinking these things as well as he could, he knew that if only he dared to look up the heavens had opened and the clear judgment on his case was written across the sky.

He knew — he knew now as much as a man can know of life. He knew he had to fight or perish.

Life had never been so clear to him before. It had always been a confused, entertaining spectacle, he had responded to this impulse and that, seeking agreeable and entertaining things, evading difficult and painful things. Such is the way of those who grow up to a life that has neither danger nor honour in its texture. He had been muddled and wrapped about and entangled like a creature born in the jungle who has never seen sea or sky. Now he had come out of it suddenly into a great exposed place. It was as if God and Heaven waited over him and all the earth was expectation.

"Not my business," said Mr. Polly, speaking aloud. "Where the devil do *I* come in?"

And again, with something between a whine and a snarl in his voice, "not my blasted business!"

His mind seemed to have divided itself into several compartments, each with its own particular

discussion busily in progress, and quite regardless
of the others. One was busy with the detailed interpretation of the phrase "Kick you ugly." There's
a sort of French wrestling in which you use and
guard against feet. Watch the man's eye, and as
his foot comes up, grip and over he goes — at your
mercy if you use the advantage right. But how do
you use the advantage rightly?

When he thought of Uncle Jim the inside feeling of his body faded away rapidly to a blank discomfort. . . .

"Old cadger! She hadn't no business to drag me
into her quarrels. Ought to go to the police and
ask for help! Dragging me into a quarrel that don't
concern me."

"Wish I'd never set eyes on the rotten inn!"

The reality of the case arched over him like the
vault of the sky, as plain as the sweet blue heavens
above and the wide spread of hill and valley about
him. Man comes into life to seek and find his sufficient beauty, to serve it, to win and increase it, to
fight for it, to face anything and dare anything for
it, counting death as nothing so long as the dying
eyes still turn to it. And fear, and dulness and
indolence and appetite, which indeed are no more
than fear's three crippled brothers who make am-
bushes and creep by night, are against him, to delay him, to hold him off, to hamper and beguile and
kill him in that quest. He had but to lift his eyes to
see all that, as much a part of his world as the driv-

ing clouds and the bending grass, but he kept himself downcast, a grumbling, inglorious, dirty, fattish little tramp, full of dreads and quivering
excuses.

"Why the hell was I ever born?" he said, with
the truth almost winning him.

What do you do when a dirty man who smells,
gets you down and under in the dirt and dust with
a knee below your diaphragm and a large hairy
hand squeezing your windpipe tighter and tighter
in a quarrel that isn't, properly speaking, yours?

"If I had a chance against him—" protested
Mr. Polly.

"It's no Good, you see," said Mr. Polly.

He stood up as though his decision was made,
and was for an instant struck still by doubt.

There lay the road before him going this way to
the east and that to the west.

Westward, one hour away now, was the Potwell Inn. Already things might be happening
there. . . .

Eastward was the wise man's course, a road dip-
ping between hedges to a hop garden and a wood
and presently no doubt reaching an inn, a picturesque church, perhaps, a village and fresh company. The wise man's course. Mr. Polly saw himself going along it, and tried to see himself going
along it with all the self-applause a wise man feels.
But somehow it wouldn't come like that. The wise
man fell short of happiness for all his wisdom. The

wise man had a paunch and round shoulders and red ears and excuses. It was a pleasant road, and why the wise man should not go along it merry and singing, full of summer happiness, was a miracle to Mr. Polly's mind, but confound it! the fact remained, the figure went slinking — slinking was the only word for it — and would not go otherwise than slinking. He turned his eyes westward as if for an explanation, and if the figure was no longer ignoble, the prospect was appalling.

"One kick in the stummick would settle a chap like me," said Mr. Polly.

"Oh, God!" cried Mr. Polly, and lifted his eyes to heaven, and said for the last time in that struggle, "It isn't my affair!"

And so saying he turned his face towards the Potwell Inn.

He went back neither halting nor hastening in his pace after this last decision, but with a mind feverishly busy.

"If I get killed, I get killed, and if he gets killed I get hung. Don't seem just somehow.

"Don't suppose I shall *frighten* him off."

⇜ VII ⇝

THE private war between Mr. Polly and Uncle Jim for the possession of the Potwell Inn fell naturally into three chief campaigns. There was first of all

the great campaign which ended in the triumphant
eviction of Uncle Jim from the inn premises, there
came next after a brief interval the futile invasions
of the premises by Uncle Jim that culminated in
the Battle of the Dead Eel, and after some months
of involuntary truce there was the last supreme
conflict of the Night Surprise. Each of these campaigns merits a section to itself.

Mr. Polly re-entered the inn discreetly. He found
the plump woman seated in her bar, her eyes
a-stare, her face white and wet with tears. "O
God!" she was saying over and over again. "O
God!" The air was full of a spirituous reek, and
on the sanded boards in front of the bar were the
fragments of a broken bottle and an overturned
glass.

She turned her despair at the sound of his entry,
and despair gave place to astonishment.

"You come back!" she said.

"Ra-ther," said Mr. Polly.

"He's — he's mad drunk and looking for her."

"Where is she?"

"Locked upstairs."

"Haven't you sent to the police?"

"No one to send."

"I'll see to it," said Mr. Polly. "Out this way?"
She nodded.

He went to the crinkly paned window and peered
out. Uncle Jim was coming down the garden path

towards the house, his hands in his pockets and singing hoarsely. Mr. Polly remembered afterwards with pride and amazement that he felt neither faint nor rigid. He glanced round him, seized a bottle of beer by the neck as an improvised club, and went out by the garden door. Uncle Jim stopped amazed. His brain did not instantly rise to the new posture of things. "You!" he cried, and stopped for a moment. "You — *scoot!*"

"*Your* job," said Mr. Polly, and advanced some paces.

Uncle Jim stood swaying with wrathful astonishment and then darted forward with clutching hands. Mr. Polly felt that if his antagonist closed he was lost, and smote with all his force at the ugly head before him. Smash went the bottle, and Uncle Jim staggered, half-stunned by the blow and blinded with beer.

The lapses and leaps of the human mind are for ever mysterious. Mr. Polly had never expected that bottle to break. In the instant he felt disarmed and helpless. Before him was Uncle Jim, infuriated and evidently still coming on, and for defence was nothing but the neck of a bottle.

For a time our Mr. Polly has figured heroic. Now comes the fall again; he sounded abject terror; he dropped that ineffectual scrap of glass and turned and fled round the corner of the house.

"Bolls!" came the thick voice of the enemy behind him as one who accepts a challenge, and bleeding, but indomitable, Uncle Jim entered the house.

"Bolls!" he said, surveying the bar. "Fightin' with bolls! I'll show 'im fightin' with bolls!"

Uncle Jim had learnt all about fighting with bottles in the Reformatory Home. Regardless of his terror-stricken aunt he ranged among the bottled beer and succeeded after one or two failures in preparing two bottles to his satisfaction by knocking off the bottoms, and gripping them dagger-wise by the necks. So prepared, he went forth again to destroy Mr. Polly.

Mr. Polly, freed from the sense of urgent pursuit, had halted beyond the raspberry canes and rallied his courage. The sense of Uncle Jim victorious in the house restored his manhood. He went round by the outhouses to the riverside, seeking a weapon, and found an old paddle boat hook. With this he smote Uncle Jim as he emerged by the door of the tap. Uncle Jim, blaspheming dreadfully and with dire stabbing intimations in either hand, came through the splintering paddle like a circus rider through a paper hoop, and once more Mr. Polly dropped his weapon and fled.

A careless observer watching him sprint round and round the inn in front of the lumbering and reproachful pursuit of Uncle Jim might have formed an altogether erroneous estimate of the issue of the campaign. Certain compensating qualities of the very greatest military value were appearing in Mr. Polly even as he ran; if Uncle Jim had strength and brute courage and the rich toughening experience a Reformatory Home affords, Mr. Polly was nevertheless sober, more mobile and with a mind now stimulated to an almost incredible nimbleness. So that he not only gained on Uncle Jim, but thought what use he might make of this advantage. The word "strategious" flamed red across the tumult of his mind. As he came round the house for the third time, he darted suddenly into the yard, swung the door to behind himself and bolted it, seized the zinc pig's pail that stood by the entrance to the kitchen and had it neatly and resonantly over Uncle Jim's head as he came belatedly in round the outhouse on the other side. One of the splintered bottles jabbed Mr. Polly's ear — at the time it seemed of no importance — and then Uncle Jim was down and writhing dangerously and noisily upon the yard tiles, with his head still in the pig pail and his bottles gone to splinters, and Mr. Polly was fastening the kitchen door against him.

"Can't go on like this for ever," said Mr. Polly, whooping for breath, and selecting a weapon from among the brooms that stood behind the kitchen door.

Uncle Jim was losing his head. He was up and kicking the door and bellowing unamiable pro-

posals and invitations, so that a strategist emerging silently by the tap door could locate him without difficulty, steal upon him unawares and —— !

But before that felling blow could be delivered
Uncle Jim's ear had caught a footfall, and he
turned. Mr. Polly quailed and lowered his broom,
— a fatal hesitation.

"*Now* I got you!" cried Uncle Jim, dancing forward in a disconcerting zigzag.

He rushed to close, and Mr. Polly stopped him
neatly, as it were a miracle, with the head of the
broom across his chest. Uncle Jim seized the broom
with both hands. "Lea-go!" he said, and tugged.
Mr. Polly shook his head, tugged, and showed pale,
compressed lips. Both tugged. Then Uncle Jim
tried to get round the end of the broom; Mr. Polly
circled away. They began to circle about one another, both tugging hard, both intensely watchful
of the slightest initiative on the part of the other.
Mr. Polly wished brooms were longer, twelve or
thirteen feet, for example; Uncle Jim was clearly
for shortness in brooms. He wasted breath in saying what was to happen shortly, sanguinary, orien-
tal soul-blenching things, when the broom no longer
separated them. Mr. Polly thought he had never
seen an uglier person. Suddenly Uncle Jim flashed
into violent activity, but alcohol slows movement,
and Mr. Polly was equal to him. Then Uncle Jim
tried jerks, and for a terrible instant seemed to

have the broom out of Mr. Polly's hands. But Mr. Polly recovered it with the clutch of a drowning man. Then Uncle Jim drove suddenly at Mr. Polly's midriff, but again Mr. Polly was ready and swept him round in a circle. Then suddenly a wild hope filled Mr. Polly. He saw the river was very near, the post to which the punt was tied not three yards away. With a wild yell, he sent the broom home into his antagonist's ribs.

"Woosh!" he cried, as the resistance gave.

"Oh! *Gaw!*" said Uncle Jim, going backward helplessly, and Mr. Polly thrust hard and abandoned the broom to the enemy's despairing clutch.

Splash! Uncle Jim was in the water and Mr. Polly had leapt like a cat aboard the ferry punt and grasped the pole.

Up came Uncle Jim spluttering and dripping. "You (unprofitable matter, and printing it would lead to a censorship of novels)! You know I got a weak *chess!*"

The pole took him in the throat and drove him backward and downwards.

"Lea go!" cried Uncle Jim, staggering and with real terror in his once awful eyes.

Splash! Down he fell backwards into a frothing mass of water with Mr. Polly jabbing at him. Under water he turned round and came up again as if in flight towards the middle of the river. Directly his head reappeared Mr. Polly had him between

302

the shoulders and under again, bubbling thickly. A hand clutched and disappeared.

It was stupendous! Mr. Polly had discovered the heel of Achilles. Uncle Jim had no stomach for cold water. The broom floated away, pitching gently on the swell. Mr. Polly, infuriated with victory, thrust Uncle Jim under again, and drove the punt round on its chain in such a manner that when Uncle Jim came up for the fourth time — and now he was nearly out of his depth, too buoyed up to walk and apparently nearly helpless, — Mr. Polly, fortunately for them both, could not reach him.

Uncle Jim made the clumsy gestures of those who struggle insecurely in the water. "Keep out," said Mr. Polly. Uncle Jim with a great effort got a footing, emerged until his arm-pits were out of water, until his waistcoat buttons showed, one by one, till scarcely two remained, and made for the camp sheeting.

"Keep out!" cried Mr. Polly, and leapt off the punt and followed the movements of his victim along the shore.

"I tell you I got a weak chess," said Uncle Jim, moistly. "This ain't fair fightin'."

"Keep out!" said Mr. Polly.

"This ain't fair fightin'," said Uncle Jim, almost weeping, and all his terrors had gone.

"Keep out!" said Mr. Polly, with an accurately poised pole.

"I tell you I got to land, you Fool," said Uncle Jim, with a sort of despairing wrathfulness, and began moving down-stream.

"You keep out," said Mr. Polly in parallel movement. "Don't you ever land on this place again! . . ."

Slowly, argumentatively, and reluctantly, Uncle Jim waded down-stream. He tried threats, he tried persuasion, he even tried a belated note of pathos; Mr. Polly remained inexorable, if in secret a little perplexed as to the outcome of the situation. "This cold's getting to my marrer!" said Uncle Jim.

"You want cooling. You keep out in it," said Mr. Polly.

They came round the bend into sight of Nicholson's ait, where the backwater runs down to the Potwell Mill. And there, after much parley and several feints, Uncle Jim made a desperate effort and struggled into clutch of the overhanging osiers on the island, and so got out of the water with the millstream between them. He emerged dripping and muddy and vindictive. "By *Gaw!*" he said. "I'll skin you for this!"

"You keep off or I'll do worse to you," said Mr. Polly.

The spirit was out of Uncle Jim for the time, and he turned away to struggle through the osiers towards the mill, leaving a shining trail of water among the green-grey stems.

Mr. Polly returned slowly and thoughtfully to the inn, and suddenly his mind began to bubble with phrases. The plump woman stood at the top of the steps that led up to the inn door to greet him.

"Law!" she cried as he drew near, " 'asn't 'e killed you?"

"Do I look like it?" said Mr. Polly.

"But where's Jim?"

"Gone off."

" 'E was mad drunk and dangerous!"

"I put him in the river," said Mr. Polly. "That toned down his alcolaceous frenzy! I gave him a bit of a doing altogether."

"Hain't he 'urt you?"

"Not a bit of it!"

"Then what's all that blood beside your ear?"

Mr. Polly felt. "Quite a cut! Funny how one overlooks things! Heated moments! He must have done that when he jabbed about with those bottles. Hullo, Kiddy! You venturing downstairs again?"

"Ain't he killed you?" asked the little girl.

"Well!"

"I wish I'd seen more of the fighting."

"Didn't you?"

"All I saw was you running round the house and Uncle Jim after you."

There was a little pause. "I was leading him on," said Mr. Polly.

"Someone's shouting at the ferry," she said.

"Right O. But you won't see any more of Uncle Jim for a bit. We've been having a conversazione about that."

"I believe it *is* Uncle Jim," said the little girl.

"Then he can wait," said Mr. Polly shortly.

He turned round and listened for the words that drifted across from the little figure on the opposite bank. So far as he could judge, Uncle Jim was making an appointment for the morrow. He replied with a defiant movement of the punt pole The little figure was convulsed for a moment and then went on its way upstream — fiercely.

So it was the first campaign ended in an insecure victory.

→» VIII «←

THE next day was Wednesday and a slack day for the Potwell Inn. It was a hot, close day, full of the murmuring of bees. One or two people crossed by the ferry, an elaborately equipped fisherman stopped for cold meat and dry ginger ale in the bar parlour, some haymakers came and drank beer for an hour, and afterwards sent jars and jugs by a boy to be replenished; that was all. Mr. Polly had risen early and was busy about the place meditating upon the probable tactics of Uncle Jim. He was no longer strung up to the desperate pitch of the first encounter. But he was grave and anxious.

306

Uncle Jim had shrunken, as all antagonists that
are boldly faced shrink, after the first battle, to the
negotiable, the vulnerable. Formidable he was no
doubt, but not invincible. He had, under Providence, been defeated once, and he might be defeated altogether.

Mr. Polly went about the place considering the
militant possibilities of pacific things, pokers, cop-
per sticks, garden implements, kitchen knives, garden nets, barbed wire, oars, clothes lines, blankets,
pewter pots, stockings and broken bottles. He prepared a club with a stocking and a bottle inside
upon the best East End model. He swung it round
his head once, broke an outhouse window with a
flying fragment of glass, and ruined the stocking
beyond all darning. He developed a subtle scheme
with the cellar flap as a sort of pitfall, but he rejected it finally because (A) it might entrap the
plump woman, and (B) he had no use whatever
for Uncle Jim in the cellar. He determined to wire
the garden that evening, burglar fashion, against
the possibilities of a night attack.

Towards two o'clock in the afternoon three
young men arrived in a capacious boat from the
direction of Lammam, and asked permission to
camp in the paddock. It was given all the more
readily by Mr. Polly because he perceived in their
proximity a possible check upon the self-expres-
sion of Uncle Jim. But he did not foresee and no

one could have foreseen that Uncle Jim, stealing
unawares upon the Potwell Inn in the late afternoon, armed with a large rough-hewn stake, should
have mistaken the bending form of one of those
campers—who was pulling a few onions by permission in the garden—for Mr. Polly's, and crept
upon it swiftly and silently and smitten its wide
invitation unforgettably and unforgiveably. It
was an error impossible to explain; the resounding
whack went up to heaven, the cry of amazement,
and Mr. Polly emerged from the inn armed with
the frying-pan he was cleaning, to take this reckless assailant in the rear. Uncle Jim, realising
his error, fled blaspheming into the arms of the
other two campers, who were returning from the
village with butcher's meat and groceries. They
caught him, they smacked his face with steak and
punched him with a bursting parcel of lump sugar,
they held him though he bit them, and their idea of
punishment was to duck him. They were hilarious,
strong young stockbrokers' clerks, Territorials
and seasoned boating men; they ducked him as
though it was romping, and all that Mr. Polly had
to do was to pick up lumps of sugar for them and
wipe them on his sleeve and put them on a plate,
and explain that Uncle Jim was a notorious bad
character and not quite right in his head.

"Got a regular obsession that the Missis is his
Aunt," said Mr. Polly, expanding it. "Perfect
noosance he is."

But he caught a glance of Uncle Jim's eye as he receded before the campers' urgency that boded ill for him, and in the night he had a disagreeable idea that perhaps his luck might not hold for the third occasion.

That came soon enough. So soon, indeed, as the campers had gone.

Thursday was the early closing day at Lammam, and next to Sunday the busiest part of the week at the Potwell Inn. Sometimes as many as six boats all at once would be moored against the ferry punt and hiring rowboats. People could either have a complete tea, a complete tea with jam, cake and eggs, a kettle of boiling water and find the rest, or refreshments *à la carte*, as they chose. They sat about, but usually the boiling water-ers had a delicacy about using the tables and grouped themselves humbly on the ground. The complete tea-ers with jam and eggs got the best tablecloth on the table nearest the steps that led up to the glass-panelled door. The groups about the lawn were very satisfying to Mr. Polly's sense of amenity. To the right were the complete tea-ers with everything heart could desire, then a small group of three young men in remarkable green and violet and pale-blue shirts, and two girls in mauve and yellow blouses with common teas and gooseberry jam at the green clothless table, then on the grass down by the pollard willow a small family of hot water-ers with a hamper, a little troubled by wasps in their jam from the nest in the tree and all in mourning, but happy otherwise, and on the lawn to the right a ginger beer lot of 'prentices without their collars and very jocular and happy. The young people in the rainbow shirts and blouses formed the centre of interest; they were under the leadership of a gold-spectacled senior with a fluting voice and an air of mystery; he ordered everything, and showed a peculiar knowledge of the qualities of the Potwell jams, preferring gooseberry with much insistence. Mr. Polly watched him, christened him the "benifluous influence," glanced at the 'prentices and went inside and down into the cellar in order to replenish the stock of stone ginger beer which the plump woman had allowed to run low during the preoccupations of the campaign. It was in the cellar that he first became aware of the return of Uncle Jim. He became aware of him as a voice, a voice not only hoarse, but thick, as voices thicken under the influence of alcohol.

"Where's that muddy-faced mongrel?" cried Uncle Jim. "Let 'im come out to me! Where's that blighted whisp with the punt pole — I got a word to say to 'im. Come out of it, you pot-bellied chunk of dirtiness, you! Come out and 'ave your ugly face wiped. I got a Thing for you. . . . *'Ear* me?

"'E's 'iding, that's what 'e's doing," said the voice of Uncle Jim, dropping for a moment to sor-

row, and then with a great increment of wrathfulness: "Come out of my nest, you blinking cuckoo,
you, or I'll cut your silly insides out! Come out of
it—you pock-marked rat! Stealing another man's
'ome away from 'im! Come out and look me in the
face, you squinting son of a Skunk!..."

Mr. Polly took the ginger beer and went
thoughtfully upstairs to the bar.

"'E's back," said the plump woman as he appeared. "I knew 'e'd come back."

"I heard him," said Mr. Polly, and looked about.
"Just gimme the old poker handle that's under the
beer engine."

The door opened softly and Mr. Polly turned
quickly. But it was only the pointed nose and intelligent face of the young man with the gilt spectacles and discreet manner. He coughed and the
spectacles fixed Mr. Polly.

"I say," he said with quiet earnestness. "There's
a chap out here seems to *want* someone."

"Why don't he come in?" said Mr. Polly.

"He seems to want you out there."

"What's he want?"

"I *think*," said the spectacled young man after
a thoughtful moment, "he appears to have brought
you a present of fish."

"Isn't he shouting?"

"He *is* a little boisterous."

"He'd better come in."

311

The manner of the spectacled young man intensified. "I wish you'd come out and persuade him to go away," he said. "His language — isn't quite the thing — ladies."

"It never was," said the plump woman, her voice charged with sorrow.

Mr. Polly moved towards the door and stood with his hand on the handle. The gold-spectacled face disappeared.

"Now, my man," came his voice from outside, "be careful what you're saying ——"

"Oo in all the World and Hereafter are you to call me, me man?" cried Uncle Jim in the voice of one astonished and pained beyond endurance, and added scornfully: "You gold-eyed Geezer, you!"

"Tut, tut!" said the gentleman in gilt glasses. "Restrain yourself!"

Mr. Polly emerged, poker in hand, just in time to see what followed. Uncle Jim in his shirtsleeves and a state of ferocious decolletage, was holding something — yes! — a dead eel by means of a piece of newspaper about its tail, holding it down and back and a little sideways in such a way as to smite with it upward and hard. It struck the spectacled gentleman under the jaw with a peculiar dead thud, and a cry of horror came from the two seated parties at the sight. One of the girls shrieked piercingly, "Horace!" and everyone sprang up. The sense of helping numbers came to Mr. Polly's aid.

"Drop it!" he cried, and came down the steps waving his poker and thrusting the spectacled gentleman before him as once heroes were wont to wield the ox-hide shield.

Uncle Jim gave ground suddenly, and trod upon the foot of a young man in a blue shirt, who immediately thrust at him violently with both hands.

"Lea go!" howled Uncle Jim. "That's the chap I'm looking for!" and pressing the head of the spectacled gentleman aside, smote hard at Mr. Polly.

But at the sight of this indignity inflicted upon the spectacled gentleman a woman's heart was stirred, and a pink parasol drove hard and true at Uncle Jim's wiry neck, and at the same moment the young man in the blue shirt sought to collar him and lost his grip again.

"Suffragettes," gasped Uncle Jim with the ferule at his throat. "Everywhere!" and aimed a second more successful blow at Mr. Polly.

"Wup!" said Mr. Polly.

But now the jam and egg party was joining in the fray. A stout yet still fairly able-bodied gentleman in white and black checks enquired: "What's the fellow up to? Ain't there no police here?" and it was evident that once more public opinion was rallying to the support of Mr. Polly.

"Oh, come on then all the LOT of you!" cried Uncle Jim, and backing dexterously whirled the

eel round in a destructive circle. The pink sun-
shade was torn from the hand that gripped it and
whirled athwart the complete, but unadorned, tea
things on the green table.

"Collar him! Someone get hold of his collar!"
cried the gold-spectacled gentleman, coming out
of the scrimmage, retreating up the steps to the
inn door as if to rally his forces.

"Stand clear, you blessed mantel ornaments!"
cried Uncle Jim, "stand clear!" and retired backing, staving off attack by means of the whirling
eel.

Mr. Polly, undeterred by a sense of grave damage done to his nose, pressed the attack in front,
the two young men in violet and blue skirmished
on Uncle Jim's flanks, the man in white and black
checks sought still further outflanking possibilities, and two of the apprentice boys ran for oars.
The gold-spectacled gentleman, as if inspired,
came down the wooden steps again, seized the
tablecloth of the jam and egg party, lugged it
from under the crockery with inadequate precau-
tions against breakage, and advanced with compressed lips, curious lateral crouching movements,
swift flashings of his glasses, and a general suggestion of bull-fighting in his pose and gestures. Uncle
Jim was kept busy, and unable to plan his retreat
with any strategic soundness. He was moreover
manifestly a little nervous about the river in his

314

rear. He gave ground in a curve, and so came right
across the rapidly abandoned camp of the family
in mourning, crunching a teacup under his heel,
oversetting the teapot, and finally tripping backwards over the hamper. The eel flew out at a tangent from his hand and became a mere looping
relic on the sward.

"Hold him!" cried the gentleman in spectacles.
"Collar him!" and moving forward with extraordinary promptitude wrapped the best tablecloth
about Uncle Jim's arms and head. Mr. Polly
grasped his purpose instantly, the man in checks
was scarcely slower, and in another moment Uncle
Jim was no more than a bundle of smothered blas-
phemy and a pair of wildly active legs.

"Duck him!" panted Mr. Polly, holding on to
the earthquake. "Bes' thing — duck him."

The bundle was convulsed by paroxysms of an-
ger and protest. One boot got the hamper and sent
it ten yards.

"Go in the house for a clothes line someone!"
said the gentleman in gold spectacles. "He'll get
out of this in a moment."

One of the apprentices ran.

"Bird nets in the garden," shouted Mr. Polly.
"In the garden!"

The apprentice was divided in his purpose.

And then suddenly Uncle Jim collapsed and became a limp, dead seeming thing under their

hands. His arms were drawn inward, his legs bent up under his person, and so he lay.

"Fainted!" said the man in checks, relaxing his grip.

"A fit, perhaps," said the man in spectacles.

"Keep hold!" said Mr. Polly, too late.

For suddenly Uncle Jim's arms and legs flew out like springs released. Mr. Polly was tumbled backwards and fell over the broken teapot and into the arms of the father in mourning. Something struck his head—dazzingly. In another second Uncle Jim was on his feet and the tablecloth enshrouded the head of the man in checks. Uncle Jim manifestly considered he had done all that honour required of him, and against overwhelming numbers and the possibility of reiterated duckings, flight is no disgrace.

Uncle Jim fled.

Mr. Polly sat up after an interval of an indeterminate length among the ruins of an idyllic afternoon. Quite a lot of things seemed scattered and broken, but it was difficult to grasp it all at once. He stared between the legs of people. He became aware of a voice, speaking slowly and complainingly.

"Someone ought to pay for those tea things," said the father in mourning. "We didn't bring them 'ere to be danced on, not by no manner of means."

≫ IX ≪

THERE followed an anxious peace for three days,
and then a rough man in a blue jersey, in the intervals of trying to choke himself with bread and
cheese and pickled onions, broke out abruptly into
information.

"Jim's lagged again, Missus," he said.

"What!" said the landlady. "Our Jim?"

"Your Jim," said the man, and after an absolutely necessary pause for swallowing, added:
"Stealin' a 'atchet."

He did not speak for some moments, and then he
replied to Mr. Polly's enquiries: "Yes, a 'atchet.
Down Lammam way — night before last."

"What'd 'e steal a 'atchet for?" asked the
plump woman.

"'E said 'e wanted a 'atchet."

"I wonder what he wanted a hatchet for?" said
Mr. Polly, thoughtfully.

"I dessay 'e 'ad a use for it," said the gentleman
in the blue jersey, and he took a mouthful that
amounted to conversational suicide. There was a
prolonged pause in the little bar, and Mr. Polly
did some rapid thinking.

He went to the window and whistled. "I shall
stick it," he whispered at last. "'Atchets or no
'atchets."

317

He turned to the man with the blue jersey when he thought him clear for speech again. "How much did you say they'd given him?" he asked.

"Three munce," said the man in the blue jersey, and refilled anxiously, as if alarmed at the momentary clearness of his voice.

⇒⇒⇒ X ⇐⇐⇐

THOSE three months passed all too quickly; months of sunshine and warmth, of varied novel exertion in the open air, of congenial experiences, of interest and wholesome food and successful digestion, months that browned Mr. Polly and hardened him and saw the beginnings of his beard, months marred only by one anxiety, an anxiety Mr. Polly did his utmost to suppress. The day of reckoning was never mentioned, it is true, by either the plump woman or himself, but the name of Uncle Jim was written in letters of glaring silence across their intercourse. As the term of that respite drew to an end his anxiety increased, until at last it even trenched upon his well-earned sleep. He had some idea of buying a revolver. At last he compromised upon a small and very foul and dirty rook rifle which he purchased in Lammam under a pretext of bird scaring, and loaded carefully and concealed under his bed from the plump woman's eye.

318

September passed away, October came.

And at last came that night in October whose happenings it is so difficult for a sympathetic historian to drag out of their proper nocturnal indistinctness into the clear, hard light of positive statement. A novelist should present characters, not vivisect them publicly. . . .

The best, the kindliest, if not the justest course is surely to leave untold such things as Mr. Polly would manifestly have preferred untold.

Mr. Polly had declared that when the cyclist discovered him he was seeking a weapon that should make a conclusive end to Uncle Jim. That declaration is placed before the reader without comment.

The gun was certainly in possession of Uncle Jim at that time and no human being but Mr. Polly knows how he got hold of it.

The cyclist was a literary man named Warspite, who suffered from insomnia; he had risen and come out of his house near Lammam just before the dawn, and he discovered Mr. Polly partially concealed in the ditch by the Potwell churchyard wall. It is an ordinary dry ditch, full of nettles and overgrown with elder and dogrose, and in no way suggestive of an arsenal. It is the last place in which you would look for a gun. And he says that when he dismounted to see why Mr. Polly was allowing only the latter part of his person to show (and that it would seem by inadvertency), Mr. Polly merely raised his head and advised him to "Look out!" and added: "He's let fly at me twice already." He came out under persuasion and with gestures of extreme caution. He was wearing a white cotton nightgown of the type that has now been so extensively superseded by pyjama sleeping suits, and his legs and feet were bare and much scratched and torn and very muddy.

Mr. Warspite takes that exceptionally lively interest in his fellow-creatures which constitutes so much of the distinctive and complex charm of your novelist all the world over, and he at once involved himself generously in the case. The two men returned at Mr. Polly's initiative across the churchyard to the Potwell Inn, and came upon the burst and damaged rook rifle near the new monument to Sir Samuel Harpon at the corner by the yew.

"That must have been his third go," said Mr. Polly. "It sounded a bit funny."

The sight inspirited him greatly, and he explained further that he had fled to the churchyard on account of the cover afforded by tombstones from the flight of small shot. He expressed anxiety for the fate of the landlady of the Potwell Inn and her grandchild, and led the way with enhanced alacrity along the lane to that establishment.

They found the doors of the house standing open, the bar in some disorder — several bottles of

whisky were afterwards found to be missing — and
Blake, the village policeman, rapping patiently at
the open door. He entered with them. The glass in
the bar had suffered severely, and one of the mirrors was starred from a blow from a pewter pot.
The till had been forced and ransacked, and so had
the bureau in the minute room behind the bar. An
upper window was opened and the voice of the
landlady became audible making enquiries. They
went out and parleyed with her. She had locked
herself upstairs with the little girl, she said, and
refused to descend until she was assured that neither Uncle Jim nor Mr. Polly's gun were anywhere
on the premises. Mr. Blake and Mr. Warspite proceeded to satisfy themselves with regard to the
former condition, and Mr. Polly went to his room
in search of garments more suited to the brighten-
ing dawn. He returned immediately with a request
that Mr. Blake and Mr. Warspite would "just
come and look." They found the apartment in a
state of extraordinary confusion, the bedclothes in
a ball in the corner, the drawers all open and ransacked, the chair broken, the lock of the door
forced and broken, one door panel slightly scorched
and perforated by shot, and the window wide open.
None of Mr. Polly's clothes were to be seen, but
some garments which had apparently once formed
part of a stoker's workaday outfit, two brownish
yellow halves of a shirt, and an unsound pair of

boots were scattered on the floor. A faint smell of
gunpowder still hung in the air, and two or three
books Mr. Polly had recently acquired had been
shied with some violence under the bed. Mr. Warspite looked at Mr. Blake, and then both men
looked at Mr. Polly. "That's *his* boots," said Mr.
Polly.

Blake turned his eye to the window. "Some of
these tiles 'ave just got broken," he observed.

"I got out of the window and slid down the scullery tiles," Mr. Polly answered, omitting much,
they both felt, from his explanation. . . .

"Well, we better find 'im and 'ave a word with
'im," said Blake. "That's about my business now."

But Uncle Jim had gone altogether. . . .

⇛ XII ⇚

HE DID not return for some days. That perhaps
was not very wonderful. But the days lengthened
to weeks and the weeks to months and still Uncle
Jim did not recur. A year passed, and the anxiety
of him became less acute; a second healing year
followed the first. One afternoon about thirty
months after the Night Surprise the plump woman
spoke of him.

"I wonder what's become of Jim," she said.

"I wonder sometimes," said Mr. Polly.

CHAPTER
THE TENTH

MIRIAM REVISITED

MIRIAM REVISITED

ONE summer afternoon about five years after his first coming to the Potwell Inn Mr. Polly found himself sitting under the pollard willow fishing for dace. It was a plumper, browner and healthier Mr. Polly altogether than the miserable bankrupt with whose dyspeptic portrait our novel opened. He was fat, but with a fatness more generally diffused, and the lower part of his face was touched to gravity by a small square beard. Also he was balder.

It was the first time he had found leisure to fish, though from the very outset of his Potwell career he had promised himself abundant indulgence in the pleasures of fishing. Fishing, as the golden page of English literature testifies, is a meditative and retrospective pursuit, and the varied page of memory, disregarded so long for sake of the teeming duties I have already enumerated, began to unfold itself to Mr. Polly's consideration. A speculation about Uncle Jim died for want of material, and gave place to a reckoning of the years and months that had passed since his coming to Potwell, and that to a philosophical review of his life. He began to think about Miriam, remotely and impersonally. He remembered many things that had been neglected by his conscience during the busier times, as, for example, that he had committed arson and deserted a wife. For the first time he looked these long neglected facts in the face.

It is disagreeable to think one has committed Arson, because it is an action that leads to jail. Otherwise I do not think there was a grain of regret for that in Mr. Polly's composition. But deserting Miriam was in a different category. Deserting Miriam was mean.

This is a history and not a glorification of Mr. Polly, and I tell of things as they were with him. Apart from the disagreeable twinge arising from the thought of what might happen if he was found out, he had not the slightest remorse about that fire. Arson, after all, is an artificial crime. Some crimes are crimes in themselves, would be crimes without any law, the cruelties, mockery, the breaches of faith that astonish and wound, but the burning of things is in itself neither good nor bad. A large number of houses deserve to be burnt, most modern furniture, an overwhelming majority of pictures and books — one might go on for some time with the list. If our community was collectively anything more than a feeble idiot, it would burn most of London and Chicago, for example, and build sane and beautiful cities in the place of these pestilential heaps of rotten private property. I have failed in presenting Mr. Polly altogether if I have not made you see that he was in many respects an artless child of Nature, far more untrained, undisciplined and spontaneous than an ordinary savage. And he was really glad, for all that little drawback of fear, that he had the courage to set fire to his house and fly and come to the Potwell Inn.

But he was not glad he had left Miriam. He had seen Miriam cry once or twice in his life, and it had always reduced him to abject commiseration. He now imagined her crying. He perceived in a perplexed way that he had made himself responsible for her life. He forgot how she had spoilt his own. He had hitherto rested in the faith that she had over a hundred pounds of insurance money, but now, with his eye meditatively upon his float, he realised a hundred pounds does not last for ever. His conviction of her incompetence was unflinching; she was bound to have fooled it away somehow by this time. And then!

He saw her humping her shoulders and sniffing in a manner he had always regarded as detestable at close quarters, but which now became harrowingly pitiful.

"Damn!" said Mr. Polly, and down went his float and he flicked up a victim to destruction and took it off the hook.

He compared his own comfort and health with Miriam's imagined distress.

"Ought to have done something for herself," said Mr. Polly, rebaiting his hook. "She was always talking of doing things. Why couldn't she?"

He watched the float oscillating gently towards quiescence.

"Silly to begin thinking about her," he said. "Damn silly!"

But once he had begun thinking about her he had to go on.

"Oh blow!" cried Mr. Polly presently, and pulled up his hook to find another fish had just snatched at it in the last instant. His handling must have made the poor thing feel itself unwelcome.

He gathered his things together and turned towards the house.

All the Potwell Inn betrayed his influence now, for here indeed he had found his place in the world. It looked brighter, so bright indeed as to be almost skittish, with the white and green paint he had lavished upon it. Even the garden palings were

striped white and green, and so were the boats, for
Mr. Polly was one of those who find a positive sen-
suous pleasure in the laying on of paint. Left and
right were two large boards which had done much
to enhance the inn's popularity with the lighter-
minded variety of pleasure-seekers. Both marked
innovations. One bore in large letters the single
word "Museum," the other was as plain and la-
conic with "Omlets!" The spelling of the latter
word was Mr. Polly's own, but when he had seen a
whole boatload of men, intent on Lammam for
lunch, stop open-mouthed, and stare and grin and
come in and ask in a marked sarcastic manner
for "omlets," he perceived that his inaccuracy had
done more for the place than his utmost cunning
could have contrived. In a year or so the inn was
known both up and down the river by its new name
of "Omlets," and Mr. Polly, after some secret irritation, smiled and was content. And the fat woman's omelettes were things to remember.

(You will note I have changed her epithet. Time
works upon us all.)

She stood upon the steps as he came towards the
house, and smiled at him richly.

"Caught many?" she asked.

"Got an idea," said Mr. Polly. "Would it put
you out very much if I went off for a day or two
for a bit of a holiday? There won't be much doing
now until Thursday."

⇛ II ⇚

FEELING recklessly secure behind his beard Mr.
Polly surveyed the Fishbourne High Street once
again. The north side was much as he had known
it except that Rusper had vanished. A row of new
shops replaced the destruction of the great fire.
Mantell and Throbson's had risen again upon a
more flamboyant pattern, and the new fire station
was in the Swiss-Teutonic style and with much red
paint. Next door in the place of Rumbold's was a
branch of the Colonial Tea Company, and then
a Salmon and Gluckstein Tobacco Shop, and
then a little shop that displayed sweets and professed a "Tea Room Upstairs." He considered this
as a possible place in which to prosecute enquiries
about his lost wife, wavering a little between it and
the God's Providence Inn down the street. Then
his eye caught a name over the window, "Polly,"
he read, "& Larkins! Well, I'm — astonished!"

A momentary faintness came upon him. He
walked past and down the street, returned and surveyed the shop again.

He saw a middle-aged, rather untidy woman
standing behind the counter, who for an instant
he thought might be Miriam terribly changed, and
then recognised as his sister-in-law Annie, filled
out and no longer hilarious. She stared at him

330

without a sign of recognition as he entered the shop.

"Can I have tea?" said Mr. Polly.

"Well," said Annie, "you *can*. But our Tea Room's upstairs. . . . My sister's been cleaning it out — and it's a bit upset."

"It *would* be," said Mr. Polly softly.

"I beg your pardon?" said Annie.

"I said *I* didn't mind. Up here?"

"I daresay there'll be a table," said Annie, and followed him up to a room whose conscientious disorder was intensely reminiscent of Miriam.

"Nothing like turning everything upside down when you're cleaning," said Mr. Polly cheerfully.

"It's my sister's way," said Annie impartially. "She's gone out for a bit of air, but I daresay she'll be back soon to finish. It's a nice light room when it's tidy. Can I put you a table over there?"

"Let *me*," said Mr. Polly, and assisted.

He sat down by the open window and drummed on the table and meditated on his next step while Annie vanished to get his tea. After all, things didn't seem so bad with Miriam. He tried over several gambits in imagination.

"Unusual name," he said as Annie laid a cloth before him. Annie looked interrogation.

"Polly. Polly & Larkins. Real, I suppose?"

"Polly's my sister's name. She married a Mr. Polly."

331

"Widow I presume?" said Mr. Polly.

"Yes. This five years — come October."

"Lord!" said Mr. Polly in unfeigned surprise.

"Found drowned he was. There was a lot of talk in the place."

"Never heard of it," said Mr. Polly. "I'm a stranger — rather."

"In the Medway near Maidstone. He must have been in the water for days. Wouldn't have known him, my sister wouldn't, if it hadn't been for the name sewn in his clothes. All whitey and eat away he was."

"Bless my heart! Must have been rather a shock for her!"

"It *was* a shock," said Annie, and added darkly: "But sometimes a shock's better than a long agony."

"No doubt," said Mr. Polly.

He gazed with a rapt expression at the preparations before him. "So I'm drowned," something was saying inside him. "Life insured?" he asked.

"We started the tea rooms with it," said Annie.

Why, if things were like this, had remorse and anxiety for Miriam been implanted in his soul? No shadow of an answer appeared.

"Marriage is a lottery," said Mr. Polly.

"*She* found it so," said Annie. "Would you like some jam?"

"I'd like an egg," said Mr. Polly. "I'll have two. I've got a sort of feeling ———. As though I wanted keeping up. . . . Wasn't particularly good sort, this Mr. Polly?"

"He was a *wearing* husband," said Annie. "I've often pitied my sister. He was one of that sort——"

"Dissolute?" suggested Mr. Polly faintly.

"No," said Annie judiciously; "not exactly dissolute. Feeble's more the word. Weak, 'E was. Weak as water. 'Ow long do you like your eggs boiled?"

"Four minutes exactly," said Mr. Polly.

"One gets talking," said Annie.

"One does," said Mr. Polly, and she left him to his thoughts.

What perplexed him was his recent remorse and tenderness for Miriam. Now he was back in her atmosphere all that had vanished, and the old feeling of helpless antagonism returned. He surveyed the piled furniture, the economically managed carpet, the unpleasing pictures on the wall. Why had he felt remorse? Why had he entertained this illusion of a helpless woman crying aloud in the pitiless darkness for him? He peered into the unfathomable mysteries of the heart, and ducked back to a smaller issue. *Was* he feeble?

The eggs came up. Nothing in Annie's manner invited a resumption of the discussion.

"Business brisk?" he ventured to ask.

Annie reflected. "It is," she said, "and it isn't. It's like that."

"Ah!" said Mr. Polly, and squared himself to

his egg. "Was there an inquest on that chap?"

"What chap?"

"What was his name?—Polly!"

"Of course."

"You're sure it was him?"

"What you mean?"

Annie looked at him hard, and suddenly his soul was black with terror.

"Who else could it have been—in the very cloes 'e wore?"

"Of course," said Mr. Polly, and began his egg. He was so agitated that he only realised its condition when he was half way through it and Annie safely downstairs.

"Lord!" he said, reaching out hastily for the pepper. "One of Miriam's! Management! I haven't tasted such an egg for five years. . . . Wonder where she gets them! Picks them out, I suppose!"

He abandoned it for its fellow.

Except for a slight mustiness the second egg was very palatable indeed. He was getting on to the bottom of it as Miriam came in. He looked up. "Nice afternoon," he said at her stare, and perceived she knew him at once by the gesture and the voice. She went white and shut the door behind her. She looked as though she was going to faint. Mr. Polly sprang up quickly and handed her a chair. "My God!" she whispered, and crumpled up rather than sat down.

"It's *you*," she said.

"No," said Mr. Polly very earnestly. "It isn't. It just looks like me. That's all."

"I *knew* that man wasn't you — all along. I tried to think it was. I tried to think perhaps the water had altered your wrists and feet and the colour of your hair."

"Ah!"

"I'd always feared you'd come back."

Mr. Polly sat down by his egg. "I haven't come back," he said very earnestly. "Don't you think it."

" 'Ow we'll pay back the insurance now I *don't* know." She was weeping. She produced a handkerchief and covered her face.

"Look here, Miriam," said Mr. Polly. "I haven't come back and I'm not coming back. I'm — I'm a Visitant from Another World. You shut up about me and I'll shut up about myself. I came back because I thought you might be hard up or in trouble or some silly thing like that. Now I see you again — I'm satisfied. I'm satisfied completely. See? I'm going to absquatulate, see? Hey Presto right away."

He turned to his tea for a moment, finished his cup noisily, stood up.

"Don't you think you're going to see me again," he said, "for you ain't."

He moved to the door.

"That *was* a tasty egg," he said, hovered for a second and vanished.

Annie was in the shop.

"The missus has had a bit of a shock," he remarked. "Got some sort of fancy about a ghost. Can't make it out quite. So Long!"

And he had gone.

⇨⟫ III ⟪⇦

MR. POLLY sat beside the fat woman at one of the little green tables at the back of the Potwell Inn, and struggled with the mystery of life. It was one of those evenings, serenely luminous, amply and atmospherically still, when the river bend was at its best. A swan floated against the dark green masses of the further bank, the stream flowed broad and shining to its destiny, with scarce a ripple — except where the reeds came out from the headland — the three poplars rose clear and harmonious against a sky of green and yellow. And it was as if it was all securely within a great warm friendly globe of crystal sky. It was as safe and enclosed and fearless as a child that has still to be born. It was an evening full of the quality of tranquil, unqualified assurance. Mr. Polly's mind was filled with the persuasion that indeed all things whatsoever must needs be satisfying and complete. It was incredible that life has ever done more than seemed to jar, that there could be any shadow in life save such velvet softnesses as made the setting for that silent swan, or any murmur but the ripple of the water as it swirled round the chained and gently swaying punt. And the mind of Mr. Polly, exalted and made tender by this atmosphere, sought gently, but sought, to draw together the varied memories that came drifting, half submerged, across the circle of his mind.

He spoke in words that seemed like a bent and broken stick thrust suddenly into water, destroying the mirror of the shapes they sought. "Jim's not coming back again ever," he said. "He got drowned five years ago."

"Where?" asked the fat woman, surprised.

"Miles from here. In the Medway. Away in Kent."

"Lor!" said the fat woman.

"It's right enough," said Mr. Polly.

"How d'you know?"

"I went to my home."

"Where?"

"Don't matter. I went and found out. He'd been in the water some days. He'd got my clothes and they'd said it was me."

"*They?*"

"It don't matter. I'm not going back to them."

The fat woman regarded him silently for some time. Her expression of scrutiny gave way to a quiet satisfaction. Then her brown eyes went to the river.

"Poor Jim," she said. "'E 'adn't much Tact—ever."

She added mildly: "I can't 'ardly say I'm sorry."

"Nor me," said Mr. Polly, and got a step nearer the thought in him. "But it don't seem much good his having been alive, does it?"

"'E wasn't much good," the fat woman admitted. "Ever."

"I suppose there were things that were good to him," Mr. Polly speculated. "They weren't *our* things."

His hold slipped again. "I often wonder about life," he said weakly.

He tried again. "One seems to start in life," he said, "expecting something. And it doesn't happen. And it doesn't matter. One starts with ideas that things are good and things are bad—and it hasn't much relation to what *is* good and what *is* bad. I've always been the skeptaceous sort, and it's always seemed rot to me to pretend we know good from evil. It's just what I've *never* done. No Adam's apple stuck in *my* throat, ma'am. I don't own to it."

He reflected.

"I set fire to a house—once."

338

The fat woman started.

"I don't feel sorry for it. I don't believe it was a bad thing to do—any more than burning a toy like I did once when I was a baby. I nearly killed myself with a razor. Who hasn't?—anyhow gone as far as thinking of it? Most of my time I've been half dreaming. I married like a dream almost. I've never really planned my life or set out to live. I happened; things happened to me. It's so with everyone. Jim couldn't help himself. I shot at him and tried to kill him. I dropped the gun and he got it. He very nearly had me. I wasn't a second too soon—ducking. . . . Awkward—that night was. . . . M'mm. . . . But I don't blame him—come to that. Only I don't see what it's all up to. . . .

"Like children playing about in a nursery. Hurt themselves at times. . . .

"There's something that doesn't mind us," he resumed presently. "It isn't what we try to get that we get, it isn't the good we think we do is good. What makes us happy isn't our trying, what makes others happy isn't our trying. There's a sort of character people like and stand up for and a sort they won't. You got to work it out and take the consequences. . . . Miriam was always trying."

"Who was Miriam?" asked the fat woman.

"No one you know. But she used to go about

339

with her brows knit trying not to do whatever she wanted to do—if ever she did want to do anything——"

He lost himself.

"You can't help being fat," said the fat woman after a pause, trying to get up to his thoughts.

"*You* can't," said Mr. Polly.

"It helps and it hinders."

"Like my upside down way of talking."

"The magistrates wouldn't 'ave kept on the license to me if I 'adn't been fat. . . ."

"Then what have we done," said Mr. Polly, "to get an evening like this? Lord! look at it!" He sent his arm round the great curve of the sky.

"If I was a nigger or an Italian I should come out here and sing. I whistle sometimes, but bless you, it's singing I've got in my mind. Sometimes I think I live for sunsets."

"I don't see that it does you any good always looking at sunsets like you do," said the fat woman.

"Nor me. But I do. Sunsets and things I was made to like."

"They don't 'elp you," said the fat woman thoughtfully.

"Who cares?" said Mr. Polly.

A deeper strain had come to the fat woman. "You got to die some day," she said.

"Some things I can't believe," said Mr. Polly suddenly, "and one is your being a skeleton. . . ."

He pointed his hand towards the neighbour's hedge. "Look at 'em — against the yellow — and they're just stingin' nettles. Nasty weeds — if you count things by their uses. And no help in the life hereafter. But just look at the look of them!"

"It isn't only looks," said the fat woman.

"Whenever there's signs of a good sunset and I'm not too busy," said Mr. Polly, "I'll come and sit out here."

The fat woman looked at him with eyes in which contentment struggled with some obscure reluctant protest, and at last turned them slowly to the black nettle pagodas against the golden sky.

"I wish we could," she said.

"I will."

The fat woman's voice sank nearly to the inaudible.

"Not always," she said.

Mr. Polly was some time before he replied. "Come here always when I'm a ghost," he replied.

"Spoil the place for others," said the fat woman, abandoning her moral solicitudes for a more congenial point of view.

"Not my sort of ghost wouldn't," said Mr. Polly, emerging from another long pause. "I'd be a sort of diaphalous feeling — just mellowish and warmish like. . . ."

They said no more, but sat on in the warm twilight until at last they could scarcely distinguish each other's faces. They were not so much thinking as lost in a smooth, still quiet of the mind. A bat flitted by.

"Time we was going in, O' Party," said Mr. Polly, standing up. "Supper to get. It's as you say, we can't sit here for ever."

THE END